YOU CAN'T BE SERIOUS!

A Royal Affair

PRAJWAL HEGDE

hachette INDIA

First published in 2025 by Hachette India
(Registered name: Hachette Book Publishing India Pvt. Ltd)
An Hachette UK company
www.hachetteindia.com

1

Section divider illustration from Dafont
('Ornament Salad' by Woodcutter)
Author picture by Om Prakash

Cover design and illustrations by Damini Gupta.

Print ISBN 978-93-5731-986-7
eBook ISBN 978-93-5731-965-2

Hachette Book Publishing India Pvt. Ltd
4th & 5th Floors, Corporate Centre
Plot No. 94, Sector 44, Gurugram – 122003, India

Typeset in Amiri/Minion Pro/Coronette 11.5/15.5
by R. Ajith Kumar, New Delhi

Printed and bound in India by Manipal Technologies Limited

FSC www.fsc.org
MIX
Paper | Supporting responsible forestry
FSC™ C043100

For those who stayed...

'Share our similarities, celebrate our differences.'

M SCOTT PECK

1.

Aaditha

There's a Boy!

FIREWORKS ARE LIVE IN MY HEAD. NOT THE SCAR-YOU-SOFTLY sparkler variety, but rockets that whoosh and crash against the cranium.

I can't remember when I dozed off last night, but I woke up early this morning, determined to work off the ire. At least some of it.

The music in my AirPods fades under the air conditioner's drone. Even at max volume, I can hear my own breathing.

I pause momentarily, something I rarely do when I work out.

Marriage. Royal, seriously?

I open my palm, flex my fingers and hold for a second or two before balling it tightly again. It's involuntary, a release almost.

I pat my leg once, twice, before getting back into position. One limb pushed back, the other lunged forward, my spine is parallel to my thigh. I slap the floor with my palms and reach with my lower extremity, cutting through the air like a flash of lightning. I am burning – my body and mind in sync.

I have been at my Kalari routine for almost forty minutes. That's when my right foot makes contact with bones. A jaw. My foot is firm as I attempt a full rotation, but before I land on my feet, I'm picked up and placed on the display riser that is my contribution to the gym.

It's where I like to hang out after a workout, my feet on different levels, sipping a double-shot bone-dry cappuccino with Raju, my friend and trainer, in that order. (post workout, of course!).

I'm staring at a pair of curious eyes and a forced smile. I'm tasting sweat.

I open my palm before balling it tightly. My nails sink into my palm. *Breathe,* I tell myself. *Repeat.* My anxiety is off the charts.

'I...'

I try to open my mouth, form a sentence, but even I, who can rattle off 250 words a minute when I'm nervous, most of them incoherent, can't manage more than one.

The last thing I expect is for my foot to find Raju's jaw.

Kalari is about reaction. The body is conditioned to be sensitive to stimuli. A still draught, a silent shuffle – nothing misses the ninja's radar.

Raju had taught me to read moves early in this journey. He is a master. Why didn't he duck?

New strains of panic kick in. I want to laugh. I want to cry. I'm bordering on hysteria.

I make my way down the rack, eyes on Raju, hands folded in apology. His perfectly ripped 6'2" body looks up at my 5'3" frame.

'Why didn't you move?' I ask finally.

'I stopped the round,' he says. 'There was a knock; I thought someone was at the door. You didn't hear the sound?'

Stopped? What sound? Have I been that out of it? 'Are you hurt?' I reach for him.

He snorts.

'What is up with you?' he asks, gesturing with his right hand. The southern roll in all its glory.

I shake my head, get on my toes and dust his left cheek before settling on the floor next to him.

My classes with Raju are at my home gym, an hour in the mornings, thrice a week – Tuesdays, Thursdays and Saturdays.

Today is Monday. I had sent him a late-night text, pleading my case to move my Tuesday class to this morning. At five minutes to six, I heard his bike and after that, the rattle of iron gates.

One of the walls of this room with an annexe is made of glass bricks. We are facing it. The other three are red stone. Except for an antique case clock, the plastered walls are bare.

'Aaditha Prathap,' Raju announces. He likes tacking on my father's name to mine every now and then as if it were a condiment he's adding for taste. 'What has happened to you?'

I can read the lines on his otherwise happy face. The more disquieted he is, the brighter his smile becomes.

'A nightmare!' I say.

His brows scrunch, replicating the ruling of a notebook.

I lounge in my room wearing my brightest smile.

My song list is playing... Dua Lipa.

Diamonds under my eyes
Turn the rhythm up, don't you wanna just
Come along for the ride?

An imaginary circlet that reads *Super Proud Mom* is sitting on my head.

COFFEE Before Books & Bras is on the verge of going international. *My baby.* I exhale – a full-body whoosh of joy.

We're in four metros – Chennai, Mumbai, Delhi and Kolkata – plus Bengaluru. We've locked locations at two major tourist destinations – Goa and Jaipur. And if all goes well, we'll be in New York in twelve months.

The intercom cuts through my euphoria, jolting me. It's late.

'We want to chat with you,' Appa says. There's an odd lightness to his voice. 'We are coming to your room.'

I spoke with my parents after I signed the papers, so I'm not sure what this conversation at almost 11 p.m. is going to be about. *Talking* isn't exactly a Prathap family pastime. We show up for each other, yes, but real conversations? Those only happen when something has to be *said*.

Appa is in customary whites, and Amma's sari is a non-committal beige. They are still in their day clothes.

'Is Akka okay?' I ask of Alia, my older sister. We are a decade apart in age and separated by oceans; she lives in sunny California. Her marriage of almost eleven years is as cold as the meat in the freezer. There's a new calm to her voice these days. I don't trust it, but it's better than the silence that filled our conversations.

'Yes.' The breathless answer comes from Amma. Alia is okay. Amma's eyes are bright as she attempts to square her sloped shoulders, the only physical feature of hers I seem to have taken after.

'Aashi,' Appa says, bringing my second name, Asha, into that the mix, before adding with a smile, 'there's...'

He pauses. A second that drags forever.

'Yes?' I urge, my heart pounding. This does not sound good.

'A boy.'

'A boy?' I shriek in horror, knowing fully well what those words mean.

It's part of the curriculum in girls' schools. The chapter is titled 'When your parents tell you there's a boy'. The legend reads shipwrecked. Guidance: Run.

My heart drops to the floor of my stomach and lies there, dead weight.

What are they thinking? I don't want to get into an anodyne arrangement. This family doesn't need another.

Who? Where? Why? The Ws rattle against my parietals. If I ask the question, I ratify the reason they walked in here for, but I need information to put an end to this.

'The boy,' Appa repeats slowly, like he is raising the bidding price at an auction.

'He has a nice, long name – Vedveer Rathore Singh – and he's an excellent young man. I believe royals have long names; it is tradition. Maybe that's why you, too, have a first and second name!'

Appa tries to slip the royal bit casually, but that's the peg he hangs his smile on.

This has got to be a joke!

'He is royal!' Amma joins in, stressing on the 'r'.

A royal? A prince? The last time I checked, we were living in an active democracy! And Appa, Appa is a senior politician!

'He's very nice,' Amma adds, shifting closer to Appa, as if to endorse the recommendation.

That's the thing about arranged matches. 'The boy' is

always bright, dazzling, copybook perfection, but the girl, 'oh the girl', there's always something sour about her. Yin and yang. Light and dark. There's only place for one piece of sublimity in a partnership. The patriarchy has long owned those rights.

Vedveer Rathore Singh. *Wait a second, I've heard this name, read this name...*

Why is Appa breathlessly jumping into another arranged match when his earlier play for his firstborn is coming apart rapidly?

The blood is draining from my face. I hear a jangle of words come at me, flaring before my eyes like teleprinter prompts.

Prince. Jaipur... Engineer from Harvard...

'*Oyi?*' I hear Raju. He wants to know why Appa has not only come up with this alliance but is also nudging me in that direction.

I brace myself. Raju is my friend, but before we became pals, Appa took him off the streets and gave him a life. Raju is nothing if not loyal.

'*Saar* made a good selection,' Raju says. He is nodding. 'Prince who is an engineer, two-in-one.' A supermarket steal deal.

'Get up,' Raju says. He is on his feet, ready to go again.

I lean forward and touch my toes. I stay in that position for a bit. I don't want to get up.

'We could've gone to your café if you wanted to talk,' Raju says. 'I would've got a free apple-carrot muffin at least.'

I laugh. I love that even at a moment like this, Raju doesn't forget 'free'. His 'Nutrition Facts Label'.

This matrimonial business, especially arranged alliances, is messy even at the best of times. For most, that's excuse enough to back out. But in my case, it's a battle I can't win unless I come up with a reason good enough to justify the no.

How can I say no to the one person who has never said no to me, the parent who has always believed in me?

Appa accepted my skeletal entrepreneurial idea when I decided to move continents without completing my graduation. COFFEE Before Books & Bras would not have seen the light of day, not this early at least, had Appa not backed me. He didn't champion my idea thinking his time would come, that there'd be payback one day. He liked the details I laid before him, but more than that, he believed in me.

I owe it to him to give this a fair chance.

Only that marriage is the last thing on my mind. It has been a while since my heart skipped a beat at the sight of someone. A man, a romantic attachment, appears so far out in the distant future, I can't even put a time on it.

'Does your sister know about this?' Raju asks.

'She does...' I shake my head. 'She thinks I should at least meet the guy.'

'This is *oyi* you wanted to work out this morning?' Raju asks. 'So that you could kick me, thinking you are kicking the prince?'

'Khadus Komal this morning would've been too much, dude,' I say.

Komal is my yoga instructor. She's a no-nonsense thirty-seven-year-old who uses her enigmatic smile sparingly. She might've been the perfect antidote for my growing frustration in that she'd guard against the mood swelling, but I don't need one more person telling me to at least meet the man before working up a storm.

'You didn't call Lavanya?' Raju asks of my best friend, the other member of the LBDs, the Lakshmi Bar Devotees group.

I nod.

According to Alia, I have 'two-and-a-half friends'. Lavanya Patil and Raju Mathew; Komal Rao is the half, in that she has the affection but not the inclination.

I left Lavanya a voice note last night but haven't heard from her. She can go without checking her phone forever, especially when she's working. I reach for my phone and dial her. She picks up on the first ring.

'Interesting,' she hums.

'I left you a note.'

'I'm checking him out on Insta.' She adds, 'Fire!'

'I'm going to come up with a plan,' I say with a

confidence I don't feel. 'A plan that will persuade this Jaipur prince to call off the alliance himself.'

'You're assuming he's on board with your dad's plan?' asks Lavanya of the many accents. Right now, it's the New York twang. It can change in the next few seconds.

'That right there is an out! That's why you are my bestie!'

I'm practically screaming. It startles Raju, who is beside me.

Which of-the-times, hotshot royal would ever agree to an arranged match so out of his orbit?

I feel a surge of hope, but the relief is brief, too brief. Because Appa can't be making plans with the desert air.

'I'm meeting him in two weeks' time, Monday after the next.' I sigh.

'Confirmed?' Lavanya asks.

'Yeah.'

Raju looks at me with a mix of excitement and alarm. 'Date set!' he says.

'Wait a minute! Is this a *roka* in two weeks?' Lavanya asks, her voice climbing decibels.

'What?' My heart is sinking. 'No way! What *roka*?' The alarm bells in my head go off.

Raju's laugh is bouncing off the walls. '*Roka* means engagement?' he asks. 'Say again, his name?'

'How does it matter?' I snap, holding the phone away from me.

'Are you with Raju?' Lavanya asks.

I put my phone on speaker when Raju announces, 'Vedveer Rathore Singh.'

'Do you have a plan to get me out of this mess?' I turn to Raju.

'No!' Raju smiles, his teeth sparkling.

'How about we find you a man?' Lavanya says. 'Some model type, who we all will vouch for. We'll tell your parents you two have been a couple for a year already.'

The idea is entertaining. I laugh.

'I'll shop on Insta and send you boyfriend options,' Lavanya adds. 'I recommend an equal degree of fire.'

'I'm not part of this plan,' Raju says, throwing up his arms as he makes his way to the door.

All I need is a believable plan. No pressure.

2.

Vedveer

Just Another Royal Morning, Until…

I EASE OFF THE TRACK; MY STRIDES HAVE SLOWED TO a shuffle, and my arms drop to the side. The morning breeze is working on my face, drying the moisture, as I make my way through the inside gates, inhaling the wholesome scent of frangipani in bloom.

The hedge shearers are on their feet; one of them is cutting the crisp morning air, aimlessly jamming wooden handles.

I've just finished a 15 km run; my watch says I did it in just under seventy minutes. The time is neither good nor bad for me.

The morning mist hangs low as it tends to this time of the year in Jaipur. The Indian winter is still receding in early February. North-western, I specify. I spent a good part of my formative years in the south, where the change in seasons could be harsh but with a whole different momentum and time.

'*Hukum*.' Pranav, the butler's gaze meets mine with an unspoken message: The maharaj is here. I nod, thinking, 'There goes my post-run stretching.'

I reach for the towel Pranav presents me with. The tray he carries is shined to a sparkle. I pull my tracks over my running shorts before picking up my unzipped jacket.

I hear Father's voice. The gardeners have heard him, too, which is why they are on their feet.

'Vedveer,' (audible pause) 'Vedveer,' (audible pause) 'Vedveer Rathore Singh!'

The pause is tetchy; waiting isn't his style. When he wants something, it has to appear before him right that very moment. The urgency is heightened by the cock crowing somewhere on these endless grounds.

The crew working on colourful beds of dahlias drop their tools and stand up. A little behind the men in green uniforms, swords of gladioli sway to a beat of their own. Only a couple of ducks are upright, flapping their wings in the pond. The rest have their heads bent backwards, catching a nap before their next meal.

The king is in the palace, not a common occurrence with this Rathore, who has a greater affinity for his New Delhi residence than Ranibagh, the seat of his throne, dubbed by a travel magazine as the Palace of Dreams. He is at Ranibagh only that many times in a year, and it's almost always for an occasion, a duty that he must carry out. Mahashivratri, for which the family gathers here, is weeks away.

Everyone on the grounds has heard Gaurav Rathore Singh, but we have yet to spot him.

'Vedveer, Vedveer Rathore Singh!'

Father's voice can rattle doors. His accent, typically British, received pronunciation, commands a ring of authority.

Whenever Father wants to have a word with me, he uses my full name. All three parts of it. We've been having a lot of talks lately. Is that why he is here, for another conversation? A telephone call would have sufficed, as it has these last couple of weeks when we demolished data. Gaurav Rathore Singh finally emerges into the open, walking out through a side entrance. He is in traditional gear, kurta and pyjamas, something of a uniform when he visits Ranibagh. The colour is brick red, and the kurta is edged in bold streaks of Leheriya.

I spot Holiday and Hope, the Shih Tzus, bounce along behind their master, yapping at his heel, enjoying the busiest morning of their lives, looking to make trouble for everyone. Even when in Ranibagh, they are rarely let out in the gardens at the rear, which are larger than the other patches of lawn, making it easy for them to disappear.

'There you are, Yuvraj!' he says, ambling across the open space, wearing a broad smile.

'Father.'

He pauses, running his hands over his kurta. His cheeks reflect the colour of his attire. Despite the traits that mark him out as a rebel, there are things local he is committed to. Among them are artisans and their craft.

His skin crinkles as he smiles, but his eyes don't light up. Usually, they dazzle like the lights at Ranibagh, which are turned on at 6 p.m. from March through to September and an hour earlier in the winter. Not this morning, though. He probably hasn't slept the whole night because of the travel in the early hours.

The people around him are energetic: staff scurrying about, a couple of them carrying servers, some wearing troubled expressions and others randomly swinging their arms, hoping to see and be seen. One of them swoops down on Holiday and Hope before I have a chance to get to the Shih Tzus, who are letting their annoyance be heard.

'How was your run?' Father asks but doesn't wait for an answer. He is shielding his eyes from the morning sun, which is yet to make its presence felt at almost nine. As he turns away, I notice a trickle of sweat running down his face, one more trail and then another. I feel my body tense. What is the matter? Why has Father made this unscheduled trip to Ranibagh?

'Where's Mother?' I ask.

He shrugs, surprised by the question. I point at his face. My expression is a giant question mark, but Father chooses to ignore it. He flicks his wrist, dismissing the staff, who are carrying the powder room on their arms. Cold towels, face tissues, sanitizer… they have it all.

Father turns to scan the surroundings, nodding in the direction of the gazebo in the eastern corner. The manpower whose hands are free rush to set the place in order. The king is not only in residence, but he is asking to be seated in a garden on his grounds he has only just discovered.

Father has a vitamin D deficiency. He has been advised by his physician to walk bare-chested outdoors to get some sun in the first half of the day. His response is a late-evening, fifteen-minute laze by the pool. He wasn't always like this, averse to physical pursuits. I've heard tales of his hunting skills as a young man, a crack shot with a bullseye reputation. Father retired from the outdoors in his late forties, hanging up his personalized hunting rifle and turning into a bibliophile. These days, he devours fiction of every hue. Academics isn't his suit; whisky and cricket on television is his thing.

He once mulled an off-road, high-power Mini to get around indoors. From his quarters to his study, I suppose. Mother shot down the suggestion with such overriding alacrity that her husband was sufficiently silenced.

I watch as he lets himself down on the cushioned seat.

His eyes are on me, my puffer vest, which I have zipped all the way to my throat, white tracks and grey running shoes. He's waiting for the staff, who are laying the tray on the table, to finish and leave. Whatever the reason for his jetting across to Jaipur is, it can't be shared before the palace staff, who are well versed with the rules we hold dear on these grounds: Hear nothing, say nothing.

As Pranav bends to fill our cups, I hear a yelp, then

another, then a shout. '*Arey unhein pakadiyein.*' It carries across the grounds. 'Haallleeedaaayyyy… Haaaapeeee.'

Holiday and Hope are speeding away on the freshly manicured lawn.

An army of uniformed men chases them. Not far from the pets, a driverless lawnmower hurtles down a landscaped slope, heading in the direction of the Shih Tzus. I'm on my feet when Pranav straightens his back abruptly and goes headlong into another of the staff, dislodging the lid of the teapot and turning the remnants of freshly brewed tea on himself. I manage to glove the lid seconds before the piece of china hits the ground.

I lurch towards the lawn when I hear Father's shout. I hold my step as staff lock down on the pets. The lawnmower hits a brick parapet and comes to a halt.

As I settle into the seat before Father, I notice that he's nervous. His left eye is twitching, and his index finger brushes against his nose, going back and forth.

'You are so quick and aware of everything around you, Veer. Nothing misses your eye, especially in the outdoors,' he says. 'I don't understand why you didn't take to hunting. You'd have been excellent.'

I nod.

If Father had his way, I'd have been named Vedveer 'Michael' Rathore Singh. Michael in honour of the elegant West Indian fast bowler Michael Anthony Holding, whose exploits Father once followed with studious diligence.

'Veer, we need to talk,' he says after tasting his morning tea.

I raise a brow, picking up my cup and inhaling the soothing scent of oolong.

'There's a proposal,' he says. He returns his cup to the tray and is looking at his palm now.

'Excellent!' I respond quickly; this is indeed a first. 'You're here for business!' This is urgent, and his travel in the early hours is fully justified.

'Not that kind of proposal,' he says, cutting through my train of thought.

'Oh!' I nod. 'A matrimonial alliance for Navya?'

My only sibling, a younger sister, is in love with a cricketer, an opening batsman for India. A tall, good-looking chap named Nalin Shah, who is on a hot streak. Only his reputation precedes him.

Father looks around him, clearing his throat. 'Not for Navya; this one is for you,' he says slowly.

I look him in the eye, and he's holding my gaze.

'We have a marriage proposal for you, Veer.'

'Ookaaay,' I return, not knowing what to make of his declaration. It's not the first. These alliances are generally mentioned during a meal whenever the family convenes and are promptly forgotten.

'What kind of a response is that?' Father is unusually sharp in going for the accelerator.

Silence, I decide, is a better option.

I'm beginning to feel the effects of this morning's run. It has sapped me, leaving me on reserve, more than I bargained for. It isn't just today. I have been at it for a while, and my body has been begging for a break. I make a quick decision against showing up at the Polo Club later in the afternoon.

'We have a marriage proposal for you, Yuvraj.' His eyes are on me now. 'And a very good one at that!' he adds with a smile. 'Lovely girl, great family.'

I place my teacup on the table and try not to laugh. My lips twitch.

'This is serious, Veer,' he says, shuffling in his seat. 'This works for us.'

I hear the morning wind rustle through the branches of the *dhok* trees that lean into the garden.

'This fits us perfectly.' Father is sweating profusely.

'What do you mean by "fits us"? And why are we reacting this way?' I ask. 'You are rushing.'

The Rathores have made an art form of taking time; if there's any doubt, see how we move. Glacial is our pace.

'She's a south Indian, and she lives in Bengaluru,' he says, looking at me intently. Pranav steps forward with a hand fan, but Father tells him off and shuts his eyes for a moment.

I feel my brows scrunching.

Marriage is inevitable in my position. I have responsibilities, heir, spare and all that, but not now.

'I was told about this family, the Gawdas; they're very respectable people. I approached them.' He is sitting up in his seat and speaks softly.

What? Father approached this family from halfway across the country, the Gowdas? He, Gaurav Rathore Singh, made the first move?

'It's okay,' I say after a while. It is time to play Father. 'Just because you approached them doesn't mean we have to go through with it. We can tell them we're not ready. That's the truth, right?'

He smiles and shakes his head. 'Why don't you meet her,' he says. It isn't a question. 'Get to know her.'

'Who is she?'

Father takes a sip of his tea and puts down the cup before wrapping his arms around his chest.

"She's the daughter of a senior politician.'

A politician! 'Name?'

'He is Prathap Gawdaji from Karnataka.'

I know who he's talking about; I have read about him. I'm not particularly enthused by politics, but I'm aware. Not everything I have read about Gowda printed in mainstream media is complimentary. I have also heard of Prathap Gowda for his coffee brand – COFFEE Before Books & Bras. His daughter is apparently the front for the business.

'Aaditha Prathap,' he says.

The name has been doing the rounds in business circles, but I can't put a face to it.

'She has a coffee business. You drink coffee, right?'

I'm laughing now, and the sound is roiling my father. I'm a tea drinker; it is what we are enjoying at this moment.

I have the occasional coffee, but I've never had Gowda's coffee.

'At least you will have good coffee to drink every day.' I hear him exhale and watch as his brows shift in exaggerated appreciation. 'Great coffee!'

Why disabuse him of his idea of the match, because that is all it is going to be – an idea. I'm equally determined.

'It's Gowda, not Gawda, please.'

'Is that how I pronounced his name?' Father's laugh carries in the morning air. 'Gowda,' he says, 'that's right?'

I nod.

'I like that you're keen I get the pronunciation right,' Father says, smiling. 'It's a good match,' he continues, nodding some more. 'You should meet the girl.'

'Good for whom? I'm not even thinking of marriage.' I'm surprised at how calm I sound.

'In every sense, it's a good match.'

I search his face for a reason to believe he is pranking me, but all I get is an expression that tells me he's on edge. He's fully aware that I'm looking at our lands, making plans to expand our agrarian projects.

'It's good. This is a very good proposal,' he says.

'Okay!' I exhale. I need to take charge and change course.

'You are okay with the proposal!' He's smiling ear to ear now.

'No! I'm not okay with getting married now; you should know better,' I say. 'Tell me you're joking, Father!'

Nothing against Prathap Gowda or his daughter. Marriage is where I don't want to go now, not for a while anyway.

'What do you mean?'

Could he be losing his mind? His shoulders drop, and his spine slackens. He's looking at his feet now.

'You know I don't want to marry for some time at least.'

Father turns away.

When our eyes meet, I see what may have triggered the rivulets that are flowing freely down his face. He has walked in here expecting me to stand my ground; he is aware the timing is off for me and that I'm determined to pursue our green dream. He's desperate to convince me. The monarch was not only looking at a proposal from outside the community for his only son, the heir to his throne, but he has taken an extreme step in his search. He has made the first move, and he is going to hold authority – father over son, king over heir – over me.

Father pulls himself up from the chair and walks up to me, unbuckling his diamond-studded watch in the two steps he takes to get to me. (He rarely wears this timepiece but has made the effort to wear it today.) He wraps it around my wrist.

'What are you doing?'

'What do you say?' he asks, ignoring my question. He steps back and looks at my wrist admiringly. 'We go to Bengaluru in a couple of weeks?'

'We can't go ahead with this,' I tell him. He is at the edge of the gazebo, and my eyes are on his back. 'I'm not even thinking of marriage. I have stuff to do before I marry.'

Father is on the pebbled pathway of the lawn. He has called for a buggy to drive him to the rear entrance of his palace.

I return to the garden furniture and look across the lawn at the colourful crotons. Someone has to give, and it isn't going to be me.

I pull out my phone and start scrolling before tossing it away.

Why would Aaditha Prathap want to go ahead with this proposal? An arranged match? She's young, wealthy and supposedly successful. Why would she want to get married into something so traditional and antiquated?

I bury my face in my palms. Did someone spike the oolong leaves, or did I just hear all that?

What is even happening?

3.

Aaditha
Cue the Meltdown

IT IS 10 A.M., AND I'M LYING ON MY BACK, EYES FIXED ON the ceiling. I'm in denim shorts and a cropped white tee; beside me, a chiffon salwar kurta, in a shade of milk cream, is neatly laid out, ready to be worn. My phone is on my stomach, face down.

The setting is just about right for someone scheduled to swipe in for a noon shift, but me, I'm stalling the day.

Workout: ☑

Shower: ☑

Breakfast: ☑

Journal: *Pause.*

I ticked boxes at regular speed, on schedule to get to my work desk by 8 a.m. My time to caffeinate and journal, but Amma wouldn't hear of it.

'Not today,' she whispered into my ear. Her voice was hoarse with hope. 'You can go later, after they leave.'

If anyone is wondering, yeah, they're the Royals. And I've been given permission to live my life once they leave. Hurrah!

The household is on high alert, help everywhere, lifting a pot, straightening a pillow, shifting furniture around, wiping an invisible layer of dust. Every now and then, you hear them – *'idalla, adu', 'heccu hoova'*. Every vase in the house is holding flowers, even those that haven't held a stem since Alia's wedding over a decade ago, which was not long after we moved here.

Even the second floor, a dead space in our home, is showing signs of life. Doors and windows are thrown open, giving the space a sun-kissed facade.

We live in a 10,000-square-foot house on Mahatma Gandhi Road. The location is not where Bengaluru's old money lives, nor is it where the powerful reside. Our home is a statement, an announcement that garners immediate attention. The sand-coloured stucco exteriors and high-rise walls might give it a palatial air, but it is more than that. Located at that precise juncture where power meets money. Newly minted.

My first steps were on slate-grey mosaic tiles, the other word for proletariat. That patchwork composite, along with the plastic indoor plants and the rainbow-hued walls of our old home, is imprinted in my memory. Two bedrooms for four people who had time for each other. The texture of my childhood. Here, in this vast space, we run into each other sometimes.

I'm expecting Lavanya to come bursting through my bedroom door any moment, spouting a hundred words a minute in some twang or the other. She has already landed in Bengaluru from Mumbai. Her message tells me that.

Lovey: *With you in a hurry.*

Like a fortress under siege, I feel pressure pressing in from every direction.

When my parents told me about the proposal two weeks ago, I was seething. But the anger quickly curdled into fear, the kind that makes your knees knock. Most days since, I've swung between those two emotions, all while wondering if I'm slowly losing my mind, thanks to parents who clearly have no idea what they're doing.

Initially, I thought it was just the two of us meeting, Vedveer and I. Two people, who I'm sure want this alliance to disappear so that they can get on with their respective lives as soon as possible. How long will it take for two smart people to come up with an exit plan?

A week later, I hear the Rathores – father, mother and son – will be here. There's a sister in the mix, but fortunately, she has a life. Of course, the family would be here; they are royals. They tread gently on a red carpet called tradition, while the rest of us arrive bouncing on a trampoline, juggling ten things at a time.

I spoke to Lavanya shortly after and asked her to bring her lovely self back to Bengaluru. I need my bestie with me today.

There's a tug at the pit of my stomach, a feeling that is keeping me company late into the evenings and nudging me awake earlier than usual.

We are new money, wealth of the shiny-new address that is becoming a landmark for all things recent, unlike the Rathores, who are as old as old money gets. Even I could go back to the time when we had little, with Appa working round the clock, trying to make ends meet.

The Rathores live in an *actual* palace. It is where they have lived for generations; even the walls know their family tree. According to the internet, they are the most landed royals in India.

So, why me?

Why would Vedveer Rathore Singh – of endless land and limitless wealth – want to marry me? I'm not even a blip on the society circuit, never mind a feature. He could have any woman on the planet. And judging by social media, he pretty much has – models, an actor, a human rights lawyer, a doctor, an heiress, a duke's daughter, society women, the works. Surely, there's someone closer to his world? A Rajput princess, maybe?

Sometimes, I think I don't even need to rack my brains to figure out how to say no to Appa; Vedveer of the bottomless coffers will probably do it for me.

I pull myself up from the bed slowly, wearing a forced smile. In the morning, Raju made me practise the bow, an exaggerated gesture to lighten the mood. We repeat the drill twelve times, holding breath and posing for fifteen seconds. He even clicked a picture of me in action. I look constipated!

I discard my shorts and pull on the salwar kurta. Just

as I reach for the kajal stick, Lavanya walks in, moaning about the security search the team from the palace insisted on for anyone entering our home.

She tosses her overnight case on my bed, which tells me she has not stopped at her apartment. It isn't far from where we live.

She takes my hands in hers, saying, 'Are you okay? I can't believe this. I really can't!' Lavanya's breath hasn't caught up with her. Her bun is coming undone over her indigo kurta. She looks just as shaken as I probably do.

Lavanya is kneeling in front of me, holding my gaze. She's wearing gold hoops in her ears and a single diamond bangle on her wrist. They are her designs.

'Why not a fake model?' she asks. I give her a weak smile. If there's anyone who knows how much I owe Appa, it is this 5'9" being, one of the pillars of my life. Lavanya is not trifling; she's trying to lift my mood.

'Supermodel is the criteria.' I play along.

Lavanya laughs. 'You've got this,' she says.

I nod. Not because I have any greater clarity or understanding of the situation I'm in, but because, at this moment, there's not much I can do to get out of this without embarrassing my parents.

'He's got to want out of this mess,' I tell Lavanya.

'There's a chance,' she says. Her nod tells me she's not fully convinced.

I feel the silence that settles on our home of three levels. The movement has stopped along with the chatter; everyone is waiting for the guests to arrive.

Amma walks into my room wearing a nervous smile. She's draped in a turquoise blue Kanjeevaram that matches her name, Neela. Her face is without a dot of make-up. After dropping a kiss on Lavanya's head, she takes a place beside us. Amma turns abruptly to Lavanya and says, 'You should make her understand that this is a very good proposal.'

'She's the best, Aunty,' Lavanya says. 'Anyone who gets her must walk between raindrops.'

Amma beams but is unmoved. 'Age is crucial. There's a time for everything in life.'

Lavanya nods and turns to me.

I'm grateful that my mother, who has no filter, didn't add, *Otherwise, Aaditha, too, will be thirty and single.*

The Rathores, I suspect, will ride the lift to the second floor, which is designed like a clubhouse, complete with guest rooms. It is built for parties we haven't hosted. The walls of our home are bare for the most part, more so on the second floor – no artwork or photographs. The flooring is marble, edged with gold, the main room has big windows, and the sofas are plush. That is all I remember of the space in my house, which I may have stepped into three or four times.

Amma is on her feet suddenly. It is almost 11 a.m.; the Rathores will arrive shortly.

'I'll hang here until you're done, and we'll head out together,' Lavanya tells me as I pull myself up. 'I want to think he'll want an out too...'

I nod. 'Is that our best bet?'

'We can make him hate you! Come on, show us some of that Aaditha sass!'

There are four animated people in the room – the maharaj, the maharani and my dear parents. They are all wearing broad smiles and sparking an effusive energy.

The two ladies have not uttered a significant word. They are beaming, nodding and agreeing with everything their husbands are saying. The other two people in this room of generous dimensions, the dude in a duck-egg-blue suit included, have other places they'd rather be.

For all the currents – the nascent and the strong – running through me these past two weeks while contemplating what this proposal could do to my life, this happy vibe is the one pressing against my trachca. I'm suffocating. It isn't just Amma and Appa who want this alliance to work; the other set of parents match tones. But why? The question pokes at me, not for the first time.

The three Gowdas in residence were in position when the Rathores entered. The visitors were also three in number. They weren't accompanied by walkie-talkie-powered security details, though a small army of men in charcoal grey had come to secure the premises at No. 5 MG Road before their arrival.

I stand up to greet the guests and am contemplating

returning my rear to the sofa when Maharani Gauri Elena (that's how she is introduced) takes hold of a gold-coloured tray from a liveried attendant, who has just walked through the doorway.

Gauri Elena steps forward in my direction, her expression sunny. I turn nervously to Amma, not knowing what to do. Amma nods before taking my hand in hers and moving it forward to accept the tray bearing gifts.

The word *roka* stings my mind; a shiver goes down my back.

The platter, covered in gold net, is carrying what looks like a large jewellery box. It is placed carefully on the table between Amma and Appa, away from me. I look down at my toes and force myself not to think of the tray. The situation can be handled, I remind myself. I have an ally in Vedveer Rathore Singh, though at this point it is only imaginary. I need to push the right buttons, and he'll bow out of this alliance.

We are seated opposite each other. The men occupy independent seats, and the two women and their offspring are in roomy two-seaters. Our eyes haven't met, but from his profile, which exceeds the pictures on social media, I can tell that this is one I would drag and drop in the supermodel folder. Not that looks or the lack of it changes anything.

I was clear at the outset itself that I'm not making a dramatic entry, balancing a tray and tripping over the hand-knotted carpet. Amma argued relentlessly, saying there wasn't going to be a tray; I was only required to walk, one foot in front of the other; they were royals. I stood my ground. This was for me; I was not taking chances. I was not about to wipe the floor with my abs with an audience in attendance.

I was warned not to carry my phone with me. It is in my tote, feeling abandoned.

The brocade curtains are drawn back, and the mid-morning light floods the room. The senior Rathore blinks; the light is too harsh for him, perhaps. My smile broadens at the sight, not because I find it funny, which I would have in normal circumstances, but because my anxiety is triggering strong reactions.

After the initial exchange of greetings, which between Vedveer and me is a couple of nods and half-hearted half-smiles, which I suspect is because neither want to appear interested (hugely encouraging), the conversation swings to geopolitics.

The senior Rathore, who is introduced simply as the maharaj, and Appa are chatting merrily, like old acquaintances. Appa, being Appa (read over-enthusiastic), tries to draw Vedveer into the conversation but is met with little or no success. Some of the baits are ridiculously plain, a cheery *What do you think, Yuvraj?* A question that may have got a nod or a smile for an answer. I don't know because I'm not looking.

And why is Appa calling him Yuvraj? Doesn't he have a name? So what if his father calls him Yuvraj? You are not his dad!

Gauri Elena's posture defines angles; her legs are folded to the side, knees touching and back erect. Her bejewelled hands are locked in a gentle clasp on her lap. She is in ivory, top to toe, a silk kurta with delicate gold embroidery. A painter's muse.

If she and I were papped, like her son regularly is, the annotation would have the word 'twinning' somewhere in it.

Amma is comfortable; her long arms are wrapped around her right knee, and she is gently rocking back and forth in her seat. She is working off nervous energy. Her head is positioned such that she has everyone except her daughter in full view. A thick string of Mangaluru *mallige* adorns her thick bun. Amma is bathed in my perfume. She had forgotten to spray herself and so helped herself to generous pumps of jasmine when she dropped by my room – not that she needed it with the flowers in her hair. That is the only fragrance I could tell in a room of mixed scents.

As our long-standing help, Yellamma, rolls the coffee cart into the room, Gauri Elena blinks before her lips lift in a smile. Is she missing her glares? Yellamma's sari sparks more colours than a Deepawali evening. My nickname for our much-loved Yellamma is '*Yella* colour'.

Yellamma is among the first helps Amma hired twenty years ago. Initially, she only did the cleaning, but as Appa's stock soared and we moved to a larger space, she started cooking, too. Now she's the housekeeper. Yellamma is in her brightest sari today, and her smile matches the drape every inch.

Yellamma, on whom every pair of eyes in the room is fixed, pauses in the middle. She tilts her head in my direction, holds up her hand and says, 'Baby, *tumba muddu*.' Very cute.

Only because it is Yellamma, I didn't wish the floors below me open and swallow me. I beam her my first smile of the morning; it is most likely my last for this AM.

Vedveer's eyes meet mine for the first time this morning, and his lips break into a smile. I don't think he, like his parents, understands what Yellamma is saying, but he, unlike them, has read the expression. No returning smiles, I'm determined.

Appa takes over from Yellamma, and Vedveer is on his feet too, handing out the beverages. Freshly baked cookies and muffins are passed around, with thank yous and pleases tossed about, but no one is touching a thing, not even the melt-in-the-mouth Mysore Pak. 'Too early to eat,' the senior Rathore says, adding that they are not a family who eats breakfast together.

Harmonious, I think, until I notice a teapot in the mix; there are teacups, too. I wonder if it is just an option or if there is indeed a tea drinker in the room.

Gauri Elena takes a sip of her bone-dry cappuccino and looks pointedly at me. She takes another sip and is glaring at me now. Are we about to come to blows?

'Excellent coffee,' she says, just as I'm about to burst

from holding my breath. She then turns to her husband and adds, 'The best I've had in a while!'

Wow! Thankfully, I only exclaimed that in my head. I try to hold back, but the smile slips out anyway.

The senior Rathore returns my sunny expression, while his son grins at his cup. I'm beginning to think he's human, but I dismiss the thought immediately. I'm not getting reeled in to that narrative.

'That's exactly what I was telling Veer,' the senior Rathore says, shaking his plump index finger.

I like this couple so much at this moment, I'm willing to exchange parents with Vedveer.

Appa's office had coordinated with the palace staff for the choice of beverages. A couple of days ago, Appa told me Gauri Elena likes her coffee just the way I drink mine.

That is my cue to ask how Vedveer likes his coffee.

I don't want to know how Vedveer has his coffee or his protein supplement. Given the size of his wrists, he is into this stuff. But I'm not playing this game.

I take a sip of the coffee Amma has handed me.

The man of the moment, posturing in dark-tan dress shoes, sips his coffee from a teacup. Like his mother, he is sitting square, while Amma and I are logged in a slouching match. I long to pull my legs up, fold them beside me and sip my beverage leisurely, just like I do in my office every morning.

This is my first cup of coffee, the one I enjoy more than the others I consume in the course of the day. I deliberately saved it for later today, for when I needed reinforcements.

Vedveer is looking around the room, perhaps wondering why the walls are bare. He drops his gaze and catches me looking at him. I force a smile.

'Why don't the children have a word with each other?' That is Appa, but why 'children'?

I study the diminishing mixture in my cup, thinking I'm better off not letting my gaze wander.

The senior Rathore coughs gently. 'We are leaving today,' he says, turning to his wife, 'but Veer will stay on. Perhaps they can meet later in the evening or even in the morning, before he flies out?'

I raise my head in time to catch Vedveer turn to his father and nod.

It feels like I'm in a theatre watching a stage performance. Only, I'm part of the cast.

This evening, I have a date with Lavanya. I'm not about to change that. A quick coffee tomorrow morning works fine. Vedveer and I need to talk. He is going to tell me he isn't interested in this alliance, and he will convey the same to the king and queen. Why he hasn't already done that, I have no idea, but I have faith in Yuvraj.

Vedveer is loved on the internet. He is everywhere; the same with his sister and her boyfriend, all great-looking people. *TittleTattle* does a piece on Vedveer every time he steps out with a new girl, and he has been stepping out with new and very alluring arm candies.

Social media's vituperative bite is for me. A rich father's daughter; what else can she be? Limited.

I'm fully aware that if not for my generous billionaire father, I could still be stuck deep in the Midwest, figuring matrix algebra and linear programming in the arid hope that I could eke out a decent living one day.

According to cyberbullies, my dad is my ATM. The higher the COFFEE Before Books & Bras graph rises, the more convinced the trolls are of my money-sucking, parasitic traits.

Yellamma – bangles clinking, anklets singing – enters the room again to announce, 'Sir, photographer *bandiddare*.' She is addressing Appa.

No one has told me anything about a photographer. I turn to Amma, who is looking at Appa.

Why is there a photographer here? What photo could possibly be needed? It's not like we're on a cruise ship in the middle of the Mediterranean.

Gauri Elena is pointing at the decorative fireplace at the far end of the room. The mantelpiece is covered with photographs of the family, including one of Alia's wedding, a reminder to its residents of how proficient we are in getting this business of arranged matches wrong.

'We can use the light to suit us,' she is saying, taking demure steps and gesturing with her long, delicate fingers.

I'm momentarily distracted by her accent, which is a mix of British and Eastern European.

The men get on their feet belatedly, while I refuse to move. Why am I the only one protesting? Why is Vedveer standing?

I'm opening out my right hand and balling it up. I don't know how long I do this, but I feel my parents' gaze on me. My anxiety therapist recommended I take deep breaths. One. Two. Three.

I decide to play along for the moment. These are my parents, and I will talk to them as soon as this royal circus exits No. 5 MG Road.

Appa is walking towards the fireplace, and Amma is following him. I'm on my feet, too; my eyes are on Vedveer's back.

'Right here,' Gauri Elena is saying to me, her eyes bright.

I'm doing everything I can to control myself and not ask the question that is maiming my insides. What is happening even?

I inhale, and my nerves are momentarily soothed by the woody scent from my right until… 'Aadheethhaa.' The voice is soft and full, but the phonetics drill a hole in my head.

I nod, but maybe I should've said 'Ra-Tho-Ray, Ra-Tho-Ray' and broken into a dance, Ra-Tho-Ray style.

Vedveer's eyes are bright, and his face is relaxed.

'Closer, please,' the photographer is saying. How much

closer? I can smell the man's perfume, for god's sake, and I'm sure he has inhaled more than a whiff of Jo Malone's Jasmine.

'Maybe, sir,' the photographer isn't giving up, 'you can put your hand on maydam.'

'May I?' Vedveer asks, before putting an arm around my shoulder. His voice is deep and distinct.

His fingers press gently on my forearms, and his breath fans my cheeks. I'm encased in a 6 ft something frame. My smile pops involuntarily.

I'm grateful that Lavanya had wittingly pushed me to wear my nude stilettoes. Wear flats, she told me! Vedveer towers over me, and I need the three inches my footwear lends me.

We pose for three photos, each more awkwardly staged than the last. The photographer and his assistant direct us like we're on the cover of the *Royal Couples* annual. Thankfully, the parent's, Gauri Elena in particular, get distracted after the first snap and stop micromanaging our elbows.

My eyes are on Vedveer, and he nods, just the slightest tilt of his head, before I link my hand through his.

'It's okay, it's just a photograph,' he says when we are done. His voice is soft, and his tone is kind.

'Thank you,' I exhale. His warm breath strokes the top of my ear, and his gaze is on my hair.

I turn to join Amma on the sofa when I hear the senior Rathore speak.

'The palace will release this picture with a two-line announcement that Ahadheethaa and Veer are to wed.'

Wed? My eyes widen in horror, and my face breaks into a violent smile. F@#king wed?

Had I not been blown away by what I had just heard, I might've strangled the man for the way he pronounced my name. He just bettered his son. No exchanging parents, thank you! These folks are equally problematic.

My eyes meet Vedveer's square. I'm silently pleading. *You don't want this; please say so, say something, anything...*

Vedveer's lips twitch. I look away.

There's something about those eyes; he is trying to tell me something. A couple of minutes pass when my eyes find his again. They are differently coloured. The right is grey, and the left is green. That is the mesmerizing part.

'I think we should hold the announcement for a bit,' Vedveer says, turning to his father.

My smile is less violent as I look into my empty cup, which I pick up only to keep my hands busy. Yuvraj has saved the day, but tomorrow, we will need to come up with concrete blueprints.

TittleTattle

Gupshup Column

RANIBAGHS IN BENGALURU (CALLING TECH SUPPORT!)

Curious so-and-so,

Soooo, the BBJ 787 carrying the Rathore insignia landed in Bengaluru today. Only for a moment, TT wondered why they were in the IT capital. For tech support, obviously. What else does one do there?

Then the doors of that hunky toy opened, and the Ranibaghs, all of them, save for HRH Navya Mrinalini, walked out looking sharper than Bengaluru's January sun. Stamped in royal sheen.

The Prince was in an ice-blue tuxedo, while his mother, HRH Gauri Elena, was in a vanilla-hued silk suit with thread embroidery in a dull gold, and his father wore a sherwani of a similar hue.

They touched down at about 10 a.m. and shortly after disappeared into the city, we think.

The Ranibaghs were overdressed, which is the norm for them, but... And, why Bengaluru? The poor dears, don't even know what dress up means down there.

Who or what do you think the Rathores of Ranibagh were dressed for? Extremely sus, wouldn't you say?

TT is tempted to declare they're here to close a business deal, maybe an IT project they're looking at. We hear they're leaving this evening.

According to Palace insiders, the gorgeous heiress from Jodhpur, Kairi Gaur, is still the lady in the dashing Prince's life. There's talk in society circles of an engagement announcement this month.

Kairi Gaur, who walked the ramp for luxury brands when studying in Paris, is HRH Navya Mrinalini's bestie and has been the constant on the Prince's sculpted arms this past year. Kairi is a fashion icon and looking to take over the family's engineering business.

TT wonders if there's a clue right there, darlings?

The last time the delicious love birds were spotted together was at the Four Hundred Club in Delhi, where they were seen leaving with a group of friends. Kairi was in a red dress that outlined her body, and they looked quite the pair with the Prince's arm wrapped lightly around her tiny waist.

1.

Vedveer

All-Action Day in Bengaluru!

I'm lounging in the Presidential Suite on the nineteenth floor of Kempe Crown, the iconic hotel that also houses the flagship Prathap's Café. I'm considering a run.

The January sun is unusually sharp this afternoon; late evening may just be right. I could go to Cubbon Park, take a couple of loops around the park and run back. It looks good on the map.

I message Ratan Singh, my secretary, who taps on the open door a few seconds later.

'Give me thirty minutes, Yuvrajji. I have to organize the support riders,' he says.

Is that a threat?

I glance at Ratan, who has known me since I was a boy. He's staring at his phone, clearly trying not to laugh.

Any remaining ambition to go for a run vanishes at the mention of support riders. I want to run, not headline a circus parade.

I start scrolling through my phone, looking for options

that don't involve an entourage, when a *TittleTattle* alert pops up, a photo of me arriving in Bengaluru. Perfect.

I toss the phone aside just as the doorbell chimes. The green smoothie, probably.

Ratan looks irritated when he appears at my door with a serving tray in hand a couple of minutes later.

'Yuvrajji,' he says, clearing his throat. 'There are two female staff members outside, requesting a photograph with you.'

Ratan knows I don't encourage this kind of attention when I'm on personal work. If he's bringing it up anyway, it must be for a good reason. I follow him to the door.

'Just one photograph, please, and off you go!' Ratan says to the beaming duo outside. 'I'll take it on my phone and share it with one of you.'

He's authoritative and clearly in charge. I stay back.

'Do you like it here in Bengaluru, sir?' one of the girls asks brightly.

Ratan's jaw tightens. He doesn't enjoy being spoken over mid-logistics.

'You're so nice, sir. Is this your first visit to our Bengaluru?' the other adds, grinning.

'Please line up quickly, or I'll ask Yuvrajji to go back,' Ratan says firmly but politely.

'May I come on the other side, sir?' one girl asks, already stepping forward.

'No,' Ratan says immediately. 'Both of you stand together.'

I offer a smile as we get into position. 'Thank you, ladies,' I say. 'And yes, it's my first time in Bengaluru.'

The photo is taken in under ten seconds, though somehow, it feels longer.

Once we're back inside, Ratan looks at me, a little apologetic.

'Sorry about that,' he says.

'It's fine. You only threatened to send me back once!'

I take a tour of the floor and arrive at a sunroom. I stand there staring at the rather large plunge pool. It is thirty metres long. The water is inviting. I look around me; it is just me and the water. I strip down to my underwear and jump in.

I need to crunch my thoughts, and I do it best when it is accompanied by cardio. Beta endorphin is my fuel.

My decision to stay on in Bengaluru was taken in the eleventh hour. When I first heard of this Gowda proposal, I hoped it would wash away. There are two weeks to go, time enough, I thought. But when everyone around me starts making plans, I'm forced to act.

I dial Aaditha because we are in an epoch where technology has simplified communication to such a degree that there should be no reason why two adults, who find themselves in a situation they've been forced into, shouldn't get on a call. She doesn't answer, and when I call again, a day later, I figure I have been blocked.

Aaditha and I need to have a conversation, which is why I decided to stay the day in Bengaluru.

Father is ecstatic. He calls my decision to extend my visit by a day 'very civilized'.

That did nothing for the questions humming in my head. The water is warm, and my arms are keeping pace with my thoughts.

Aaditha was straight-faced for most of the morning, arms folded just below her chest, except for when she tugged at her clothes or drank her coffee. Then came the wedding announcement, and she startled visibly.

Our eyes met across the room. It was only a moment, but it was enough to tell her that I'd handle it.

Father hadn't said anything about a photograph to me, much less a palace announcement about the wedding. His words knocked me off my feet for a moment. I looked daggers at Mother, who had obviously lit up on some cue from her husband. She even suggested a spot for the photograph, like some creative director summing up options. It wasn't even her home; she was the guest. Mrs Neela Prathap was content rocking back and forth in her seat for most of the hour we were there.

Aaditha went along with the photograph, even though she took her time leaving her place on the sofa.

Nomenclature – COFFEE Before Books & Bras – is the prime reason I think Aaditha may have had more of a role in the business than just being the front for it. It's not an ordinary brand name; it has personality, someone's personality. Too many words and way too much love for it to be Prathap Gowda's call.

There was something in the way Aaditha sipped her brew – not just pleasure but pride. Her shoulders lifted, and her eyes brightened when the parents praised the beverage.

It's possible that Aaditha wants out, too.

Why would a south Indian heiress, an industry leader seemingly, be agreeable to an arranged match with Rajasthani royalty?

We are disparate as societies go, and by all accounts, the Gowdas know serious money. So why tie yourself up in royal traditions that mean nothing to you when you can live freely?

The Gowdas and the Rathores are poles apart, geographically and culturally. We love to show, even if the show is sophisticated, while the Gowdas are vanilla in a healthy way, much like their walls. No art, no souvenirs from places travelled or traces of a life lived, no photographs of the family, save for a few on the mantelshelf. Maybe that's the part of the house they open for occasions and have deliberately left it sparse. It's refreshing that there's no pretence, no hiring of an interior decorator to jazz it up.

I know it is Father who reached out to Prathap Gowda, but Karnataka's finance minister could've easily said no, come up with any number of excuses without offending anyone. That he didn't says something. Prathap Gowda probably wants it more than his daughter. I wonder why? What's Mr Finance Minister's plan?

As we exited their home, Prathap Gowda told me his daughter would be at her office in Kempe Crown by 8 a.m. and if that hour suited me, I could see her then. I turned to tell Aaditha I would be at her office by 8.30, but her back was to me. She was in conversation with her mother.

The time, so early in the AM for a meeting, took me by surprise, but it suited me. I could leave for Ranibagh immediately after.

I sleep through the rest of the evening. It is past 9 p.m. when I wake up.

My phone tells me more accounts have copied/reposted the *TittleTattle* pictures. Their Instagram handle, @TittleTattle, has more pictures of 'the Ranibagh Royals' getting off the airplane. Someone even has a picture of our jet arriving in Bengaluru, but I can't tell if it is Bengaluru or even if it is this morning's photograph.

Ratan arranges for private dining. I have barely eaten today, and my stomach is rumbling.

I pull on jeans and a freshly ironed black dress shirt and head for the elevator.

The elevator opens into a dimly lit corridor that separates the living quarters from the rest of the property. At the end of the passage is a brightly lit foyer. I'm getting my bearings slowly. It is a large, open space over which a chandelier hangs low. There are quite a few people milling around, given that it's a Monday evening.

I decide against stepping out for dinner and retreat. Ratan has the doors open and is waiting for me. I spot Aaditha just as I pull back; she has seen me, too. I curse under my breath and walk out of the elevator.

What is she doing here? She can't be working this late. Even if the flood of vitriol on social media isn't the full truth, this is way past the school bell. Especially if your workday began at 8 a.m.!

As I make my way towards her, I realize that Aaditha hadn't seen me earlier. Her rear is facing me now. Whoever it is she is with, a statuesque lady, identifies me.

I recognize Aaditha because of her hair, straight and heavy, a fall of ebony, which she has drawn in a heap over her left shoulder. Just like she did earlier in the day when we were done with the photographs.

The friend sounds her out. Aaditha turns to face me, wearing a recharged smile. I see that she has changed from her traditional attire. She's wearing ripped jeans and a bustier blouse. A large handbag hangs from her shoulder, and a black wrap is draped on her arm. She appears taller than she did in the morning.

I couldn't tell earlier because of the situation, but now that we are face to face in a more relaxed setting, she looks nothing like in the antediluvian photos doing the rounds on social media. That's the problem with an anaemic digital footprint; it can give wrong first impressions. Not that Aaditha cares; if she did, she'd change it!

Aaditha's gaze shifts to the residential quarters behind me. She doesn't know I'm staying here.

The person she is with looks familiar. I might've crossed her on social media, or she could be someone known. I didn't have a name for her, though.

'Aaditha,' I say.

She's giggling; it's a soft, bubbly sound, but it doesn't stop until she finally says, 'Maaaan! The way you say my name.' More tee-hee follows before she sings, 'Aahdeethhhaaa.'

I'm embarrassed, and I apologize quickly. Only I don't know which part of her name I have mispronounced.

'Aaditha,' she says, stretching out her hand, 'nice to meet you.'

'Aaditha,' I repeat with a prayer, 'likewise.'

She nods. I exhale.

'You didn't tell me you're staying here.'

'You didn't ask.'

A late evening breeze sweeps across the slowly filling foyer; the decibel level climbs each time a car appears on the circular driveway. It is beginning to feel crowded.

She points at my wrist. 'You have rolled up your sleeves,' she is saying, following it up with a rush of tee-hees.

'Hello,' her friend says, introducing herself as Lavanya Patil.

'Vedveer.'

'Sorry! I forgot!' Aaditha says gayly.

The name is familiar, but I can't tell who exactly Lavanya Patil is.

Aaditha opens her palm and stretches her fingers and rolls them back in. She was flexing her palm in the morning, too. Is she injured? Is this physio?

A horn blares, out of tune on a quiet night, and Aaditha steps back involuntarily. She's under the chandelier, and that's when I notice her eyes. They are glazed, as are her friend's. They have obviously enjoyed their drinks.

I turn to Aaditha. Her lips are quivering. Is she cold?

'Are you cold?' I ask.

'Have you had drinks?' she asks.

I take the wrap from her arm and drape it around her shoulders. She is cold.

'Chivalrous!' Lavanya says.

'I forgot I had it with me,' Aaditha coos, her hand going up to her head and massaging it lightly.

I'm beginning to feel the crowd around me.

'Have you ladies had dinner?'

Aaditha throws her arms up and laughs. 'All done,' she says.

'Are you here for coffee?' she asks.

Whatever it is Aaditha Prathap and Lavanya Patil knocked back this evening, it has triggered a memory lapse while loosening tongues.

'Dinner,' I say, pointing randomly behind her.

'We'll walk with you,' Aaditha says. Lavanya Patil nods; she seems happy to play along.

As Aaditha transfers her weight to one leg, her jeans ride up, and I notice her chunky footwear; she's on a platform, literally. 'You're giving me a complex,' I say as we dodge our way through the crowd.

Aaditha's laughter is a roar.

As we move, I hear a commotion behind us. A man is shouting, 'Sir, please, please stop.' Aaditha tugs at my arm, and I turn to face a man madly waving his cell phone at us, asking us to stop.

'Please, can you stand for a picture, sir, with ma'am and ma'am?' he asks. He is addressing me, but he is no one I know.

I hold up my hand and look around for Ratan. He's nowhere to be seen.

Aaditha slinks her arm through mine. 'Don't be a snob,' she says, nudging my ribs with her elbow.

This is a whole different Aaditha Prathap, a 180-degree turn from the person I met in the morning.

We line up for a photograph. I'm at one end, and Lavanya is on the other. I inhale Aaditha's seductive perfume; it fills my nostrils. Nodes of gardenia, or is it ylang-ylang? Jasmine, maybe?

I don't know how many photos the man and a couple of others took before Aaditha's phone rings. She answers and says something in Kannada that sounds like *Batra idly, bartha idi*.

'Kannada?' I ask.

'It's Kannada,' she replies, laughing.

'That's what I said.'

Her shoulders shift. '"A" is not silent.'

Ratan appears miraculously and sweeps us past a ginormous doorway that shuts behind us. He is marching us towards the dining area, along the secluded passage. Once we make ground, he steps back. We've lost Lavanya, too, somewhere behind the giant decorative pillars we have crossed.

Aaditha and I stop simultaneously. I'm facing Aaditha, whose palms are on my arms. She's on her toes, gripping me hard; I feel her nails through my shirt. I'm drinking her scent; it's definitely jasmine. I lower my head just as she reaches up and brushes her lips against mine, back and forth, her hips shifting against my crotch. She is looking at me now, smiling, admiring her handiwork perhaps. Her hands are still on my arms, digging deeper into me; her eyes are speaking a language I'm unsure if I should decipher.

I hear my groan as I wrap my hands around her back, my fingers knotted in the silken strands of her hair. I claim her lips in a kiss.

It is slow at first, lazy strokes, our mouths tasting each other's spaces. Then the urgency grows with the little sounds coming out of us. We are each lost in the depths of the other, going hard and reaching for more. She exhales, and I inhale her breath. My legs part, and I pull her into me. We are hanging onto each other, unaware of the seconds that have swollen into minutes.

When I open my eyes, my lashes fan her face, tickling her. Aaditha opens her eyes and blinks.

I break the moment and step back, my heart thumping in a manner it had no business to. Aaditha's smile is luminous.

'You've had dessert before dinner, Your Highness,' she says.

5.

Aaditha
What Happened Last Evening?

My head is so heavy, I'm having difficulty keeping it straight. I look at the clock on my office desk sideways.

There is a good twenty minutes to go before Vedveer Rathore Singh comes knocking. The Rathores were punctual yesterday, but that could be because of the parents.

I pull out my phone to message Lavanya.

We had a bottle each of some ridiculously expensive red last evening. Lavanya's idea of a celebration after I tell her the prince is just as uninterested in this archaic match as I am.

The elitist snob, who spent most of the hour at our place pretending I didn't exist, condescended to throw an arm around me for the photograph. Not that he had a choice; the photographer was practically begging. *'Please, sir, Aaditha Maydam, come close.'*

Lavanya and I said cheers to jailbreak.

In the next hour or so, the prince and I will put finishing

touches to our hitherto unspoken plan before he does the good deed for the day and calls off this *roka*.

Lovey: *It was nice running into VRS last evening.*

ME: *Easier to bury the body now!*

Lovey: *What body? You were giggling away with him last evening! You'll make a handsome couple BTW!*

ME: *Savage! I must've laughed once or twice. I had to be cool. We just bumped into him.*

Lovey: *Right. Maybe I was high and seeing things, but I thought you guys smooched.*

ME: *Have you been drinking again this morning, Lavanya Patil? No more than half a bottle for you next time!*

Lovey: 😂

ME: *We must've air-kissed! Get serious! What were you doing when we were smooching? Standing and watching? Weren't you and I together the whole evening?*

Lovey: 😂 *There's an image in my head of the two of you full-on kissing! You think I dreamt it?*

ME: *Obviously!*

My hands tremble as I slip my phone into my tote.

I kissed Vedveer? I?

My fingers are on my lips; they feel fuller this morning. My heart is racing, and the room is turning. It cannot be true. Lavanya's fertile imagination has conjured this scene.

I look at my watch; there are a few minutes to go for the half-hour. I dig out my phone, hit on Instagram and start scrolling.

I don't have to scroll far; there it is. A photo of Vedveer and I.

Our hands are linked. Just like yesterday, during that impromptu photo session at home. Only, this time, I'm leaning into him, wearing ripped jeans and a bustier, with my wrap carelessly thrown on top. I'm smiling. *Smiling.*

Vedveer stands still, face unreadable.

Lavanya's in the frame, too, but she's cropped badly.

My heart takes off. Not racing, bolting.

What is this? How did this happen?

I can feel the breath rush out of me like I've been punched.

Did Vedveer ask me to pose for this?

Did I just… instinctively link my hand with his?

Who took this?

Did Vedveer have this photograph posted?

Did he mean for it to look like this?

A handle called @cholethings posted the picture; the profile pic is a plate of *chole*.

I'm opening and closing my palm between patting my chest, trying to calm myself down. Okay, I pose for a picture with Vedveer. That doesn't mean anything. Most definitely doesn't mean we smooched!

So, what exactly happened? The social media timeline?

The Rathores announced their arrival in Bengaluru in that gossip rag *TittleTattle*. Fortunately, they left me out of that little skit I saw that last evening before Lavanya and I headed out.

Question: Why were the popinjays (read Royals) in Bengaluru?
Answer: Dialling tech support.

I'm gagging as I troll *TittleTattle* in my head. Absolute scandal sheet, that! Royals this and royals that! People have names for a reason; use them.

My head is a chaotic mess. Why can't I remember what happened last evening? I know we ran into Vedveer, we chatted some, maybe... What time was I home? I wasn't late. I had a full night's sleep!

When I walk through the café to my office a little after 8 a.m., I notice some of the staff is particularly chatty. Smiles everywhere. They may have seen the photograph, and now they will see Vedveer when he walks in.

F@#k! F@#k! F@#k!

A gentle knock cuts through my panic-heightened state.

Vedveer is at the door; he is wearing a broad smile. I try to return it, but I can't go beyond a twitch. Why is he smiling? He hadn't smiled a whole lot yesterday when he visited with his parents. He nodded for some before massacring my name.

Vedveer pauses, assimilating the space before him. My gaze shifts to his gait as he moves; it is a slow, almost lazy step.

The collar of the button-up shirt is open. Navy flannel

on grey denims and suede shoes. In the photograph, he's wearing a black shirt on blue jeans, but that could just be a colour tint. Navy/black, grey/blue. Who carries that many clothes for an overnight trip? I assume he leaves today.

I type on an already open email on my desktop; it is addressed to me. I complete the unfinished sentence and press send. I needed time to compose my appearance.

Rahman's '*Chhoti si Asha*' is buzzing in my ears. I tug at the AirPods and place them in their case, which I return to the drawer.

I summon that professional smile I save for customers reaching out to tell me how good my coffee is.

'Come in,' I say, fortunately more to myself. Vedveer is well inside the room.

His mood is a little too sunny for my liking. What happened to the man who acted swiftly in stopping his over-enthusiastic father from making a wedding announcement yesterday? He's supposed to be my ally, not friend! My teeth sink into my lips.

I watch as his hands reach for the only other seat in the house. Vedveer pulls the winged chair back and walks around it. He stops before my desk and puts out his hand. 'I hope you're well rested,' he enquires.

I nod wanly, giving him my hand.

He settles into the chair, and I push back on my Ikea wheels.

'Tha... thank you for making time,' I say.

Vedveer nods. He's looking around my office, taking in the nuances, maybe.

'You have an interesting name for your café. What's the story behind it?' he asks.

The question surprises me, coming from him, at this juncture of getting to know each other, but if there's one thing that calms me down, it is talking about my caffeinated chain.

I exhale.

'I think of books and bras as support staff,' I say. I laugh sometimes when I put it that way, but not today. It's a conscious decision.

My eyes are on Vedveer. I can see he's listening.

'I'm not alone in feeling this way. The second B, the bra, isn't spoken about or referred to freely. I want to put it out there in a public space, on a nameboard. Bra. I want girls and women in every section of society to say the word boldly, without being forced to blush.'

They can choose to blush, but that's a different thing entirely.

Vedveer nods. I feel the weight of his gaze on my cheeks.

'It helps that my sister has the talent to hold that part of my brand up.'

'She's a designer?' His brow doesn't shoot up. Just a slight shift of muscle on his forehead, suggesting he's curious.

'Alia sourced pieces for us initially; now she's assembling them.'

Vedveer is quiet for a while. He seems comfortable in the silence, but I feel it.

'You are staying here?' I ask.

Vedveer is taken aback. I asked him the same question last evening. I can read it on his face.

He nods. 'Pruh-thaap*ji*,' he breathes out, 'recommended it.'

I want to plead with him never to use Appa's name around me unless he learns how to pronounce it. It's a simple name, not some polysyllabic crime story.

Ra-Tho-Ray is ringing in my ears.

I pick up the intercom. 'Coffee?' I ask.

There's a knock on the door, and it opens immediately. Rachael, one of our older staff, is all smiles, carrying an elaborate floral arrangement – white lilies and red roses.

I'm trying to make sense of what is happening, when Vedveer turns to face Rachael, who looks dotingly at the prince.

Is Vedveer sending me red roses?

'This has just been delivered for you, ma'am,' Rachael says. Her eyes are on Vedveer, who now looks at the book rack before him.

'Who sent it?' I ask. I'm not shrieking, thankfully!

'The sender is anonymous, ma'am,' Rachael says, placing the vase on the long side table.

Rachael exits my office, shutting the door behind her, but I'm still agape mentally, trying desperately not to show it.

It has got to be Vedveer. Who else would send me red roses this morning?

Vedveer's eyes are still on my book rack. I hope he's not encouraged by Indra Nooyi's *My Life in Full: Work, Family, and Our Future*.

I pick up the intercom again and cough to get his attention. 'Coffee?'

'Of course! Coffee!' he says, smiling brightly.

'Cappuccino?'

He nods.

'Breakfast?'

'I don't eat breakfast.'

His Royal Highness probably only surfaces at noon.

I want to put this out there: I didn't ask for an early AM meeting to inconvenience VRS, though that would've been a sweet touch. The only reason I told Appa that I'm at work at 8 a.m. is because I wanted to get this over with at the earliest so that I could get on with my day.

Appa, whose day begins at 4.30 a.m., didn't think the hour unreasonable. He is several filter coffees down by then.

I turn to my right and face the only window in the room. The blinds are down. They are always down; that's how I like it.

My eyes shift to the flowers. Who is this anonymous sender?

Was Lavanya serious about Vedveer and me kissing last evening?

Is Lavanya pranking me?

Butterflies are flying free in my stomach.

'Do you write code? For a lark?' I ask Vedveer. There's a plan the both of us need to hammer out. I haven't forgotten.

Vedveer stops smiling, and his forehead scrunches into folds.

'I studied environmental science and engineering,' he says. Then, almost as an afterthought, 'Atmospheric chemistry.'

What the hell.

I bury my face in my hands and let out a laugh, loud and slightly hysterical.

Environmental science?

That word didn't even register when my parents first mentioned VRS two weeks ago. I must have tuned it out.

Vedveer's eyes wander to the flowers.

Prem, the server, enters the room. He is carrying hot cups of coffee and a bakery basket – muffins, pain au chocolat and our signature confectionery, mango Danish.

Vedveer pushes back his sleeves, exposing toned forearms. I give in to the image of them wound tightly around me for a nanosecond. Is that what happened last evening?

He takes a sip of his coffee, ignoring the deliciously laid-out basket.

'Good?' I ask stiffly, knowing immediately I should specify what exactly I meant by good. 'Hot enough?'

He nods. 'Hot, yeah. Very hot.'

'Too hot?'

Vedveer is smiling. 'Right hot.'

I laugh.

Maybe he, too, likes his coffee hot like folks down south do. Generally speaking.

Vedveer's posture is all lines, starch stiff and straight.

I draw up my bare feet and fold them next to me before picking up my cup and taking a sip. My brain is crying for caffeine.

Vedveer reaches for the mango pastry.

'Good ch-choice,' I say. 'It's our speciality.'

'It's good,' he says.

His sleeves have ridden up on his right arm. An entire subculture on Instagram is dedicated to his forearms. They are wholly brawny, but that's not why we are facing each other across a table this morning.

I stop thinking about his arms.

How can we call this *roka* off?

I'm playing with words in my head, arranging and rearranging, aiming for the right tone.

'I called you a couple of times,' Vedveer says, leaning back in his seat.

'When?'

'A week ago? I thought we should at least speak before we meet.'

'I don't know, I'm not sure…' I may have blocked his number.

'I'm probably on your block list,' he says, nodding.

'Apologies.'

I feed his number into my phone and send him a message.

Me: *Hi* ✋

'I should have messaged first, maybe,' he says.

His phone is in his pocket, probably. I haven't seen it.

God, oh god! I call out to the powers that be. Please tell me we did not kiss. I will not ask you for anything ever again.

'Did you send the flowers?' Of all the million ways I could have worded that question, I choose preposterous.

'No,' he says, before asking, 'You don't know who sent you those?'

I shake my head.

'Anonymous admirers, casually slipping red roses into the mélange.'

'What are your interests?' I blurt out. 'Do you have hobbies?' I ask like a kindergarten teacher.

'Organic farming,' he says, his smile brightening.

'Environmental science and engineering,' I say.

His head bobs.

Dung. Cow Dung. Soil chemistry. I try to perk myself up. We reside in parallel universes. I could tell Appa that we are very different. That has got to count as a good reason!

'Aahdeethaaah,' he says, pausing to smile. 'I hope I am saying it correctly? I was sufficiently schooled on pronunciations last evening.'

It is an improvement. 'Aahdeethaaah' didn't drill a hole in my head like it did yesterday when the Rathores came calling. But that may also be because any mention of 'last evening' is sending me on a tailspin.

'Last evening,' Vedveer is saying.

My head is turning. My fingers threaten to cover my mouth, but I clasp them tight and leave them on my lap.

'You were bright and bubbly, a whole different person,' he finishes.

I try to smile. 'We met socially,' I say. I know I'm sounding unhinged, but what happened last evening? 'We ran into each other,' I correct myself. 'Lavanya, my friend, was there too.'

Vedveer nods. His eyes move away from me. He is considering what to say, maybe searching for my surname. I hope it has been wiped out of his memory. Phonetic atrocities should be remanded.

He is on his feet. He peers into my two-shelf library cupboard. 'Are these for sale?' he asks, picking up Robert Iger's *The Ride of a Lifetime*. His eyes are on me. I shake my head.

This tiny 150-square-foot space is my escape, my Himalayas, where I can disappear. Door bolted and phone switched off.

My strip of an office space has a library cupboard, and the top bracket holds an assortment of books I like, from Nooyi to Robert Iger and *Shoe Dog* by Phil Knight, *To Kill a Mockingbird* and Matthew Perry's memoir, *Friends, Lovers and the Big Terrible Thing.*

'No. These are my books. We have contemporary fiction on our shelves outside.'

The café itself is a large, wide-open area with pots of greenery and loads of natural lighting. The seating is spread out across the floor, which is standard in all our outlets. We have three 10x10 shelves of books, and just behind the books, we stock Alia's lingerie selection. That is always a crowded space.

'Would you rather sit in the café?' I ask out of politeness, knowing he'll turn it down. Who needs one more picture of themselves on social media?

'Yes,' he says enthusiastically.

My eyes widen in horror. *Do you want to be photographed again with me, you dolt?* TittleTattle *already has a photograph of you preening in Bengaluru, as if that wasn't bad enough. I'm clinging to you like some shrinking violet in a photograph a freaking fan has clicked. Now what, you want us to walk the ramp for them?*

'I like open spaces,' he says, 'the outdoors.'

The man couldn't think beyond his royal nose even if he was commissioned to.

I get on my feet reluctantly.

'You don't want to go out.' It isn't a question. Vedveer settles back on the sofa and picks up the coffee cup.

I exhale.

'You've never been photographed in your café,' he says, nodding to himself.

His tone is gentle, but I miss it because questions are coming at me in my head like traffic in this city, from every possible direction.

'Never?' I counter too quickly.

'Yeah. I looked quite a bit on social media and didn't see a single picture of you in the café,' he says. He's facing me.

'Why social media?'

'Because I wanted to know something, anything about you before I came to Bengaluru.'

'What did you want to know?' I ask. I feel the sharpness of my tone.

'Get a sense of who you are,' he says. 'We are practically engaged, Aahdeethaaah!'

'It was the *roka* then yesterday at my place?' I ask.

He nods.

Roka is not my custom. When we get engaged, rings are exchanged, we send out invitations and put out a feast.

'Why are we here?' he asks. His shoulders straighten, and for the first time in the morning, there's an edge to his tone. 'We are very different people.'

Chalk and cheese. I couldn't agree more, but why is he playing innocent? How did *TittleTattle* know he's in Bengaluru? He's probably tipping them off and providing them photographs.

I exhale. I listen to the air that escapes me. 'How did we even get here?' I ask, laughing.

Vedveer's shoulders drop to a relaxed position. 'Our folks find us well suited!' he says, adding, 'That's how well they know their children.'

I want to give him a high-five, but I'm not sure if I will be breaking protocol.

'The question is, how do we end it? It doesn't matter how we got here!' I say.

He nods. He wants to say something, but he's holding back.

'But you were almost already engaged,' I say, giving him an out.

'Someone else also likes to scroll, I see!' he says. 'But rookies must be warned not to believe everything they see and read.'

Tittle Tattle

Gupshup Column

CODE APART, WHOEVER THOUGHT ANYTHING HAPPENS IN BENGALURU!

Curious so-and-so,

A little birdie confirmed that the Ranibagh Royals had called on Prathap Gowda at his Bengaluru residence a couple of days ago. Bear with us, we are a little confused here! Was the dhoti-kurta-wearing Finance Minister of Karnataka the reason why the Rathores were dressed to the nines?

Did the Royal contingent zip down in their finery just to secure a business deal?

Meanwhile, a photograph of Aaditha Prathap in ripped jeans clinging to Prince Vedveer has gone viral.

TT's question: Is Aaditha, the daughter of

Prathap Gowda and CEO of COFFEE Before Books & Bras, a fan or a friend of the Prince?

Hit us up if you have an opinion.

Aaditha hasn't been snapped with either of the young Ranibagh Royals before this. It's possible that the families know each other. The photograph did spark familiar vibes.

TT is guessing Aaditha is a fan because of how she's turned out. She must've been on an evening out with Lavanya Patil, heiress to the Patil jewellery empire (who has been conveniently cropped out of the frame). Aaditha and Lavanya must have run into the Prince. She probably quickly linked her arm with the dashing Royal for one to show Papa or save for posterity. Because who knows?

Somebody be kind and tell the girl extreme rips are out; it's the subtle abrasions and the lived-in looks that are in, but even that is a no-no if you want to pose with royalty!

The only reason TT is wondering, darlings, is because the Crown Prince consented. He's not known to pose with random people, unless, of course, they're friends, which is a possibility here.

Just to keep this guessing game going a touch longer, Aaditha Prathap was photographed last evening in her café with another toothsome gent.

They were having coffee together! And this time she is dressed in a dull, shapeless co-ord set (her wardrobe is crying for a stylist, and god knows she has the money to invest in herself).

TT has learnt that the gentleman even had a floral bouquet delivered to Aaditha in the morning. Listen up, people, the bouquet had a smattering of red roses!

TT can't help but wonder if Aaditha is making a point to the Ranibaghs. Did she slip that photograph with the Prince into the hands of a hanger-on? I'm single, come get me, but hurry up or... there's someone waiting in the wings!

6.

Vedveer

Delhi Darbar

It is eighteen minutes since I pulled back the curtains and let the early-afternoon light flood Father's study. Gaurav Rathore Singh huffs behind his glasses, which Rajkumar, the butler in attendance, swiftly procured from the other end of the room.

Father hasn't mentioned Aaditha in the interim. That's a relief.

He shifts his position, turning away from the window.

'It feels like I'm sunbathing in Mykonos in August,' he mutters. 'Too much light, wattage, heat!'

I chuckle.

In general, Rathores prefer curtains closed; we don't like to be seen, except on occasion. 'We are not on public display' is father's common retort whenever the drapes are drawn apart. This afternoon, he is holding back. It is twenty minutes now, and his cheeks are cooked to a piquant pink.

I'm an exception to that Rathore rule. I drift organically towards natural light.

I had come up with something to distract Father, and the sun became my abettor. He tosses Aaditha and marriage at me every three minutes.

'She's a lovely girl,' Father says again. It didn't take him long to snap back – three minutes short of thirty.

It has been ten days, and that rich, redolent scent of jasmine still swirls around me in circles.

Her hair! I exhale like it's the only thing I know how to do. That hypnotic cascade of black silk spilling around her shoulders.

I shut my eyes. I can still taste her, feel the echo of her mouth on mine. That kiss, it is the first thought that drags me out of sleep every damn morning. And yet she acts like it never happened. Like it didn't shake the ground.

She teases, brushing my lips with hers, stokes me awake and steps back to view the havoc she has wrecked. Her smile, sweet, unholy perfection.

'You must think about this, Veer.' Father's words interrupt my thoughts.

'They are a respectable family. Prathap Gowda is a senior politician…'

'Why does Prathap Gowda want this proposal to work so badly? What's in it for him?'

The extremes I swing between – the pull, and the question that nags.

Father stares at me like I've lost my mind. 'Are you

seriously asking why any father would want his daughter to marry the crown prince?'

That also.

He scoffs, shaking his head. 'Good god, Veer. We're the Rathores. And they, they're a fine family. Decent, dignified. A good match for us. The young lady runs a successful business. What more do you want?'

I nod, but the unease doesn't leave me. Still, I let it go, for now.

Instead, I pick up my teacup. 'So successful that she cannot see beyond her cappuccinos,' I say.

Aaditha hadn't picked up that I sipped my beverage from a teacup when there were extra coffee cups on the trolley at her home.

Father laughs. 'That's a nice way to put it.'

I shrug.

My gaze rests on the window that overlooks our eastern garden, which changes with the seasons with flower beds of the ornamental variety.

I have spent a part of my childhood in this room. It is where my grandfather, Maharaj Rawal Rathore Singh, retired to at the end of a day when he was in Delhi.

Grandfather looks down at us from an oil painting just above the grand fireplace. The only source of natural light for the room is the large, rectangular window, which at the moment is causing great distress to his son. This is where Grandfather drank his morning coffee when he was in Delhi. He was the only coffee drinker in our family until Father married. Mother and Navya have taken it to a whole different level.

What would Grandfather have made of the Aaditha Prathap situation?

How do we end it? she asked.

'What are you looking for in a matrimonial match, Veer?' Father is on a mission. 'What qualities does young Aaditha lack that you're looking for in a wife?'

What now, a shopping list?

If I could just go back in time and leave that kiss behind in that Kempe Crown corridor, I would be fine. I could move on as easily as she has.

'Marriage is not a conversation I want to be having right now.'

'Why not? It's about time we have that conversation.'

'We've let our lands waste away for too long!' I say, holding Father's gaze. He is across the room from me.

We are looking to upscale our considerable acreage into 100 per cent organic ground. The Green Dream is Rawal Rathore Singh's vision. Grandfather was before his time.

I've been immersed in our holdings since returning from Bengaluru. We have records dating back to the early 1600s. The plan is to survey the palace property first so that we have an estimate of what is required to transfigure our lands. About 60 per cent of our agricultural assets have been wasting for decades, since Grandfather's health deteriorated. That we haven't already owned and serviced the land that is ours is a crying shame.

'Why are you resisting, Yuvraj?' Father asks. 'This is the right age, and we are fortunate to have found a suitable match.'

He is toying with a colourful crown-shaped paperweight that is part of the palace memorabilia collection. He is trying not to make eye contact.

Father is so caught up in his own dance – books and whisky – that he wouldn't know a mall rat from a tree hugger, never mind if Aaditha and I are suited for each other or not.

Gaurav Rathore Singh worships at the altar of indulgence. He's not a collector of the uber-luxe; no, he lives it. Wheels, wings and whisky, especially if it's rare, refined and ruinously expensive. But he's not curating a museum; he's savouring an experience.

His dopamine rush hits the moment his back sinks into the buttery Italian leather of his sofa or when a Yamazaki single malt glides down his throat.

Father won't put a name to it. Won't call it excess, or even desire. Because to define it would be to limit it, and to rein it in would mean denying himself the one thing he truly loved.

It wasn't just a taste for the finer things. It was an affair. A full-throttle, all-consuming one.

He heaves himself up from the chair and steps away from the desk. He is preparing for the next question – you can tell by the intensity of the activity. He continues standing, hands crossed over his chest.

The door to the study opens, and Holiday and Hope stroll in. They try to settle against their lounging pillows by the divan before finding spots at the feet of the two humans in the room.

'Aaditha is a very smart young woman,' he is saying, 'to have come up with this idea of a café chain and make such a roaring success of it.'

Prathap Gowda had burnished Aaditha's abilities to such a fine shine that it reflects in Father's eyes. There's no other way he'd know anything about her. There's nothing much on her anywhere; I have looked.

As far as I can tell, it is the same set of three photographs of Aaditha that are doing the rounds on social media. They are old shots. One is an airport picture, the second one also looks like an airport image, but it could've been at a restaurant or hotel, and the third is definitely at a Bengaluru restaurant. They aren't complimentary shots, but she has done nothing to change the image.

That is the only content on her. COFFEE Before Books & Bras has a tonne of reels, but Aaditha isn't in any of them. She has chosen not to.

Aaditha Prathap is a looker. Social media has got it so wrong, the joke is on them.

Her dark hair, parted in the middle and tucked behind her ears, frames her face. The bulk of her hair is swept over one shoulder and left there in a heap, like some industrial arrangement.

Father's eyes fix on me. It's as if he's trying to read

my mind like those mentalists in the works of fiction he devours.

Holiday arches his back.

Father walks to the chaise and settles on it.

'Tell me, what is your impression of Aaditha?' he asks.

'Yes, yes, please tell us.' Mother waltzes into the room, adding to the clutter. 'I like that picture of the two of you; you'll look good together,' she says, waving her index finger at me.

'What picture?' Father asks. He's surprised.

Mother promptly opens her phone and passes it to her husband, who she is seated next to. Her eyes are on me.

'Charming!' Father says, looking pointedly in my direction. 'You are protesting after taking the lady out to dinner?'

'Protesting?' Mother asks.

'We didn't go out for dinner. We bumped into each other in the hotel lobby, and we spoke.' I've had years of practice at being strait-laced. It comes easy now.

'This photo doesn't look like two people who have just bumped into each other.'

I shrug. Father has read too much fiction.

'And who is this fellow she's having coffee with at her café?'

'What fellow?' My tone is even, but the question breaks out before I have time to consider what I'm saying.

'There's a picture of them in the gossip pages your mother reads.' Father huffs.

'That's the last time you're getting any intel from me.' Mother looks at her husband adoringly.

'It seems,' Father drawls, looking at his wife, 'our son knows nothing about his fiancée's other meeting!'

'Are we playing snakes and ladders here?' Mother is all smiles.

I'm wading through social media, looking for *TittleTattle.*

Who is *this* guy she's having coffee with in the open while I'm shoved deep into a bunker-like space she calls an office? I read the piece and learn that the same bloke sent her the roses.

Why did Aaditha pretend like she didn't know who the flowers were from? There were lilies and verdant fronds, but there were red roses, too. She even asked if I had sent them to her.

'He's a good-looking chap,' Father is saying. 'Maybe Vedveer is losing his charm!'

'No way!' Mother says and ambles across the room to throw her arms around me.

'Do you like her?' Father prods.

'We are very different people.'

'Opposites attract, right?' That is Mother sounding like a giddy sixteen-year-old on a night out. 'I like her, her coffee is great, the family is lovely, even though their house is so bare. Didn't you think?'

She is looking at me. I nod.

'I couldn't get over the interiors. Did you spot a curio even?'

Father laughs.

'Also, her dressing, very plain, like the walls of her home,' Mother says.

I didn't want to counter because that would take this conversation out of orbit.

Aaditha's style is understated; it goes well with her personality, which is powerful.

Her apparelling is straight and simple, even on a night out with her friend at Kempe Crown. Not the ripped jeans, though, which is more rebel schoolgirl than pathbreaking CEO. Her lips were glossed but shorn of colour. Lush and 2× lovely.

'I dropped by only to check if you're here,' Mother is telling her husband. 'I'll be back.' She pats his hand, and he takes hers to his lips.

I let the room settle.

'I'm here to talk about our land, Father,' I say after Mother's perfume follows her out of her husband's study. 'It's high time we start farming on the acreage that has been wasting away for decades.'

I got on a call with a friend of my grandfather – Prakash Chandra, the last word on organic farming. The octogenarian had visited us for the last time before Grandfather's health took a turn for the worse in the late 90s.

Prakash Chandra advised that while organic farming

afforded sustainable growth, it is only in the long run that it would pay. For now, while it would improve soil structure, water retention and nutrient content, it would send the budget through the roof. Especially given the expanse we are looking at.

The good thing about Father is that he didn't pretend to be anything he isn't. Titled and entitled. He takes care of his people and hopes that they take care of the land that is assigned to them. He's never out in the fields or where the action is; he goes by all that is listed when the accounts come to him at the end of the week. As for the estates that are wasting away, he doesn't even want to look at those because that might mean accepting their existence. The reigning monarch is generous and much loved among staff and tenants. He has little or no expectations from them.

'I've been speaking to Prakash Chandra.'

His expression tightens at the mention of the name. 'The nonsense the old man fills your head with. He is senile. He chews on every piece of leaf he can lay his hands on. What do you expect?!'

'Not leaves, Father, medicinal herbs,' I say. 'He is a little slow these days, maybe, but far from senile.'

Hope barks; it is a high-pitched sound, and a second later, Holiday joins in.

Father leans forward; his feet are on the floor, and his elbows rest on his knees. His back is bent. He stays in that position for some time.

'You have some thinking to do,' he says, straightening his back and tapping the cashmere beside him. 'Think about the proposal and weigh it all.'

A lot of decisions have been made in this room in the horizontal. Legend has it that I was conceived on this very chaise. Might've been an uncomfortable exercise.

'Veer!' Father calls.

I hear the desperation in his voice; it drags and bounces off the walls. He is faced with a mountain of a problem. His only son, his heir, is going crazy over organic farming.

'She's a lovely girl.'

And just like that, we are back to discussing Aaditha. The door to the study opens, and a valet walks in with Father's pre-prandial whisky.

I push myself up from the chaise and walk up to an ornate mirror that breaks the layout of a stack of books. I stand there for some time before returning to the chaise, which is vacant now. I pick up my phone and unconsciously hit on Instagram and start scrolling. There are a tonne of pictures and reels of Navya and her beau; there's growing anticipation of a wedding announcement.

I keep scrolling, ignoring the bulk of the reels, until I see Aaditha in one of them.

She's attacking a plate of fries; this is a recent take. She is at a nightclub in Mumbai. It is an unfair clip, and the comments are worse.

She's so fat.

Aloo jaisi.

Rich father, no manners or culture.

Look at her eating.

Eating job she has.

Money to spend.

Bonda hai!

Spoilt rich girl. I feel sad for her.

Suddenly, there are more photographs and reels of Aaditha, a medley that includes old pictures, accompanied by various Bollywood soundtracks. The uncropped image of us on that January night has also surfaced.

I go back to that particular picture and hit on the comments. There are quite a few vile ones, but there are an equal number suggesting something is brewing, and pinning my visit to the city to Aaditha.

I go to *TittleTattle* and stop at the photograph of Aaditha and the mystery man. If the piece is anything to go by, this meeting took place the same day we met.

I'm breathing hard. It bothers me that I couldn't pin down Aaditha Prathap.

Who is she: CEO or nepo baby? Single or attached? I try to regulate my breathing. It shouldn't really matter who she is. I'm looking to put an end to this shoddily scripted charade. I should have done it ten days ago, but I was distracted by the exchange of the previous evening.

Father clears his throat to get my attention. 'Since it's all out there now,' he says softly, 'you and Aaditha and photographs of your late-evening outing, why don't you invite her to next weekend's polo match when we play the Rest?'

What is he saying?

The polo match is an annual palace event, where the Royals take on the Rest. It is a Jaipur tradition, a marked date in society circles. It is when every known face in the country descends on our city. On second thought, it might actually be a good idea to have Aaditha in the same cloud space; it gives us a chance to talk face to face.

'Not next weekend; it's in two weeks' time, Father.'

'Even better!' he says, bringing his hands together in a loud clap. Rajkumar, who is dozing on his feet, opens his eyes in a startled reaction.

'We should invite the whole family,' Father adds.

I nod. It's unlikely that she'd come alone.

This is an opening for me to find out who the real Aaditha is.

Is she the woman I met at her house – self-assured, composed, every bit the business head her father would have us believe? Or the Aaditha I ran into in the colonnade, the one who knew exactly how to kiss a man back so completely that I can't get her out of my head even weeks later? Or maybe she's the Aaditha of the morning after, nervous, unsteady, like a stage performer who has forgotten her lines, who then goes out for coffee with Romeo, which she promptly advertises.

'I'll call Prathap Gowdaji right away, and Mother would like to spend time with…'

'Neela,' I offer. 'Her mother's name is Neela.'

'Yes! Mrs Neela Gowda,' he says, before raising his

voice and adding, 'The day after the match, the palace will release a wedding announcement. All these photographs circulating without context aren't good for anyone. We have to keep Aaditha's reputation in mind; she's a young girl.'

'Maybe inviting her to the polo match isn't such a good idea,' I wonder aloud.

'Why?' Father asks, his brow crinkling.

'Having Aaditha at Ranibagh will stir unnecessary media speculation.'

Father is staring at me and nodding like he gets the point I am making. But is he?

The Gowdas at the polo game, if anything, will confirm the relationship, after which the palace will be hounded for interviews. The traditional interview of the newly engaged couple done by the national broadcasters will be next on the agenda. We don't need this attention, not Aaditha or I, not now.

7.

Aaditha
Not the Mint!

THE WOMEN OF THE PRATHAP FAMILY – AMMA, ALIA AND I – arrive in Jaipur beneath an afternoon sun nearing its 2 p.m. arc. We are an hour behind schedule, courtesy Bengaluru's moody weather. But really, late for what? A bunch of grown men on ponies chasing around a ground?

The world is tilting around me, my heartbeat thundering in my ears.

My left hand finds Alia's right. I grip her tight. She nods; her smile is calm and steadying.

I focus on Amma; her seat faces mine. She is draped in a sap green Kanchi cotton sari, her face is bare, no expression, no make-up, and her topknot is couched in *Mangaluru mallige.* This is how Amma is dressed most days, save for the emerald and diamond studs and matching bangles.

I like that Amma owns who she is, right down to her clothes – no edits, no second guesses. Alia tries to suggest a Mysore silk sari, but Amma brushes it off with a shrug.

Classic Amma. Akka is home for a couple of weeks; she has been drafted in for this affair, and she signed on with zero protest. The bright side? We had a good time over the last few days, after the shopping stress was behind us.

Shortly after Alia's arrival in Bengaluru, I laid out my tried-and-true pale yellow co-ord set and even presented a few backup options for her approval. She didn't so much as glance at them. I offered a second outfit, same colour story, but that didn't merit a look either.

Alia is the family's style CEO. We'd love to say we aspire to her level, but it takes more commitment than we care to admit.

Amma boarded in her six yards, and Alia, who, like Amma, is lean and tall, also has her game outfit on – a belted houndstooth linen jumpsuit. She wears a diamond bracelet on her wrist and solitaires in her ears.

I changed into a candy-striped off-shoulder dress somewhere mid-air on our hired jet. Alia had chosen it – an almost knee-length chiffon number from a Mumbai designer – after several tedious telephone conversations, where she did all the talking and I was only required to nod.

It arrived two days ago, hand-delivered in a fancy box.

I blink as the doors of the Falcon 20 open. A flood of light flushes into the jet. A strong gust tousles my hair as we head out. I take it as a warning, pressing down the dress that is eager to float at the slightest excuse. This is exactly why I stick to practical clothes. Ruffles are cute until the wind picks up. Salwar, slacks, jeans, now that's real-world fashion.

We are greeted by a lady whose name escapes me. She apologizes that the maharani isn't able to receive us herself. (As if! I don't do the eyeroll.)

Three burly men in ash grey uniforms bearing the Rathore crest stand behind her. They're apparently our security details for the polo match. Imagine that.

I force myself to take in the surroundings. The air is clean, and the sky is a lively blue. Somewhere in the distance, the Aravallis reach up majestically, merging with the expanse of azure.

A couple of Mercedes are parked a few hundred yards from us.

We are escorted to the coffee-brown Maybach limousine. My knees knock as I climb into the vanilla-hued interiors; it smells of fresh peach. I close my eyes and drop my head back. This is a little too much!

I'm a working girl; there's a tonne of stuff piled up on my desk. But here I am, flying private, to attend a polo match! Something in my life is totally off; my kneecaps agree.

I walk into Appa's study with nothing more than Chinese takeout on my mind when he makes the announcement. It is a completely ordinary Sunday evening.

'We're invited to a polo match. Our Royals side is playing the Rest.'

Our Royals side? We've been associated with Ranibagh for but five minutes. And polo? I've seen pictures and sketches of men on horseback, swinging mallets, but I didn't know people still play it.

'Aaditha and Alia will go to Jaipur to watch Vedveer play,' he is telling Amma, who is nodding dutifully.

'Vedveer is playing,' Appa says, turning to me.

'So?' I ask. My mind may be swinging between flat noodles and men with mallets, but I notice Appa has not only roped in Alia but also got her on the guest list. This has been cooking for a while, obviously.

'Why are you arguing all the time, Aashi?' Appa asks.

'It's a question, Appa, not an argument. I'm allowed to ask a question.' Even if he thinks it doesn't merit an answer.

Some five days later, Alia arrives, big bags and bigger smiles. That's when the weight of it all lands – hard. Until now, I was only thinking awkward conversations and uncomfortable footwear.

I accost Appa in his study later that evening, where he's mid-conversation with Alia. She is offering him fashion advice, naturally.

'You know I don't enjoy watching sporting contests live. I get nervous.' I break into their conversation. 'The place will be swarming with photographers, trying to capture my every expression.'

'She gets very nervous,' Alia agrees. She's beside me now, arranging my hair, tucking it behind my ears.

Appa nods. 'I will let the Rathores know. You don't have to watch it live.'

Hmm... If I don't have to watch it live, why are we going to Jaipur? I can watch this episode of men and ponies on my phone.

'Why are we doing this?' I ask. 'We've had no communication with them after they were here. So why are we going to some society circus we have assiduously steered clear of all these years?'

'What communication is needed? That, too, after Vedveer and you were photographed together at a dinner party. What is there left to say?'

'It wasn't a dinner party, Appa!' I come back. 'And Vedveer has been photographed with at least a hundred different women!'

'But he's not marrying them! Or, you know, standing very close to all of them...'

'Appa, you can say making out. Aaditha is not a child any more,' Alia chimes in. She has moved away and is looking at me triumphantly.

I give her a dirty stare. 'We were greeting each other!' I say.

Appa clears his throat. 'Whatever. Behave yourselves when you're there, both of you.'

Alia is all smiles.

'And don't give Amma tension. She has agreed to go with you two despite my not being able to make it.'

'This polo whatever is not important enough for you?' I turn to Appa.

'I'm not the one getting married, Aashi.'

No. And it's not going to be me either.

My eyes open as the wheels slow to a crawl. We are turning into the gates of the Ranibagh Palace. My breath catches in my throat; it is a rough knot. I feel my eyes widen. What is this, a township? A whole damn planet? My gaze can't get to the end of it; it is mightier than I could grasp, beyond anything words can hold. Pale pink exteriors, red accents, golden sun-kissed domes, tall archways, stucco ornamentation… It climbs into the clouds.

We roll down the pathway. On my right are lush green fields edged with sparkling white canopies. The stage is set for my execution!

Little rivulets are running down my face. I don't need a mirror to tell me that I look exactly like I do every morning after my workout, face puffed and glistening.

Amma looks like she wakes up in a palace every morning, and Alia, chic in a Ralph Lauren suit, fits the part.

My eyes are on the army of photographers who flank a short flight of stairs. They are jostling for space behind rope barriers, and their cameras are trained on the Maybach. I feel my body cave into the leather. My head turns to face Alia, who points at the opening car door. A light afternoon breeze brushes against my bare legs, and my hands splay across the skirt of my dress instinctively. The thought of pulling my sling over my face crosses my mind, but my hands are otherwise engaged.

There's a buzz of noise all around me. People jostling, voices shouting instructions and the constant click of cameras. '*Abhi nahi, baad mein.* Photo *ke liye* time *hoga*.'

Security personnel open tall doors that lead to a huge hall, where we are greeted by Gauri Elena. She is styled very differently from the last time I saw her. Her rose-red, tea-length linen dress has wide arms and a long side slit. She wears uncut rubies on her ears but nothing on her arms – no bracelets, no watch, just a lone ring catching the light.

'I love the flowers, Neela,' Gauri Elena tells Amma. 'So fragrant. I wanted to tell you when we were in Bengaluru.'

'I wish I'd known. I would've brought some along.'

I inhale the familiar scent of jasmine, holding on to every comforting note it offers.

'Alia, so nice to finally meet you; you're every bit as gorgeous as I'm told.' Gauri Elena embraces Alia before stepping back, her gaze fixed on my sister. She's taking in the details. They are about the same height. As if 5'9" isn't tall enough, they're perfectly poised on stilettos. I hang behind Amma and Alia. I'm playing for time.

'Darling,' Gauri Elena breathes while enveloping me in a hug. I stay in her arms longer than necessary, mostly because I don't know what else I am supposed to do. The eyes of the room are on me; I feel it.

'Hi,' I say, not knowing how to address her. 'How are you?' I ask.

What do I call her? Aunty? She's not my aunt. Ranisa? Gauri Elena? It is a nice enough name, an east-meets-west combination, Guntur-red chilli ravioli, but I'm not sure what the proper way to address these folks is, and I am not about to guess.

Gauri Elena takes me around the room, which has a fashion parade vibe to it, a match-mine-if-you-can bend. As far as I can tell, there are no photographers around, not even an official one. I find my shoulders relaxing. There are Bollywood A-listers, models, television anchors, musicians, leaders of industry and even some retired cricketers. The ladies are mostly in dresses; there are some onesies and formal shorts. A supermodel, whose name is at the tip of my tongue, lets her eyes roam the room.

Vedveer has been romantically linked to more than one woman in this space, something that malicious rag of a publication *TittleTattle* will race to confirm.

Vedveer has had his share of women. The one he is most often seen with is Kairi Gaur, who is of a noble lineage from the region. He has been photographed with her multiple times at events all over the country, at Bollywood parties, movie premiers and Delhi society dos.

She on his arm, his arm around her waist. There are shots of them holding hands, firmly, hers in his, which to me is a clue, not if people hold hands but the way couples hold hands. There's a difference when it's a declaration.

My pulse is racing. Why should it matter when and where Vedveer is photographed with Miss Whoever? It has nothing to do with me. I only have to push that button that will force him to bow out of this ridiculous act.

'This is Aahhdithhhaa,' Gauri Elena is saying, lending to the carnage of my name. 'This is her sister, Alia, and Mrs Neela Gaaaudaa.'

'How pretty you are, wearing a sari,' someone is telling Amma, pointing at her drape, like Amma doesn't know what she's wearing. The voice is squeaky and over the top in decibels.

I can tell Gauri Elena is the only one from her family in this space. Her husband has excused himself, and the daughter is travelling with her beau; the son will be on a horse in less than an hour, trying to score.

The hall is huge; it could probably take in a city. I look around me. This is the by-invitation crowd, I gather, and there are some five hundred people. The seating is banquet style, and above every table, a rose gold circular ring lighting drops. The rear wall is laden with photo frames of what look like polo games through the ages. At one end of the floor is a bar. Servers in black and white are carrying trays of champagne glasses.

'You should sit with me and watch the game,' Gauri Elena tells me, her hand on my wrist. 'I will be right by you; we'll have a good time together.'

My heart is thudding erratically. Where is she watching the game from? Unlikely that it is from the privacy of her chambers.

I made it clear to Appa that I'm uncomfortable watching the game in person with dozens of paparazzi cameras pointed at me. I didn't want my anxiety to be turned into a public spectacle.

This was the condition I set before agreeing to make the trip. I'm barely here, and we are already negotiating. I feel Alia's grip firm on my elbow. I read her gesture.

'Come, come now, there's nothing to worry about,' Gauri Elena presses.

I nod. What else can I do? If I stand my ground, I'll be called dramatic. Difficult. Problematic.

I manage to give Amma and Alia the slip. I need a breather.

I head to the back of the room, my skirt swishing about my bare legs as I move away. I pick up a glass of champagne and position myself behind a pillar. A gulp of liquid courage hits the back of my mouth and burns my throat. I take another gulp and feel my engines rev. I leave the crystal on an empty serving trolley and walk away.

It is a crackling February afternoon, bathed in warm, golden light. I'm flanked by the mothers, Gauri Elena on my left and Amma on my right. Alia is on Amma's left.

Amma looks swish in her new sunglasses. She has never been one for glares, preferring the sun directly on her face. She owned a pair once, years ago. It was rarely worn and has long since vanished. Alia brought her a trendy pair this time.

'Sunlight is good for the eyes,' Amma mutters but makes the effort to wear it today.

Amma is about to watch an actual match – one that doesn't take place over the dining table or involve family scores – for the first time in her life.

I pick up a glass of champagne on my way to my seat. Despite my best efforts to avoid the spotlight, I have ended up in the front row. I sip my drink slowly this time. I haven't eaten all day, but my stomach is adequately lined with anger. I sink into my seat, disappearing behind vintage sunglasses.

So… did Vedveer and I actually kiss that evening?

It's the fan's photo that's throwing me into an existential crisis.

I mean, did a kiss actually happen? Why am I leaning in like that? Why do I look so weirdly comfortable with him?

Maybe he pulled me closer. Or maybe I was just being my usual overly agreeable self.

Angles are deceptive – they can turn fleeting moments into stories that never happened.

Amma leans into me to tell me I'm twisting my lips. My hand moves to cover my mouth instinctively. As I pull it away, I notice nude lipstick on my palm.

Since when has Amma started paying so much attention to me? Most of the time, I'm the adult in the relationship.

'Alia told me,' Amma says. I glare at Alia, who shoots me an angelic smile.

Umm… excuse me, what?

'Are you comfortable?' I ask Amma.

'No!' she says. 'I'm here only because we couldn't send you girls alone.'

I nod, blinking back tears. My emotions are riding the roller coaster, fuelled by expensive champagne. I'm the reason for Amma's disquiet.

I watched a recording of some polo match last evening to prepare myself; ten minutes was all I could take.

My eyes are on the players on the other side of the grass pitch now, tracking the red shirts. I can't tell which of them is Vedveer. I look for the tallest man on horseback, but from the distance at which I'm seated, height isn't easily distinguishable.

I don't even know why I'm looking for him. The reason I'm in Jaipur is to finish a conversation we left hanging two weeks ago.

The sound from the microphone blasts across the grounds. I turn a deaf ear to it until I hear my name. 'Aaditha Prathap, Ranibagh's princess-to-be, is in the audience this afternoon.'

Wait! WHAT just happened?

The champagne turns in my head, and the colour rushes to my cheeks.

Photographers from every nook of this sprawling space turn their lenses at me.

In the last weeks, my popularity has grown to such an extent, I can hardly recognize myself.

Gauri Elena looks at me from under her wide-brim raffia hat. She is smiling, but it is clear from the slightest shift of her brow that emerges from behind her shades that the announcement has surprised her.

I'm breathing hard. I taste the moisture that lines my upper lip.

Amma's eyes crinkle the way they do when she's pleased, Alia is beaming, and Gauri Elena puts a comforting hand on me.

There are gasps in the audience, audible sighs. I feel eyes drilling a hole in the back of my head. Is that a wail I hear? Some princess wannabe?

'Watch where you're going?' That's a shriek from somewhere behind me. A clatter, then silence, the shatter of glass hitting the floor. 'You've ruined my dress!'

Do I get up and see if everyone's okay, or do I just sit tight, given that an announcement has blown my brains? And maybe that of a few others, too!

Gauri Elena turns to her right and summons her wingman. He's swiftly dispatched to take care of whatever it is that is happening in the rear of the tent.

There's a roar as the teams – one in red tees and khaki breeches and the other wearing navy on white – take the field. Gauri Elena claps, and I join her in the genteel exercise.

I'm careful not to contort my face, or worse, bite my lip like I sometimes do when watching a cheesy romcom.

Vedveer leaps into my vision; he cuts a regal frame on horseback.

My eyes cover his length, the width of his shoulders, pausing at his ripped arms. He stops for a moment and looks my way. His lips widen slightly in a hint of a smile, as if to say thanks for coming, for watching.

Is it just my imagination, the smile bit?

Okay. No. No feelings! My throat is tight, and I exhale a rough gruff.

Gauri Elena turns to see how I'm doing. She has caught the exchange between her son and me. I try to smile but manage a nod. This is exactly why I didn't want to be seated here, before all of Rajasthan. If that wasn't enough, they even had an announcer introduce me as the 'princess-to-be'.

They might as well have fed me to the paps with complimentary champagne!

I pick up my glass; it has been replenished.

I need to message Lavanya, but nobody in the row I'm seated in is fiddling with phones. In the other dome-shaped enclosures that flank ours, almost everyone is recording the action. There's something else I notice about the other guests as my eyes search the stretches, first on our right, then to the left. My stomach plunges, taking my heart along with it. We Prathaps are the only ones without hats.

Alia asked me if she should get us hats, but I shot her down, saying, 'We're going to watch a polo game; we're not invited to some cosplay party.'

I raise the binoculars briefly, catch some of the action, then drop them back into my lap. I don't really need them. Quite a few of the guests, including Gauri Elena, used these viewing lenses that were placed on our seats, when play shifted to the far end of the field.

The setting is spectacular. The sun has cast its glow on the expanse, lined by blooming bougainvillea in shades from white to plum. The action is swift – horses and men. It plays much faster in person than it did on my computer screen last evening, which was more of a jumbled mess, horses and riders clashing, mallets ripping through the air without making contact, more noise than play.

Gauri Elena has been in conversation for the most part with her sister-in-law, who is seated next to her. She leans into me now. I inhale her perfume for the first time. I can't detect the notes, but it is an exotic scent. Rose and burnt wood, maybe.

'He's running a fever,' she says of her son, 'but he had committed to play the game today. Vedveer doesn't go back on his word.'

I nod. Of course! He's burning up, yet he's on horseback like a hero from some Victorian novel. As if being annoying isn't enough, he has to be heroic, too!

The early chukkers are exciting in terms of action, though Vedveer doesn't appear to be in the thick of it. Even an amateur could call that. Gauri Elena can't help herself, spouting gobbledegook in my ears. It takes me a bit to get into the match, the sound of hooves thundering across the field, mallets meeting, and the crowd erupting in waves of excitement that hinge on the primordial.

The Royals strike first, scoring within the first five minutes. The Rest recover quickly and counter with successive goals. By the end of the third chukker, the score is 4–3 in favour of the Rest.

The sun is warmer than when we arrived, and the helmets the players wear are not helping.

Sweat trickles down Vedveer's flushed face; his red shirt clings to his sweat-soaked frame.

I take deep breaths and remind myself not to get too involved in the action. I don't need my face, with its range of comic expressions, to add to the entertainment.

It is a challenge, however, to stay out of it in the fifth chukker as Vedveer gets into the thick of play.

The crowd is on its feet, egging him on with shouts of 'Yuvvvvvrraaaaajjjjjjjj! Yuvvvvvrraaaaajjjjjjjj!' bouncing off the Aravallis.

He strikes once, and a couple of minutes later, he latches on to a pass from a teammate. As he manoeuvres his pony to get into position near the goal, Gauri Elena's fingers sink into my forearm. In the next second, Vedveer sends the ball sailing through the goalposts, sealing the match.

Meanwhile, I try to shake my hand, which is bruising badly.

Chants of 'Caaaaappptttaaaaan!' echo across the grounds.

Joyous scenes break out all over, with players congratulating each other, shaking hands and tapping helmets.

'Oh, dear,' Gauri Elena says, her eyes wide in horror, looking at the nail art she has left on my skin.

I'm breathing hard.

'I'm so sorry. I got carried away.'

'It's okay. It's not as bad as it looks,' I say, summoning a smile I didn't know existed in my reserves. 'Great work!' I add, looking at the field.

A section of the crowd are out of their seats and almost on the field, celebrating the victorious Royals. Gauri Elena is also on her feet; so are Amma and Alia. I climb out of my chair hurriedly and start clapping (because everyone else is).

The winning team ride their ponies together, doing a slow victory pass, with Vedveer, their captain, leading the way.

'There is going to be a prize distribution ceremony,' Gauri Elena leans into me and says while looking adoringly at her son. 'I will be handing the Rathore Challenge Cup to Vedveer again. The Royals haven't lost since Vedveer started playing for them when he was just eighteen.'

Gauri Elena's cheeks are blush pink. 'You have to join

me now,' she says. 'We'll walk to the middle. Next year, you can do the honours.'

I exhale. Next year I won't be anywhere near here.

I follow Gauri Elena to the dais for the presentation ceremony. I hear wild cheering from one end of the ground, shouts, screams and a lot of noise, but I don't lift my head. My eyes are on the turf I cover step by dainty step. The last thing I need is to go headlong and embrace the grass.

Vedveer walks towards the dais as the announcements are being made.

'Mother,' he says as he leans over and places a kiss on her cheek. She reaches up and presses her lips on his forehead and hands him the trophy.

Vedveer steps aside and faces me; our eyes lock for a moment before he lowers himself and brushes a kiss on my cheek. I hold myself still, inhaling his scent. He smells of energy.

'Thank you, everyone, for joining us today,' Vedveer says, pointing the trophy at the spectators, who are still cheering lustily. 'Rest, you absolute legends, you pushed us to bring our best game. Great show, guys! Royals, I wasn't sure how today would go, but you rose to the occasion and made this victory possible. Let's celebrate before we remember how sore we are going to be tomorrow,' he finishes with a laugh.

There's a general rush of activity soon after the prize distribution. The crowd begins to move in, looking to be a part of the celebration, while the staff swiftly clears the ground. A teammate relieves Vedveer of the trophy, and Gauri Elena drifts towards the society folk.

Vedveer reaches out for me, his hand finding my elbow, motioning me to walk with him.

'You look lovely,' Vedveer says. I feel his breath on my neck and the flutter of butterflies in my stomach.

'Aren't you wet?' I shout out above the noise. *What am I saying? What am I saying?*

Vedveer lets out a chuckle.

'I mean, aren't you sweating? You are definitely sweating.' I'm out of control.

Vedveer smiles. 'The sun is out. I was playing. It happens.'

I nod, letting the rush of words that escaped my mouth settle on the grass around us.

You are hot, and no, the weather has nothing to do with it, I think as we stand facing each other. His arms are folded across his chest, legs parted in an easy, open stance. The red tee, sweat-stained and heavy, hangs on him, while the breeches cling low at his waist, drawing the eye. The riding boots pull it all together.

Vedveer's gaze travels slowly over me before settling on my eyes. We snap out of the moment when his palm cups my elbow, coaxing me away from the others.

'Thank you for coming,' Vedveer says. 'I'm not sure if sport or polo is your thing, and I hope you weren't bored!'

'You are welcome,' I grin, my eyes meeting his, 'but don't expect me to start wearing your jersey!'

'Fair enough, for the moment! But someday? Is that too much to hope?'

'Don't push your luck, Captain!'

Vedveer feigns dismay, his lips dipping in a pout.

'The mint with a hole is suing, copyright infringement and all,' I say.

Vedveer's head tips back, laughter bursting from him. A little behind, Jaipur's late afternoon sun hangs.

Hmm... God must look like this.

'We'll have our legal team look into it,' he says.

Vedveer's eyes are like the sea, which changes colours with the seasons. Or reasons.

'The match-winning goal was fantastic,' I say. I'm laughing hysterically now.

'You had fun?' he asks. The light in his eyes is soft.

I'm opening and closing my right palm.

'Why do you do that?' he asks, reaching for my hand hesitantly and then looking at my palm as if he were reading it.

My palm curls and flexes on its own whenever I'm nervous, but that's not something I'm going to enlighten Vedveer about.

His eyes drift up my forearm, where the marks his mother's nails left on me are still visible.

'What's this?' he asks, his gaze sharpening.

'Your mother was... very nervous,' I say lightly.

'No. That's ridiculous.' His voice tightens, and his eyes darken. He presses his fingers gently against the marks.

'Does it hurt?'

'Not now,' I say, offering a smile. 'It's fine, Vedveer. I am fine.'

My stomach lurches, and my heart is beating erratically.

'Are you staying the night?' he asks.

I shake my head. We aren't staying.

'We need to talk, you and I,' he says. 'There is going to be a wedding announcement soon.'

And just like that, the champagne fizz is lost. Another announcement? I rock back on my pointed footwear.

Vedveer's hand is firm on my elbow.

'Whose wedding?' I ask.

'Ours,' he says, 'yours and mine.'

I hear the silence. It's banging on my eardrums.

'Excuse me?'

He nods once. Barely. 'Tomorrow, or the day after, the palace will make the announcement.'

This is a hostage situation! 'Why?'

Vedveer exhales.

'We both knew this was coming,' he says. His shoulders drop to a resigned slant.

'I knew they'd push; I didn't know you'd fold,' I say.

Vedveer doesn't answer. I hear the rattle of his breath.

'So that's it?' I ask, leaning into him. 'No conversation? No choice? Just… congratulations, Your Highness, you're now engaged to someone you barely know?'

His eyes are locked on mine as he steps closer. Too close.

'Is that what you're angry about?' he asks. 'That I barely know you?'

I stare at Vedveer like I'm seeing him for the first time.

Vedveer and I are not and never will be a couple. This mighty palace, these great grounds, this antiquated sport he excels in are so far from my world that we may as well be living on different planets.

I excuse myself from Vedveer as his friends gather around him; my fingers linger on his arm a touch longer than would pass as cordial. I break from the crowd and walk towards the restrooms. I need a moment.

I head to the last stall of an empty restroom, bolt the door and click on Instagram. There are loads of pictures of Vedveer atop a chestnut pony. Photographic evidence that he can exist without female accompaniment!

I hit the message icon to start a conversation with Lavanya.

Me: *They introduced me as the 'princess to be'. Can you imagine?!*

A chat bubble pops. Lavanya is writing. Amen.

Lovey: *What?*

Me: *So VRS tells me the palace will make the wedding announcement soon. As in the next day or two.*

Lovey: *What? Why is everything moving at such a dizzying pace?*

Me: *I don't think VRS is interested in this alliance, but I don't think he's doing anything to back out.*

Lovey: *Why do you say that?*

Me: *I tried to push him to take a stand, but he somehow seems reluctant.*

Lovey: *Hmm... That doesn't mean he's not interested. Listen, I think you guys did kiss.*

Me: *Maybe we did. But how can I have no recollection of it?*

Lovey: *Where are you?*

Me: *In the ladies' room, sitting on the throne and messaging you. Anyway, laters. I think I have company!*

I hear voices, hushed words and laughter. It is getting closer.

I look down to check if the door is full length when I notice the flooring; it is eye-catching, white and gold vitrified tiles with a streak of indigo running through it.

'Ozempic, you think?' Speaker A is saying. 'I read a comment from a post, quote, "She is onto something; no one changes so much in such a short time." Maybe surgery to woo the prince, who can have any woman.'

That's when I decide not to walk out.

Speaker B: 'Possible. This is not how she looked even a few months ago. I'm tempted to say weeks. She generally wears really funny clothes. Auntyji-type clothing.'

Speaker A: 'What she's wearing today is decent, though. How old do you think she is?'

Speaker C (male voice): 'Thirty–thirty-five maybe; she looks that.'

Did I wander into a common restroom?

Speaker B: 'Must've bought it today.'

Speaker B: 'Wait a minute, who is the chaperone? 1970s streetwear fashion!'

Giggles and laughter.

Speaker C: 'So out of place for a polo match.'

Speaker A: 'The other two were her mother and sister. Not one of them was wearing hats. It's like they googled what to wear for a polo match and forgot to buy hats from the Bengaluru market!'

More mean-people laughs.

Speaker C: 'In that Instagram pic where she's all into him, she looks about the same size. Maybe she cleaned up in time for him. Her dad is new money, and she's the face of the café chain.'

Speaker B: 'Does she grow the beans?'

Right at that moment, my music app comes alive. Justin Bieber is singing, 'You think I'm crying on my own, well I ain't...'

I let Bieber run for a bit before I open the door and walk out to a trio of frozen faces.

Tiffany Govind, a supermodel, dark-haired, light-eyed, with legs that run for miles, is leaning against the sink. She is wearing a body-hugging dress. Standing beside Tiffany in a pale pink ensemble is Kavya Aulakh, heir to Aulakh Steel. She is Speaker A. Speaker C is Aroon Pai, a notorious cross-dresser with a raspy voice.

I now know the society crowd, thanks to social media and Vedveer.

'Cosmetic surgery, ah? Not that important. Also, people, Ozempic is last season,' I say before turning to face Aroon Pai. 'Women tearing down women – tiring. Men chiming in – embarrassing.'

I'm seething. Things are exploding in my head, and my feet are barely moving. I purposely did not bring up Amma and Akka; we are so above this shoddy lot.

This is precisely why I didn't want to be here in Jaipur, on royal territory, parading for a position I DID NOT want, dragging my family through the mud in the bargain. We don't need this. I'm more determined than ever to push Vedveer to break it off.

Next year, there will be a different 'princess-to-be' at the Rathore Challenge Cup.

Tittle Tattle

Gupshup Column

HATLESS AT THE POLO GAME, PRINCESS-TO-BE MAKES HEADLINES

Curious so-and-so,

Ranibagh Royal Tea: The Princess Has (Unofficially) Arrived!

Coffee Queen Aaditha Prathap was introduced by royal announcer Samuel Verma as the 'Princess-to-be' at the Rathore Challenge Cup this weekend. Yes, you read that right. And no, we're not breathing normally either.

If there was any lingering doubt about these two being a thing, TT suggests you put your conspiracy theories to rest.

Now, we agree it's odd that the Palace didn't

roll out the velvet carpet for an official announcement first. But let's be clear, this wasn't some over-enthusiastic emcee settling social media debates. Slips like that simply don't happen at Ranibagh. That is one tightly run ship. And Samuel Verma? He's no amateur. If he called her Princess-to-be, someone very senior signed off on it.

So, how did we get here? After a dating roster that reads like a who's-who of elite society, Prince Vedveer is basically engaged to Aaditha Prathap, a woman who is desperately seeking a crash course in Ranibagh dressing protocol.

That said, this afternoon's candy-stripe dress was a step in the right direction. We approved. Except that she showed up to a royal polo match without a hat. And she wasn't alone; her sister Alia went hatless too.

Is there a hat embargo we weren't told about?

Mummy Gowda kept things real in a Kanchi cotton sari and chappals, thankfully not the Hawai type, or TT might've had to revive the Maharani with smelling salts. She wore a string of jasmine in her hair and her bank balance on her ears and wrists.

But let's get back to the main act.

Despite the fashion fumbles, the Prince looked completely smitten. After the match, he was seen leaning into Aaditha during a hushed conversation, her hand in his. He, sweaty and sexy in polo gear. She, looking like a subtle summer dream. It worked. We felt things.

On the field, however, the Prince was clearly elsewhere, glancing over at his 'Princess-to-be' more than once. We thought it was adorable and perfectly in sync with the bombshell announcement from earlier.

Make no mistake: This is the closest the Palace has come to a wedding announcement. TT's not in the mood to wait; we're circling a December date. Ranibagh in all her glory on a winter night is the stuff of dreams.

Oh, and while we're on outfits and accessories, there were polo hats galore, from wide-brimmed classics to feather-fitted chaos, but supermodel Tiffany Govind absolutely stole the spotlight. Dressed in an off-white halter-neck number that hit just below the calf, she looked ready for the runway (and probably needed to be, since her prince is officially off the market).

8.

Vedveer

You've Got Mail!

PAINTED PORTRAITS OF KINGS AND QUEENS LINE ONE end of the Maharaj's Library, a section that may have served as a tea room in earlier times. By the rectangular window that overlooks the koi pond stands a delicately carved settee. In the centre, a deep-red Persian rug anchors the space, surrounded by an arrangement of plush seating.

I use the Maharaj's Library more as a study, a place I retire to when there is work to be done. This morning, I'm buried in paperwork, trying to figure out what exactly it would take to convert our properties into organic land.

Raj Kiran, the valet, is at the far end of the room.

The analogue mechanics are pushing towards 10.30 a.m., and Mother and I are scheduled to meet for lunch at noon.

It is four days since the polo weekend, and Mother is yet to return to her husband.

Over lunch, we'll inevitably rehash last weekend; Mother never bores of a story she's already told six times. She lives for the details and has the memory of a surveillance drone.

She's quite fond of Neela and finds Alia 'TV-beautiful'. (Which, in Mother-speak, is high praise.)

Aaditha? Summed up in two words: book smart. According to Mother, 'Social media hasn't even begun to scratch the surface of Aaditha's… let's call it "low-visibility charm"'.

As for anyone pitching her as the face of her father's business savvy? Mother calls that 'a marketing tragedy'.

'The only thing she isn't is the face of the brand; she's its whole and soul. The child is nowhere in the media. She gets so little credit,' Mother says.

Raj Kiran spins around the moment the doors to the library swing open. 'Ranisa,' he says, stepping back and bowing.

Mother is in blue denims and a white shirt. She is carrying the morning newspaper, which she places before me.

'Good morning, Mother.' I'm on my feet. 'It's okay to knock, you know.'

'What? I didn't knock?' She gives me her broadest grin, pointing at the announcement.

His Royal Highness Gaurav Rathore Singh is delighted to announce that Crown Prince Vedveer is to wed Aaditha Asha Prathap later this year at Ranibagh.

Palace Spokesperson

The Ranibagh Palace, Jaipur

A photograph of Aaditha and me, taken at the Gowda residence in Bengaluru, was dispatched along with the palace announcement last evening.

Aaditha's middle name took me by surprise when I read the draft yesterday. At first, I thought it was a mistake, but that was not the case, obviously.

In an interview, Prathap Gowda revealed that his wife named their second daughter Asha. But their firstborn, Alia, thought the name sounded old-fashioned.

Alia had her own suggestion, Aaditha. A name she'd picked up at one of her school birthday parties and lobbied for relentlessly.

There is more of an explanation in the newspaper this morning, which details the wedding announcement.

Neela watched her husband slave, trying to make ends meet, and named her daughter Asha (hope in Hindi), with a wish that her birth would herald better days for their family.

I move away from the desk and walk to the back of the room, where my eyes find the koi pond. It is a soothing sight.

Aaditha and I couldn't be more different. We are polar opposites, with clashing personalities, conflicting cultures and lives shaped by separate worlds. And yet, somehow, those worlds have collided. I am next in line to the throne living in a modern democracy; she is the daughter of a senior politician, raised in the heart of power, fluent in its language.

It's a rare kind of fire that burns when the world is handed to you, and still, you choose to create something that's entirely yours. She's probably had huge help from Prathap Gowda, but people are not buying her coffee because her father has money.

Aaditha. I say her name in my head.

Aaditha has had chances to end this, too, but hasn't.

She says we should call it off but hasn't acted on it. She accuses me of folding but is equally guilty of toeing the line. She even watched the polo game, sitting beside Mother, despite her father saying she gets extremely nervous and 'didn't want to be on display'.

There might have been some passive–aggressive coercion from the Rathores, but Aaditha could've stood her ground. She's capable of it.

Then there's the kiss that burned itself in me, which she has forgotten. And yet, when we're together, I can't believe she feels nothing.

My fingers are tapping my elbow rhythmically.

Is there another man in her life?

The one who sends her red roses, whom she later has coffee with, yet pretends not to know who the flowers are from.

What about me? Why can't I, who sees our differences so clearly, be the one to say no? What's stopping me from calling it off?

A small voice cuts through the noise because, deep down, I don't want it to end, maybe. Not after the kiss.

I return to my desk and ask Raj Kiran to ring for coffee and tea and give us some privacy.

Mother waits for Raj Kiran to close the door behind him. 'I feel bad we didn't advise them to bring hats for the game. We have a whole collection in the cloakroom for guests who may have forgotten hats,' she says.

I shrug. I'm not sure the Gowdas really cared.

'It didn't strike me until the game started, and then, I didn't want to make a show of it,' Mother pushes ahead. '*TittleTattle* has gone to town on the Gowdas not wearing hats.'

'I'm not sure the Gowdas are overly concerned. They have lives, Mother.'

'It's different for a woman, Veer. When people gossip about our choices, it becomes personal.'

I nod.

'I feel bad for the child; she gets such bad media.'

'Social media. Media and social media are two different things.'

'I know, I know, but optics. Maybe we should hire a style-savvy intern to help Aaditha,' Mother suggests, leaning back in her seat.

'Help her with *what*?'

'Clothes, primarily; her style is too plain. We're royals; she's got to look like she belongs. Candy stripes are juvenile,' she says, her eyes moving expressively. After a long pause, she adds, 'And also maybe protocol; we need to brief her.'

'I'll do the briefing if and when required,' I say quickly, 'but I'm not sure we can thrust a stylist on anyone.'

Mother is smiling. 'Even someone who is almost family?'

'Mom, stop!' *She wants to end it.*

Mother's eyes widen.

'That's why I said an intern. Maybe we can pick someone from a design school.'

I shake my head. This business of wanting to change her wardrobe is completely over the top. We need to dial down.

It is time to shift the conversation, take it away from style and dressing.

'I haven't checked with Ratan, but I'm sure we are already inundated with interview requests from media houses.'

Mother's face lights up. 'Oh yes! I forgot that; I was so nervous. We did it right here in this room,' she says, looking around her and pointing at the wall adjacent to the window. 'You should plan that soon, Vedveer, for reasons of security.'

I nod. Mother raises a valid point; only, I'm not sure if this is what Aaditha and I need right now.

The wedding announcement has just been made. We need to deal with that, especially Aaditha. Then, to appear on national television, answering questions together about each other, would be too much at this stage. It will keep the media at bay for a while, sure, but at the moment, she needs her space.

'Lunch at noon,' Mother says, tapping her dial. 'It is our last on this visit. I leave tomorrow.'

I'm on my feet to walk her to the door. She has obviously waited only because the wedding announcement was to appear in today's newspaper.

My phone pings. It's an email from Aaditha.

From: Aaditha (aaditha_is_aaditha@gmail.com)
To: vrs-rathore@ranibagh.co.in
Subject: Pros & Cons of the Annoying VRS situation.

Calling in some.

Pros

- *Loves his family.*
- *Wants to get out of this marriage as much as I do!*
- *Treats staff well!*
- *Smelled really nice even after polo (ugh!)*
- *Not a yapper. (Not a fan of yappers.)*

Cons

- *Can't say my name or Appa's without sounding like he's at war with vowels and consonants.*
- *This royalty stuff is not for me. You just can't be yourself, and I don't know how to live with so many rules! How you sit, who you talk to, how you talk, photographers jumping out of bushes to snag a picture. It's constricting. I feel something close around my throat whenever I'm around them.*

- *Too many exes, and all of them look like influencers posing for their next selfie. Like, seriously!*
- *Average kisser, I mean, I have zero recall. (I've had more chemistry with my toothbrush. Duh!)*
- *I'm willing to bet he has never experienced the heartbreak of a broken flip-flop.*
- *May own matching monogrammed towels with his initials. I didn't ask. I just know.*
- *Calls his mom 'Mother' and dad 'Father'. That's a level of posh I'm not spiritually equipped for.*
- *Probably rehearses speeches in the mirror. Shirtless. With lighting.*

I read and re-read them.

One of the cons sits heavy.

Aaditha is not happy with this alliance; that is as clear as a bell. I hoped that for all the protocol and noise around me, she would see me somewhere.

I shake my head and smile as my eyes fix on the moniker. Has she saved my contact details on her phone as Annoying-VRS?

I look at my watch; it's not yet 11 a.m. Aaditha is at her office, maybe, dark hair dropping around her shoulders, fingers on a keyboard, punching out a pros and cons list on me.

But who is the mail meant for? Who is she going to call?

An hour slips by before my phone tears through my thoughts. It's Aaditha.

'Hello, Vedveer, Aaditha here. Is this a good time?'

Her voice is soft and businesslike, but even at the best of times, there is an edge to her tone.

I don't realize it, but I'm smiling.

'Hello, Aaditha, how are you?'

'I'm good,' she says after a longish pause, before adding, 'and you?'

'Not bad.'

'This has been a crazy day!' she says.

'Has it?' I can't stop smiling.

'Can you ignore the mail I sent you? I mean, delete it from your memory, pretend you haven't read it?' The words come out in a rush.

'What mail?' I feel like giving her a hard time. You can't just have no recall of *that* kiss?

I hear the breath that escapes her lips. For a moment, she buys into what I say, only for a moment.

'Please,' she says, 'can we at least pretend? I'm so embarrassed. I don't think I have ever done something like this.'

'What? Lists?'

Aaditha laughs. 'Stop it, Vedveer! You are evil.'

'No! Come on! I make lists, too!'

Her laugh hits a soft, musical note.

'How have you been?' I ask.

'Not bad. Busy. The usual, just some stuff to be done, put together,' she says.

'Like lists?'

'You are not going to let me forget this, are you?'

I shake my head. I know I am on an audio call.

'Are you in Jaipur?' she asks.

'Yeah,' I say before throwing the question back at her. 'Are you in Jaipur?'

'No, no,' she replies a little too quickly.

'Are you in Bengaluru?' I ask.

'Yeah, in my office.' she says.

She's probably wrapping and unwrapping her fists. Her nervous tic is relentless.

'Just checking,' I say. 'Didn't want to bump into you by accident and owe you a tea I didn't sign up for.'

There's an audible silence at the other end before she goes, 'Teeeaaaaa?'

I laugh out loud.

I'm not sure when I get on my feet and start walking around the room, but that's what I'm doing now. I move towards the lounge chair on the other side of the desk and settle on it.

My finger accidentally hits the Instagram app; notifications are popping up like corns in an oven. Our wedding announcement is everywhere.

@TittleTattle has posted another picture of Aaditha; this was three minutes ago. It is another old shot from her college days in Ohio. She is wrapped in a puffer jacket and walking hand in hand with the same dude she had coffee with at her café.

'I just saw the announcement,' she says.

Just saw? Prathap Gowda hadn't told her about it two days ago, when the palace got in touch with his office?

'I saw it earlier yesterday, before it was sent out to the media.'

She is about to say something but holds back. I can tell by the sharp intake of breath. 'It's all a bit crazy,' she says slowly.

'The pace is whirlwind,' I agree with her. I wait for her to talk, to tell me something about how she feels.

'I'm worried I'll be married off before I inhale again!'

I nod. I laugh. It is a light sound.

'It is gratifying to know that it isn't the case,' she says.

I nod and let the silence stretch, willing her to speak.

'So, you're really going through with it?' she asks in the same tone she'd use to enquire about the weather.

I hold back for a few seconds, letting the charged quiet settle. 'Is this you pretending you've never taken a decision and hoping I'll blink first?'

I hear her inhale.

'This engagement can't work.' Her voice bursts through the line. 'We come from completely different worlds, Vedveer. Yours… your life is alien to me.'

I inhale. The midday air feels heavier than it should.

'Right,' I say, keeping my voice level. 'Alien is one way to put it.'

She doesn't reply.

'You didn't choose this, Aaditha, I get that. Neither did I,' I say. 'But we're in it now.'

The silence is loud and telling.

'Don't you want out too?' She asks a question I'm not ready to answer.

'Who takes the fall?' I ask after what feels like an eternity. I feel a pull somewhere inside me; it's physical. If she's choking, then it has got to be me; that goes without saying.

'Both of us! Let's figure out how to end this,' she says. 'This arrangement, planned by our families, is suffocating me.'

I pause. A beat too long, maybe. 'Okay!' I commit. 'Let me know when you have a plan.'

Tittle Tattle

TO ALL THE GIRLS I'VE LOVED BEFORE...

Curious and so-so,

With wedding bells now officially ringing for Prince Vedveer and Coffee Queen Aaditha Asha Prathap, what better moment to take a walk down the memory lane of His Highness's love life?

Yes, darlings, before sealing the deal with the heiress to your morning caffeine fix, our Prince left behind a glittering trail of 22 known women (that we could confirm, and match with photographs), each more headline-worthy than the last. We're talking beauty queens, fringe royals and a human rights lawyer (because of course), before the bride-to-be, the queen of a business empire. (Is it hers or Daddy's? Debatable. But the paperwork says CEO, so who are we to judge?)

From charity balls to polo sidelines and Bollywood parties, these former flames have lit up society columns for years, only to be ghosted once the royal spotlight shifted. The one TT will miss on his muscular arms is Kairi Gaur. The best arm candy in the business!

Stay tuned, darlings. This tea practically serves itself.

A lot of *who-is-she* (read Aaditha) was doing the rounds in society circles, following last weekend's polo game.

Psssttt: most of them drink her coffee.

So, she may not be a looker (she's not bad-looking, trust us; it's the sad sack clothes she wears that give off old lady vibes), so unlike perfection on two legs, Ms Gaur. But Aaditha is raking in the moolah, folks, so let it drop!

A little birdie tells me Aaditha's new addition to the coffee table is a dark drink called envy. Drink up, girls! Not on an empty stomach, please.

Now, darlings, we had to be fair to the Prince (who has been TT's long-time favourite). Because we were running this feature on him, we had to do some digging into Aaditha's past (not enough that we judge her simplistic style). So ordinary it breaks us!

It doesn't look like there's much of a past, though, except for this dude she was snapped having coffee with in her café. His name is Arjun Mahesh; he's an Indian-American, and like the Prince, he's a looker. Outside of the fact that they're holding hands in the picture from their college days, which we posted on our Instagram handle, there's not much to tattle, sadly.

The 'Princess-to-be' has her own set of problems, though! It begins with her wardrobe.

9.

Aaditha
Thundering in the Head

I'M STANDING ON POINTED HEELS SO SHARP I'M IN DANGER OF going right through the flooring. I use the foot rails of the bar counter to hoist my rear onto the high chair. It is only after I settle into the seat that I exhale and let my shoulders relax.

The onyx-topped bar counter, on which I place my phone face down, sparkles under the lights. My phone is all I'm carrying. No cards, no lipstick, no bag. It is in my room on the twenty-third floor.

I'm in Delhi on a rare overnight trip for the final day of the annual India Initiates Business Conclave. It ends with the awards ceremony, and this year, I take home 'The Initiator' award.

I'm looking for a little getaway, which is why I rode the elevator down to this decadent set-up – the Four Hundred Club. A blatantly elitist piece of real estate.

The only way you can walk these marble floors is by paying an XXXL membership fee or if you happen to stay at the Lodhi Road Hotel itself. Hotel guests can't just show up at the doorway and demand a table; reservations should be made at least an hour in advance, and requests can be turned down without explanation.

Earlier, when I was going through the guidelines, I deliberated whether I really wanted to go. The welcome is so reluctant.

The Four Hundred Club, launched on speakeasy lines in the early 70s, is now an escape of sorts for Delhi's super wealthy. The image of the club is contoured by the financial flex of the membership.

An attractive thirty-something in a navy suit greets me as the lift doors part.

'Aaditha Purthaapji.'

He knows my name; I'm guessing he could recite my business portfolio, too. I look for a name badge but can't spot one.

Navy leads me to an exclusive seating area. I'm standing before burnished wood, thinking this table for four has three places too many for me this evening. It has been a while since I have been out on my own, not since my college days in Ohio. I have a great time whenever I go out with friends, all two-and-a-half of them, but there's a different energy to going solo.

The centrepiece of this bustling two-floor economy is a sleekly designed bar counter, with backlit shelves displaying an extensive selection of premium spirits and liquors.

I tap Navy on the shoulder and point in the direction of the bar, informing him of where I'm headed.

Harry Styles's 'Adore You' is on the audiovisual system. It blends with the customizable lighting that fires up screens.

'I'd walk through fire for you

Just let me adore you.'

I'm feeling good, even if the sensation is ephemeral.

That ludicrous Pros & Cons list from two weeks ago? Still living it down.

Lavanya, in her Psych Goddess mode, pushed me to make a list, which I did, and proceeded to send it to her, or think I sent it to her address. The plan was we discuss the list. I was so impressed with my work that I hit the send button and called her immediately, but she hadn't got my mail. I checked my sent folder only to see that I'd sent it to vrs-rathore@ranibagh.co.in instead of Lavanya.

The undo window is for a maximum of thirty seconds!

I wanted to roll myself into a bread loaf and disappear into a freezer. Days and weeks later, I still do.

Most of the points are okay, I think. Not something I would invite Vedveer to read, but… I had been stupid, and I'm paying.

He's going to make me sweat!

It's the point about the kiss that is driving me crazy. The problem is, I really don't remember it.

Average kisser, I mean, I have zero recall. (I've had more chemistry with my toothbrush. Duh!)

I take about an hour to compose myself and call Vedveer. He doesn't sound too perturbed by the words he has read (it is unlikely that he'd let it show even if he did), but there's something... A heaviness in his voice?

He doesn't bring up the kiss line... So, then, Lavanya didn't dream it up?

As if the wedding announcement and that email weren't enough for one day, I place the responsibility of calling off the engagement on him. He doesn't refuse; he asks me to come up with a plan. Like it was something that could be fit into the day's agenda, scheduled between ribbon cuttings and some royal do-gooding project.

I take a sip of sangria that is placed before me by a mixologist whose name badge says Toddy. I put the burgundy glass down and give Toddy a thumbs-up.

Freakin' *TittleTattle* also wants to join the party, so they dig up an old photo of Arjun Mahesh and me from our Ohio days and blast it on their Instagram like it's breaking news. A relentless February day that was!

Where did they procure that photograph from? I don't think even I have that picture with me.

Arjun Mahesh was a master's student in finance when I met him. He's tall and broad-shouldered, with soft, silky hair that falls across his face, hiding features that don't need a veil. Sometimes, he pulls his hair back in a man bun. Lushest lips ever.

His face is a light bulb in a dark room. He knows it but pretends that he is unaware. And does a damn good job of the show. That's the dull part, I learn later. Confidence is one thing; giddy awareness of physical features one is born with is a disservice to self.

I pick up the burgundy glass and eye the bowl of nuts before me. I decide against helping myself. Not even a single nut, I tell myself.

My eyes are on my phone. I'm scrolling through Instagram and click on the *TittleTattle* link (because I have time to kill). I hit on the latest edition and turn the pages. I pause at a layout that resembles a university annual. On the left is a column titled 'To all the girls I've loved before'. The headline is a giggle. The piece, well... I count some twenty-two pictures. The tile is captioned: 'Casanova Prince's Class of 22!'

Has Vedveer actually dated all these women? Twenty-two? Is it even possible? Why then does this Collective King want to get into an arranged match?

I open WhatsApp and message Vedveer. I attach the *TittleTattle* page and ask: *Who is your favourite?*

I get a reply in five minutes.

VRS: *I was hoping you hadn't seen that.*

Me: *Oh please! It is everywhere. So? Any frontrunners? The human rights lawyer? The beauty queen?*

VRS: *Tempting, but no. I prefer the one who has a thing for matching monogrammed towels.*

Me: *Excuse me??*

That damn list!

I'm careful not to contort my face weirdly; I don't need to entertain bartenders.

VRS: *Custom-stitched. Initials perfectly aligned. She pretends it's not a big deal, but trust me, she'd know if someone swapped the hand towel.*

Me: *I feel very seen.*

VRS: *You are!*

Me: *Haha!*

I put down my phone and shut my eyes. I wonder where Vedveer is. I don't know much about his life, but whatever I learnt from that first conversation we had in my office, he's probably at Ranibagh.

I ran into Navya at the Conclave. Vedveer's sister looked like she'd walked out of a *Vogue* spread... That's her staple.

'Yours is the only coffee I drink,' she told me and then leaned over and whispered, 'Welcome to the family. We're all so proud of you.'

When we broke from the hug, she added, 'My brother is lucky, but why isn't he here?'

Before I could even shrug in response, I got whisked to another part of the room. When I went looking for Navya Mrinalini later on to apologize, I was told that the princess had just left. I used that as an excuse to get away from the cocktails and dinner. I desperately needed some me time.

I swivel around in the high chair, the full 360-degree turn, and notice that the place has filled up.

I feel my face swell with a smile.

I'm finally being acknowledged as more than a rich father's daughter. At least in circles that count.

The champion of COFFEE Before Books & Bras.

Tomorrow morning, I'll be in the newspaper. And this time, it won't be for how plainly I dress or how ordinary I look.

I've won an award. A real one. I earned this.

Toddy places a bowl of potato wafers before me. My eyes circle the crystal bowl. My tongue is wet, and my stomach is alive. My eyes shift from the untouched cup of nuts to the chips. I can almost taste them. The salt, the tang, the crunch. I'm so ready for them I giggle.

Toddy turns. 'Anything you need, ma'am?'

I shake my head. My smile is ear to ear.

I'm not going to eat in an adrenaline rush.

I shift on the barstool, putting a distance between me and the eats. The table of eight that faces the bar counter has one woman in the mix and an empty chair. That particular bunch looks younger than the rest of the crowd; they are about my age, maybe.

My phone lights up. Alia is messaging.

She is on a break from her marriage and work, sourcing bras from factories while putting together some of her own creations from some resort in Kingston, Jamaica, I suspect.

She sends me her latest bra designs: the lace collection, Guipure, Brussels lace, eyelash lace and hand-drawn embroidery. Alia is working on outspoken, vibrant shades. The one she calls 'Rouge Noir' takes my breath away. It is made of eyelash lace, and it plunges. Another called 'Chartreuse' has a floral motif and is without lining.

Me: *Rouge Noir & Chartreuse* moi.

Alia: *34C, right?*

Me: *B with silk satin.*

I'm too bored to type, so I send Alia a voice note telling her that I'm loving the colours and that it will look great on Indian skin tones. Besides COFFEE Before Books & Bras, Alia also had a sizeable clientele that included Hollywood stars.

Alia: *I want to be bold this time.*

Me: *Tired of predictable shades.*

Alia: *This collection has no blacks.*

Me: *Call it 'No Blacks' or 'Bright and Beautiful'.*

Alia: *I like the second one. It sums up the collection.*

I wonder if Alia's choice of colours reflects her mood. We had a video call earlier in the day when she showed me some of the lace she is considering. She looks as good as the lace.

Me: *How are you, Akka?*

Alia is engaged with needle and thread. I can tell by the timing of her responses.

Alia: *How is the prince?*

Me: *He's alright, I guess!*

I haven't told Alia about the Pros & Cons list because of the kiss, obviously!

I don't want to talk or think of Vedveer right now. He and this wedding are all I seem to be thinking about lately. These brassieres are Alia's escape, getting them and making them. For now, I'm going to use it as my distraction, too.

Alia: *Are you at TFHC?*

Me: *Yes*

Alia: *Bar snacks?*

Me: *Yes.*

Alia: *Eat the nuts.*

Me: *Eating it slowly.*

I haven't yet started eating them, but that is exactly how I'm going to do it when I start.

Alia: *That's the way to do it. Be aware that you are eating.*

Me: *Trying to.*

I zoom in on the Rouge Noir. It is fabulous workmanship. I want to wear it immediately.

I take my eyes off my phone momentarily and pop a single nut into my mouth. I feel the texture, taste the tang. I could do this, I think, not for the first time.

I start to feel the room around me, sounds of chatter and laughter, along with the music.

I hear a 'sexy back' comment come from behind me. Is it the table of eight? It can't be my back they are talking about. I laugh to myself.

Alia: *But most important is to eat it the way you want to eat it. It's not like you binge every day. You only overdo it at times.*

My sister has no idea about my bingeing; in fact, no one in my family knows. She uses 'binge' casually in her text. That's not on her, though. Addictive personalities know how to cover their tracks. Until they can't.

My phone buzzes.

Alia is sending me more pictures of bras. This time, she's branching into underwear, too. She has chosen a combination in matching and contrasting shades for the first instalment.

There's some commotion at the door. I can hear it, but I don't turn. The door opens. I feel a stiff draught fan my bare back.

I pick up my glass and take a sip. I feel a dryness on my tongue.

I hear more voices, an accent, furniture being shifted just behind me, someone saying, 'Your Highness,' and there is laughter.

I feel a shiver go down my spine.

I start attacking the bowl of nuts, alternating between chips and nuts. Two at a time. Three. Four. More. The pace is feverish. I'm barely crunching, much less chewing. I can't stop, nut after nut, chip after chip. I have lost control.

Me: *I'm attacking the nuts.*

I don't tell her why.

Alia: *That's my girl!*

The word 'distraction' flashes in my head, and this evening, like a malfunctioning doorbell, it persists.

My first therapist had told me the first step to pause bingeing is to make yourself conscious of it and then come up with a distraction.

I hit WhatsApp and click on the exchange from an hour ago. We were in the same city when we were messaging. I feel my stomach tighten. I go to Instagram and scroll through Alia's collection again.

I hear 'cutie on the high chair'. I look around the counter; there is no one else on a high chair. It is just the odd word that comes through the din of the music.

Taylor Swift slays:

It's me, hi,
I'm the problem, it's me
At teatime, everybody agrees
I'll stare directly at the sun but never in the mirror
It must be exhausting always rooting for the anti-hero

I couldn't agree more with Taylor.

That's when I hear the name 'Vedveer'. I strain my ear. Someone is saying, 'The prince.'

I will the ground below this barstool to open up and close right after me.

I feel everyone's, or is it someone's, gaze caressing my almost bare back. My cheeks are warm, and my stomach turns. I'm wearing a belted deep green and black midi dress with a slit that does a lot of climbing. I'm breaking into a cold sweat, and my legs knock involuntarily.

What are the odds that I'm in Delhi on a rare overnight trip and I run into the crown prince of Jaipur?

I met his beloved sister, and even she never told me that he's in Delhi.

The chances are pretty good, actually. I don't need a round of cartomancy to tell me that.

With some luck, you can get out of here unnoticed, I try to tell myself. Maybe crawl out on all fours.

I'm back on the snack carousel, going harder and harder at the nuts. The replaced bowl of chips is almost over. I'm not thinking; I'm reacting. My breath is hard; it feels like a storm.

Toddy places another slightly bigger bowl of nuts before me and nods at my half-finished sangria when I ask him for a refill.

I want to disappear from here now, right at this very moment. I reach for my phone.

The Pour Homme EDP envelops me. I take in air and try to hold it within.

Why am I so jittery around this man?

The marriage announcement.

That juvenile Pros & Cons list.

The latest WhatsApp exchange was meant to settle my nerves. All it did was tighten the noose.

Toddy picks up a glass to stir; his eyes meet mine. Maybe he recognizes me.

'Aaditha.' A voice I know from behind me.

I turn to face Vedveer. He's in a pale shirt that sparks his eyes.

I swallow the barely crushed nuts in my mouth. I wonder if the salt is all over my painstakingly done make-up, standing out like some debased glow cream.

I shift, trying to get on my feet. Vedveer gives me a hand, and we're both on our feet.

'Congratulations!' he says, drawing me closer and placing a kiss on my cheek. 'Well done! It's a big one!'

I stare at him in disbelief. Why hadn't he come if he had known I was getting an award?

If Vedveer were the one getting this award and I happened to be in Delhi, I'd absolutely show up and cheer for him. It's a prestigious plaque, he said so himself. The only reason my parents aren't here is because Appa felt his presence might steal the spotlight from me.

'Navya tells me you won "The Initiator" award,' he says, answering the question my eyes echo.

'I just got into Delhi, like an hour ago,' he says, his lips slanting in a smile.

We were WhatsApping an hour ago. He doesn't mention it deliberately. We are in a public space.

'I ran into Navya on the way here, and she told me about The Initiator award. Sorry! I've not been up with the news. I wish you had told me.'

Vedveer's eyes are warm, but everything else about him is buttoned up and closed off. The business suit isn't just a look; it's the mood. Not that it should matter to me, given that we know where we stand with each other now.

'I should have,' I say sweetly, 'but I didn't know you'd be in Delhi, and I didn't want to trouble you.'

I feel the room close around us, and I turn to see everyone on their feet, thumping their hands together.

I step back and lean against the bar, and my right hand reaches for my still half-finished glass of sangria. I'm breathing hard, and Vedveer's eyes are on the hollow of my neck.

'I would've called and congratulated you if I'd known you were still in Delhi,' he's saying, closing the gap between us. 'I thought you'd be travelling back home. I was planning on calling you in the morning.'

My shrug is nonchalant, but my face breaks into a smile.

A little behind Vedveer, the folks who were seated at the table closest to the bar are now standing. Among them is a tall, impeccably styled woman, whom I now recognize from photographs as Kairi Gaur. Are they still seeing each other? My grip around the glass of wine tightens.

One of Vedveer's friends brings his hands together in a loud clap. 'I have a suggestion that His Royal Highness make a speech on account of his fiancée's victory today,' he says.

His fiancée? We're not engaged, dude, not yet! Victory? I hadn't won a war… though it felt like one. I retreat and allow myself a smile. It matches Kairi's in sweetness.

A loud roar drowns the music.

'Come on, Your Highness,' his friends cheer. 'We want a victory speech.'

What victory speech can Vedveer give you, boys? I'm the one who won the award. It's sitting on my bedside upstairs.

'Yeeeeesss!' someone else shouts from one of the corners.

There are more cheers, and as if on cue, the room aligns in a chant. 'Vedveer, Vedveer, Vedveer...'

I join the clapping, only because I don't know what else to do. My eyes find Vedveer, imploring him not to pander. We barely know each other. What is he going to say? He, too, probably thinks I got here riding on Appa's coat-tails.

The music is turned down, and Vedveer signals to the bar, ordering a round for everyone in the house.

'Vedveer, Vedveer, Vedveer.' More chants.

His Royal Highness raises an arm, and cutlery crashes to the floor somewhere in the room.

Vedveer pauses. His eyes are on his suede shoes, before he turns abruptly and looks in my direction.

I haven't rehearsed, he mouths.

For a moment, I don't know what he's saying; then the list comes to mind. The damn cons.

Probably rehearses speeches in the mirror. Shirtless. With lighting.

I pull up my phone, turn on the torch and point it at him.

I keep my face still, even as everything inside me twists. He grins.

Vedveer clears his throat and starts speaking to the room, before shifting slightly to hold my gaze.

'To Aaditha. "The Initiator" award is proof of the strides you have taken in the business world. Here's to more accolades and even stronger coffee!'

Vedveer's eyes linger on me for a touch longer than necessary. I mouth a thank you to him. He spoke honestly, and that is compliment enough.

People are raising their glasses, and another round of cheers goes around.

I hang back, away from the people, who rush towards Vedveer. This is his ground, his fraternity, even if the award I claimed earlier in the evening is mine.

As I watch the rush and roll around me, I wonder if this is a good time to announce the location of my Jaipur store, just beyond the gates of Ranibagh. I'm drumming my fingers on my glass.

Just to set the record straight, this store was planned well before my life became entangled in this circus.

The location… A genius idea dawns on me!

Having their to-be–daughter-in-law do business just outside the palace gates will doubtless anger the mighty Rathores. They'll push me to make a choice.

Vedveer Rathore Singh, I didn't even have to come up with a plan!

I turn hastily, and the heel of my shoe catches the back of the barstool, and I come down in a heap, the barstool on the ground beside me. Whatever is left of the sangria is on me. My phone pops out of my grip and falls face up.

Vedveer rushes to my side while motioning the waiter

to bring him my phone. He wraps his hand around my bare ankle. 'Are you okay?' he asks, his voice strained.

I nod. I think I'm okay.

Vedveer's eyes are locked on mine as he scoops me off the ground. 'We need to get you out of here,' he says.

10.

Aaditha

Welcome to the Circus

MY HEART IS HEAVY, AND MY PULSE IS RACING LIKE THE WHEELS we are riding on, speeding through New Delhi's near-empty streets at 8 a.m. on a Sunday.

Amma is next to me; her eyes are on the road. My parents flew in last evening. Appa had dinner with us and left. He was here to check on me. Appa doesn't worry too much about Alia. She is the sensible one. But his younger daughter, I have a tendency to slip and slide. He keeps an eye on me. Always...

Amma is doing the chaperoning, the heavy lifting. I feel for her. She has never really been away from her husband since they married, but recently, she's been forced to do more and more of it on my account.

We are headed to No. 9 Lodhi Estate. The driver informs us that we'll be entering through the back gate, generally used for staff and service vehicles. Charming. He apologizes repeatedly, conveying the Rathores' appreciation of our understanding of the situation.

As if.

My life as I know it is over; it is a full-blown media circus now. All that I have taken pains to steer clear of. The only thing left is to be seated on a decked-out elephant and troop around.

Vedveer asked me to shift to his place after we were papped at the Four Hundred Club two evenings ago.

One moment, my rear had come down hard on the cold marble floor, and some ten minutes later, we got photographed. The next thing I know, my return date to Bengaluru is pushed back and my parents are 'invited' to Delhi.

Vedveer tells me television channels have been chasing the palace for an interview with 'the couple' since the polo game. There have been hundreds of calls, apparently (like people have nothing to do with their time), but the good prince has been deferring to 'give us space', and that is no longer possible.

He has pushed it too far already, it seems. The Rathores 'traditionally' do the engagement interview at Ranibagh, but Vedveer (thankfully) thought flying to Ranibagh would be asking too much of me at this point and that Delhi was the practical option.

Never mind that we are not yet formally engaged. Vedveer has decreed, which means I couldn't fly back to Bengaluru on Saturday.

The interview is to be recorded at noon today. Molars have jammed against molars, and my fist is opening and closing like the jaws of a shark.

When we launched COFFEE Before Books & Bras, I didn't do a single interview, not one. Though there was no dearth of requests, courtesy Appa's position. I didn't want to put myself out there. I know the difference between media and social media, but I wasn't giving the trolls any information on me. I believed my baby had a life of its own, and I was confident the brand would talk for itself one day.

And here I am now. Karma is not kind.

The Rathores had parked a Maybach at the hotel for Amma and me to leave well in advance, just to confuse the media, who, they suspected, would gather around No. 9 Lodhi Estate at about 10 a.m., a little after the broadcaster announced the interview. I had an eye on the rearview mirror; it was all clear.

Vedveer put me down on a lounge chair in the near-empty reception area of the Four Hundred Club two evenings ago. The lighting in the salon is brighter than the ambient lighting inside the club.

'Your ankle may be slightly swollen,' he said, kneeling for a closer look. 'It could be the shock,' he added, his hand wrapped around my joint like a brace. He loosened his grip to check flexibility, shifting my foot gently.

'I think you are going to be fine,' he said.

'Yes, Doc.'

Vedveer smiled.

He placed an ice-pack on the ankle with his right hand and summoned a waiter with his left. He asked for a glass of water. 'Your lips are dry,' he said. I drank up as soon as the water arrived and requested a second glass, this one iced.

We sat there silently for about ten minutes, his expression settling with his thoughts as the clock behind him ticked.

'How does the leg feel?' he asked, moving the ice-pack and cradling my foot in his palms.

In his hands, my foot felt good.

'I'm not used to wearing footwear like this,' I said, looking down at my black shoes. 'I'm comfortable in kitten or block heels or just plain flats. You need a whole different skill set to walk in these!'

'I'm aware,' Vedveer said, his lips lifting in a smile. 'More like self-destructive weapons than footwear.' He gestured to my shoes.

'The Conclave has a dress code, and this place, too, has a similar one,' I said. 'Though coming to the Four Hundred Club was a last-minute decision. I didn't have any other footwear that would pass muster here.'

I patted the skirt of my dress.

I was speaking quickly; my tone was rushed.

'Do you want to try and stand, maybe take a few steps, just to see if you're okay?' he asked.

I pushed myself up slowly. Vedveer put out his hand

and took mine in his. He stood before me like we were prepping for a waltz to the tune of our ragged breath.

I took a couple of steps. I was not in pain, but I felt my ankle.

I returned my rear to the chair and watched as Vedveer rearranged furniture around me, the sight of which had staff scurrying to help, but he dismissed them. He lifted my leg and placed it on the table.

'The incline will help your foot,' he said.

I nodded. That's when I remembered that Vedveer was on a night out, for which he had flown all the way from Jaipur. Kairi Gaur must be waiting.

'Those are your friends?' I asked, pointing in the direction of the club.

He nodded.

'Don't you want to return to them?'

'I'm good,' he replied.

'Not very interesting, ah?'

Vedveer laughed.

It was at that moment that we noticed a camera flash. Vedveer was on his feet instantly, reaching for his phone and muttering under his breath. He walked away, phone in hand.

When he returned a few minutes later, he was followed by security, who formed a cover at the far end of the salon.

'We can't allow this situation to continue,' Vedveer said, kneeling before me. He was breathing hard. I could hear him.

'If we ignore this, the paparazzi will be hanging outside your hotel window.'

I was about to say that the only thing to do was to stay away from places like this, but I bit my tongue.

'Right now, you're okay in Bengaluru, but that could change, too.' His voice was rough. 'We need to act, throw them a few crumbs, do whatever it takes to keep them off our backs for a while.'

'What do you mean?' I asked. It was a photograph, one more on social media. There were more pressing matters in the world, surely?

'We have to do the interview! We can't push it back any more.' The decision was made.

Vedveer is at the door, waiting to greet us as we pull up at their rear entrance. He gives Amma a hand as she climbs the steps and then takes her arm in his as we walk through the pantry and the kitchen. His gallantry makes her blush.

The place is swarming with staff in sparkling whites, who stop their tasks and step aside as we pass.

As soon as we are out of the kitchen area, Vedveer hangs back and apologizes. Our eyes meet, and I nod.

He takes a unilateral decision to do a television interview. No discussion, no 'Are you okay with this?' I get his argument; the media is everywhere, and privacy is a joke. But the chaos isn't new. Waiting a few weeks wouldn't have changed a thing.

The reason I didn't protest Vedveer's POA is that had I insisted on going back to Bengaluru and scheduling the interview for another day, convenient to both of us, my family would've been on my case. Appa raised security concerns when I told him I'm staying the night in Delhi. He actually thought I would need security.

Amma and I are shown to the 'Parivaar Suite', which apparently is the only guest quarters on the floor the royals live on. It is the size of a spacious two BHK (bigger than my first house). It has two bedrooms, a lounge area with an upholstered sofa set, a coffee table with two chairs and a walk-in wardrobe, where the dress I am to wear for the interview is being aired out.

I find this so intrusive – a stranger unpacking your bags! I'm not sure, however, how I'm going to make anyone understand.

I look at Amma, who is settled on the sofa. I ask, '*Enakke maduttiddare idella?*' Why are they doing this?

Amma smiles. '*Talekedisikollabeda idkella.*' Don't break your head over all this.

Navya Mrinalini – (that's how I'm introduced to her, and that's how her name is imprinted in my head) – had accompanied me to a designer to buy an outfit for the interview today.

The outing took about an hour, after which we headed to the Four Hundred Club for coffee. On weekends, it is apparently open in the afternoons. A recent thing.

'We should make a booking?' I said, remembering the conditions for booking a table, at least an hour in advance.

'No booking is required,' she replied, her palm resting gently on my arm as if to make a point.

'Nice to have some leeway, for coffee at least!'

'Says the Coffee Empress!'

'Hmmm... More like for a Rathore!' I said.

Vedveer was waiting for us at the Four Hundred Club. He was seated at a round table near the bar, not far from where I had tripped. A couple of waiters hovered around him.

'How is your leg?' he asked, his eyes on my footwear.

I was in flats. That's when it dawned on me that it didn't fit the dress code. The lady at the reception was so enamoured by her royal guest that she didn't bother to check if what I was wearing fit their guidelines.

Vedveer apparently finished his coffee before we arrived, and we barely settled into our seats when two COFFEE Before Books & Bras' bone-dry cappuccinos arrived at the table.

I liked that they served the coffee with two button-sized biscuits, one savoury and the other sweet. I complimented the waiter.

'That's a really nice touch,' Navya Mrinalini agreed.

I felt Vedveer's gaze fan my left cheek; it was naked without a spot of make-up.

I lifted my eyes and met his. The grey-green palette was a shade deeper than usual, like a storm brewing.

'How are you feeling?' he asked.

I nodded. I inhaled.

'Does she know the pick-up point for tomorrow?' Navya Mrinalini asked.

I was given a detailed briefing on how to get to the car park in the morning and at what time. Not for the first time.

Some twenty hours later, I'm settled on a sofa in the lounge area of the Parivaar Suite, considering a coffee. Amma is seated beside me; she hasn't said much this morning.

The chambermaids are fluttering around the room, complimenting me on the dress I will wear later. They tell me a make-up artist will be here in an hour to get me ready.

I'm doing a lot of inhaling and exhaling.

There's a knock on the door, but before I can react, the door is pushed open. It is Gauri Elena. She sweeps into the room, dropping compliments as she walks – Amma's sari, the cut of my (non-distressed) jeans. Amma and I are on our feet, and Gauri Elena's hand is on Amma's bony arm. She asks us to join her and her son in the breakfast room. Navya Mrinalini is apparently out for a photo shoot.

I excuse myself respectfully. I want a moment on my own. I need to catch my breath.

I pick up a coffee and settle on the sofa in the bedroom as soon as they are out of the door.

I remember the launch of COFFEE Before Books &

Bras. Appa had done everything he could to get me to do some interviews; he said the brand could do with the publicity and I could fix my public image that way.

I'd rather take whatever vitriol they throw at me than twist myself into an impression that isn't me.

The landline rings. I let one of the staff get it.

'This is for you, Rajkumariji.'

I blink. Rajkumari? It is the palace staff. They apparently want to give me a protocol briefing. There goes my 'me time'.

There's a light knock on the door, and two women walk in. One of them is slightly older and is draped in a sari, and the other is wearing a salwar, both of them with prominent name badges.

I'm on my feet, coffee cup in hand.

'Please sit down,' I say and take a seat opposite them in the lounge area.

They smile and nod but continue to stand, which is making me uncomfortable.

The older lady, whose name badge reads Smita, starts talking. 'We have to brief you about a few things – like how to sit and stand when you're in public, how you exit a vehicle and how to climb into it,' she says, looking at my posture. I'm sitting on my left leg, which I have drawn up. 'Also, what to wear when you're in public. The Rathores have a legacy in style, so certain attire, especially for female members of the family, is better to leave out of the wardrobe.'

'What about distressed jeans?' I ask. A rebellion is brewing inside me. 'That is only for common people,' Smita says, 'and you're not common any more.'

Who decides that I am common and not common any more?

'What about underclothes?' I am intent on pushing the knife deeper.

Smita's face contorts. 'Only things that can be seen,' she says. 'If you have any doubts, please run your clothes by us at any time, and we'll let you know if they meet palace standards. It is not a problem.'

It is a problem for me!

'There are royal titles that you need to be aware of so that you address people appropriately. Also how you bow to the king and queen. The Rathores don't like excessive bowing, but there are rules you need to follow.'

Smita takes a breath, and I try to summon a smile.

'Rajkumari, if you will please stand up,' she says, walking towards me, to maybe take the cup from my hand. 'Sapna will give you a demonstration, and you can practise it.'

I put up my hand to tell Smita I can handle a cappuccino cup. I'm resorting to hand signals only because I can't trust myself to speak. I feel the tears at the back of my eyes.

As Sapna steps back to prepare for the demonstration, there is a knock on the door, and before I can respond, the eight-foot slab of teak is swung open.

I stare at Vedveer's advancing figure. His eyes spark a question. The women bow promptly.

'Yuvraj, we are here for the palace protocol briefing. How the rajkumari needs to address the maharaj, ranisa and you, how she needs to bow,' Smita says.

'Not required.'

'We were told—'

'Leave now, please.' His tone is polite but firm, and his smile has hit sub-zero temperatures.

'We'll come back a little later when the rajkumari is free.'

'No,' he says. 'Listen to me very carefully. Anything to do with the rajkumari has to go through me, and only me.'

Vedveer turns to the ladies-in-waiting and requests them to leave the room. 'Thank you for attending to the Rajkumari,' he says as they bow to take their leave.

'I'm sorry about this,' he says, turning to me as the doors close behind the staff.

I nod.

'Cappuccino?' I ask and turn quickly. My back is facing him.

'Yes,' he says slowly, 'coffee.' He may be smiling now.

When I turn to face him, coffee cup in hand, considerably more in control, he takes the cup from me and places it on the side. He takes my hands in his and makes me sit down. I feel a tremor in my palm; his are firm around mine.

'I apologize for the manner in which I have disrupted your life, Aaditha,' he says.

'That's meant to scald you,' I say, pointing at the coffee with my eyes.

Vedveer laughs. It sounds like relief.

'No kindness for the wicked.'

His eyes carry questions that bore deep into mine. I can never tell what he thinks and why he leans a certain way. He is a man of few words and even fewer expressions. Except when he laughs. That is a dangerous thing.

Vedveer reaches into his pocket and pulls out a box, which has two rings in it. One is an emerald piece studded with diamonds, and the other is a rock, a solitaire.

I inhale his perfume, wondering what this is about. We can't be exchanging what looks like engagement rings in the Parivaar Suite when it is just the two of us.

'We can't go into the interview without rings,' he says, returning to his feet.

My emotions are on a crazy roller-coaster ride.

'I think the size is right. It's my grandmother's.'

On one hand, this feels natural, an intimate moment for which Vedveer made sure we are alone... but that is only one part of the story. I try to smile.

Vedveer puts the ring on my finger; it fits perfectly. Like his grandmother, I have scrawny fingers.

'This,' he says, pointing at the rings – I see the brief flicker of hesitation in his eyes, but he decides to plough ahead – 'is a tradition, something I would not foist on you, but I hope you come to appreciate it.'

His eyes meet mine, and for a minute, I forget to be mad at him.

Vedveer's hands shake; my finger is firm as we exchange rings.

I slide the solitaire on Vedveer's finger. His eyes are on mine, and my heart has fallen to the pit of my stomach.

His thumb brushes my finger momentarily before I pull it back.

'Umm… sorry. I…' He is on his feet, looking away. 'I'll let you have a moment and wait for you outside.'

I take in what just happened. He put a ring on my finger because we were papped and not because there is anything else at play. Only because it is tradition… It turns in my head like a whirlpool, dragging me down the dark end.

I really like what I'm wearing. Navya Mrinalini does have great taste.

Vedveer's sister spotted it even before the designer, Sara Khiani, brought it out and placed it on the display table.

'This is a good colour,' she said, turning it over and looking pointedly in my direction. Navya Mrinalini was meditating.

I wasn't particularly impressed at that point. It is a pure silk sleeveless dress in the palest green.

'It's inspired by the spring forests of Rajasthan,' Sara told us, pointing at the embroidered pears and falling leaves of different shades that were pinned with sequins.

Just as well Amma had brought her emerald earrings along; they go perfectly with the dress. They also match the ring Vedveer put on my hand.

As I pat down the dress, it occurs to me that the Rathores might have sounded my parents out about the ring Vedveer put on my finger. Maybe that's why Navya Mrinalini had chosen this dress for me.

When she was looking at me, she was deducing what I made of the outfit, not how it would look on me, which is something fashionistas (read: Alia and Lavanya) do when they help you pick a dress. They're imagining how it looks on you. There was no other dress in green at the Khiani home outlet. There were a lot of plums and yellows, blacks and the white family, but no greens, not in Western attire.

I hear Vedveer at the other end of the room, but even before his voice reaches me, I can tell by the shift of energy on the floor that he is here. He is in a suit of a similar hue.

I wonder if it is also new or if he had picked the ring after looking at his wardrobe.

'Aaditha.' He breathes my name, and his breath fans the top of my ear.

I don't know why, but I get the feeling that he says a prayer before saying my name every time.

It's a simple name, three syllables.

Vedveer's hand is on my back as we walk together into his father's study a little after noon. The room is dark for the most part, except for where we are to be seated, a cream-coloured two-seater on which light pours.

We are introduced to our interviewer, Naveen Sharma, with whom we chat briefly before the cameras roll. Sharma, a senior (political) journalist, speaks for a few minutes, making introductory remarks, before he turns on us.

Sharma sits upright, holding up his height, which almost matches Vedveer's, whose posture is relaxed.

He starts engaging by making a show of the rings we are wearing. Sharma says the ornaments are 'steeped in tradition'. The solitaire wasn't presented by the Gowda family, as is custom for some communities, but was worn by Maharaj Rawal Rathore Singh, while the emerald ring belonged to his wife, Maharani Pavitra Hansa.

Pavitra Hansa's parents likely gifted her the ring, which the Rathores are now claiming as their precious tradition. I try not to smirk. Vedveer's eyes are on my hand.

Sharma goes straight to Vedveer. 'How did this proposal come about?' he asks.

Vedveer smiles and turns to look at me, like he is checking if I am okay.

I nod. Just the slightest shift of my head.

'This is a match arranged by our families. Our fathers are well known to one another; that's how it began. It was Father who raised the topic of marriage to Mr Prathap Gowda, and everyone was happy with it,' Vedveer says.

There was just the slightest hesitation when Vedveer said 'Father'. Is it because he should have referred to his dad as Maharaj in a public interaction?

'How long have you known each other, Yuvrajji?' Sharma asks.

'We've been chatting since January, getting to know each other gradually,' Vedveer says, looking away from the camera and directly at me, lifting a brow in question. 'We use all forms of communication, even email. It's been a fun experience. My fiancée is an extremely intelligent, smart woman, and we like to spar.' Vedveer concludes with a soft laugh.

My fiancée? I don't understand this energy spike, but I feel it.

Sharma decides to up the ante. 'You are the crown prince, and you have various palace responsibilities that include the charities your family runs. Do you think the princess-to-be will be able to share your load, given that she's also a career woman and is very different from you culturally?'

'This is a conversation we have obviously had,' Vedveer says, pressing his palms together. He's not impressed with the question.

'Aaditha is aware of her role and responsibilities as much to her own family as to the one she will be marrying into. She's been leading from the front with her coffee chain these last years, doing a very good job. It's clear that when she commits, she has worked out all that it entails. Besides, she'll have all of us supporting her. If you remember, the ranisa also embraced a culture very different from hers, and she has done quite well.'

Vedveer turns and looks at me like he is passing the ball to me in a game of field hockey, cheering me to go score.

My breath is ragged, and I'm flexing my palm unconsciously. His gaze shifts to my hand, and his face lights up with a smile. Vedveer closes my palm with his, like he is simply taking my hand in his instead of covering a nervous tic.

Something in me melts in that moment.

I take a deep breath and begin. 'I don't see why one cannot *try* to do it all. A full-time professional, daughter, sister and *wife*. I'm not the first person to attempt this; it is an everyday thing in most households. Not everything will go like you planned; a lot of days are a struggle, but it is okay.

'I'm aware that I come from a different cultural background to the Rathores. There are a lot of things about my culture that Vedveer will have to fine-tune himself to. I speak Hindi, so that's already a beginning; he will start learning Kannada, I'm sure.'

Vedveer's smile is so broad it spreads to the dark corners of the room. Not so much Sharma's smile. With no scandalous scope so far, he is positively sour.

'What was your first meeting with the Rathores like?' he asks, shifting in his seat.

Vedveer looks at me and nods, his grip on my hand firm.

'Very pleasant. They're good people. The ranisa enjoys my coffee, and Navya Mrinalini has been drinking COFFEE Before Books & Bras coffee for a while now. We bond over coffee. Most of all, they're kind people and made my family and me comfortable instantly.'

Vedveer's brow shoots up, and his eyes are boring into me. I turn away and look at my footwear.

'Can I ask if you always wanted to be a princess? How young were you when you first heard of the Rathores?'

I sit up, my shoulders snapping back instantly. This question is a hailstorm, disruptive at so many levels.

I look at Vedveer, who is equally stunned.

Sharma is so impressed with himself that I hear his smile more than see it.

'I don't have a date for you, unfortunately, but I guess about the time I learnt to read and write.'

As I speak, headlines dance before my eyes – five-year-old Aaditha, fan of HRH Vedveer.

'Indian history is curriculum in the school I studied in,' I finish.

Sharma has the good grace to laugh at least.

He turns to Vedveer. 'How is your Green Dream project going, Yuvrajji? How much time do you spend in Jaipur?'

'The wheels are already in motion. It is a project that's very dear to me. I hope to fully cover it in a couple of years, get it off the ground, 100 per cent organic. I'm in Rajasthan most of the year, at either Ranibagh or Aranya

Mahal, and that's how it is going to stay for a while at least,' he says.

'Yuvrajji, I have to ask. How did you miss the princess-to-be's award ceremony in Delhi?'

Vedveer doesn't miss a beat. 'That was clumsy on my part. I got the date wrong, and I'm still making it up to her,' he says, his eyes stroking my cheeks.

That was a heck of a comeback, given that he is being roasted for no fault of his.

'What about your business?' Sharma asks me. 'How do you think you'll be able to run it from Jaipur?'

Vedveer nods. I realize he is trying to tell me he'll take the question.

'COFFEE Before Books & Bras is Aaditha's baby; she knows the ins and outs of it. I'm certain Aaditha will be able to manage it from wherever she is based,' he says and turns to me.

I nod.

'While we are on the topic of careers, I must reveal my expansion plans for COFFEE Before Books & Bras,' I say, looking down at my nails, determining that I have to play the exit strategy now.

It is getting too cozy between Vedveer and me.

'I'm delighted to announce that we will be debuting in Jaipur in a couple of months. Our first store will be located just outside the gates of Ranibagh. That way, I can keep a close eye on my business. I hope that will put to rest your fears, Mr Sharma! Coffee is on us anytime, of course!'

I turn and look at Vedveer, who is nodding. His eyes are bright, and his cheeks light up in a warm glow.

TittleTattle

Gupshup Column

SAY IT LIKE THE PRINCESS-TO-BE AADITHA!

Curious so-and-so,

So, TT is doffing hats to Coffee Queen Aaditha Prathap, who gave the national broadcaster a royal snub. Imagine asking a CEO if she wanted to be a Princess, and that too in 2024!

Naveen Sharma's patronizing question: Can I ask you if you always wanted to be a princess? (No, you cannot!) How young were you when you first heard of the Rathores? (None of your damn business!)

The tone of her response was lazy, a resounding slap that echoed across the country from New Delhi to Bengaluru - and TT is applauding the crash-boom.

Aaditha wasn't done. She even invited the hapless Sharma for a coffee at her 'coming soon' store in Jaipur, which TT confirms is located opposite the gates of Ranibagh.

The tea is boiling, dearies. Just like we promised.

Aaditha's first television interview - remember she hasn't done any interview before or after the launch of her coffee chain - shut down the doubters. She handled herself admirably and spared no one, not even the royals.

'I speak Hindi, so that's already a beginning; he will start learning Kannada, I'm sure.'

TT loved what Aaditha was wearing, an absolute showstopper. About time, baby!

A little bird tells us HRH Navya Mrinalini picked the outfit (but of course) from her favourite designer, Sara Khiani. The dress, in swathes of pure silk, costs INR 1.7 lakh. We don't have a price for the bauble on her ring finger, a timeless classic. A Rathore heirloom. Suffice it to say that the figure carries half a dozen zeroes!

They were quite the couple on the couch, and TT hopes you didn't miss the moment when the Crown Prince took Aaditha's hand in his, midway through the interview. It floored us.

The glances they exchanged during the 17-minute exercise carried a quiet intensity; sparks danced in the silence between them. It is hard to believe they have only known each other for two or three months.

Why would HRH Vedveer, with such a tall dating resume, agree to an arranged match?

We have a burning question, dearies. Is it possible they were already in love? From the way they looked at each other, it certainly seemed so.

There was some *gupshup* that the interview was hastily arranged, given that it was announced only an hour or so before the recording.

The Rathores do what they want to do, when they want to do it.

The interview was rescheduled from the traditional prime-time slot to noon at the behest of the Palace. No explanations were given.

11.

Vedveer
Seasons and Reasons

For most adults, 1 p.m. is lunch hour, time to break for midday sustenance. But for Gaurav Rathore Singh, even though the clock flipped to PM an hour ago, it's still the early hours of his day. He generally retires around two or three o'clock in the morning and rarely surfaces before noon.

I haven't seen Father at a breakfast table ever. If we are to travel early, he grumbles at the world, having spent the night resenting the morning in advance.

It is at breakfast that Mother tells me that her husband wants to have a word. It is to be the first order of business. She asks Navya to be there too.

'One o'clock in the study?' I ask, wondering what this is about. The family is in Jaipur to oversee Holi preparations.

'*Hanji*, Yuvraj!'

Navya nods. I doubt she has heard Mother; she is busy punching her phone keyboard.

Mother's Hindi is heavily accented, a strain of Russian

and British accents standing out like a linguistic palimpsest each time she opens her mouth.

It cannot have been easy for her to not just learn a foreign language but also embrace a culture that was foreign to her. The world wasn't so connected in the '80s, and distance is real. Gaurav Rathore Singh, whom she calls Gaurav, with a little lisp, enjoyed a Western lifestyle, which also means Mother didn't have much of a warning of what to expect when she arrived in India.

Hindi is a tonal language; the retroflex and nasal sounds also take some getting used to. Just as well that Mother is uncommonly good with languages. Her diligence in trying to remove every trace of her 'foreignness', from how she dressed to what she ate and drank, to how she moved in a crowd, isn't unnoticed, especially by her husband. If not for her colouring and accent, it would be hard to tell her apart.

The breakfast room at Ranibagh is a happy space. The angled sunroof allows for a flush of natural light, not something Navya enjoys. This morning, she is wearing oversized sunglasses.

I'm standing by an arched window, teacup forgotten in hand, watching the late-morning light flood the garden that is starting to stir – jasmine buds, gulmohar blossoms and frangipani in full bloom.

My mind goes to Aaditha. The outdoors doesn't call out to her like it does to me; she made that amply clear on our first meeting at her office, but she likes flowers. The vases in her house and workplace are full.

Would she stop to smell the jasmine?

I exhale. I have watched trees change with the seasons every year, how the green deepens and then darkens. Autumn arrives quietly here. Would she notice how the bougainvillea clings to summer, defiantly pink? I imagine her walking these paths – not as a guest – wrapped in a shawl, the winter breeze stroking her cheeks.

The palace has always been mine, yet suddenly, it feels like something I want to share with her.

There's only the small matter of her wanting us to come up with a plan to break this engagement.

I never expected to bump into Aaditha in Delhi, not even after Navya told me she had won 'The Initiator' award.

It was a regular Friday meeting with friends at the Four Hundred Club.

I greeted the familiar faces as I entered the room, making my way to our table. Kairi had ordered my drink, and I took a sip even before I took my seat. I felt rushed for no apparent reason.

I was momentarily distracted by the almost-naked back on a barstool. I tried to look away, but I couldn't. The posture was defined, and the shape was striking.

I took another sip of Jaboulet Red and tasted the grenache, feeling the sweet burn of liquid in my mouth.

It is not like I knew the back, even though the frame

was familiar. Tiny. Slightly rounded scapula, upright. An earthenware pot placed upside down. I struggled to stay put in my seat.

Onyx. The colour of the dress was the red herring. I had only seen Aaditha in quiet tones of white, echoing a promise of committing to a nunnery. I had no problem with the colour. Butter is lip-smacking, but to restrict yourself to one colour 90 per cent of the time is a bit skewed.

I have no idea how she ended up sprawled on the ground, though. She said her foot got entangled with the leg of the stool. I'm not sure about that, but she came down hard, and we're lucky there were no broken bones.

Aaditha wasn't pleased with the hurried scheduling of the interview, even though she didn't contest it. Her expression said it all – lips tightened and a shutter dropped over her eyes. She wanted to say something, but her determination overrode her instinct.

The point is, the interview had to be done. It is tradition, but the reason I pressed ahead, after stalling for weeks, is because it was the best way to get the press off our backs. I felt we could give them something and walk away. They would hound Aaditha otherwise, late in the evening, early in the morning, and that was not something I was willing to risk.

I walk into the Maharaj's Library just after 1 p.m. Father is seated behind the grand desk at the far end. He has sheets of paper in his hands but is staring at the heavy curtains that cover the window that faces him.

I walk up to the curtains and tap the switch that draws the drapes apart. 'You need the sun,' I tell him, even as he scrunches his nose at me.

'What's this?' I ask, picking up the papers he places on the table. There are a couple of numbers scribbled on the first sheet – 5,000 and 50.

'That's what they are offering us,' Father says. He is signalling to Raj Kiran, for sunglasses, which are duly placed on him.

I'm looking at Father with a question I haven't asked.

'Five thousand crores for a fifty-year lease for a section of Ranibagh and the grounds at that end.'

My brain is doing the maths.

'My title and all it encompasses,' he says, his hands behind his head as he pushes back.

He takes a sip of his whisky and returns the glass to the coaster, placing it perfectly in the centre. He is silent.

'A section of Ranibagh and the grounds that run alongside,' I say.

I turn the figures over in my head. This is our best shot at a sustainable future. We can't continue financing our exorbitant lifestyle just by relying on smart investments, most of which are gained from disposing of land.

We'd need a gold mine just to raise the capital to start cultivating our lands. The acreage is vast, and nearly 60 per cent of it has to be prepared from scratch. Some estates are in serious decay; others, in more favourable locations, have reverted to forest. It could take anywhere from five to ten years before we see any kind of return.

'Lease is a good thing; at least that way, we don't lose our land,' I say.

Father throws a curious glance my way before shifting some ten degrees in his seat.

'This way, we can at least hit a pause button on selling our land.'

'That happened a long time ago. I put a stop to it long ago,' he insists.

The time he stresses on is five years ago, to be precise.

'I give Ranibagh away, just like that?' he asks, his voice unusually subdued.

Somewhere in this vast space we are treading – properties, legacy, tradition and custom – I meet my father and feel for him.

For as long as I can remember, he only travels to Jaipur twice or thrice a year. Still, it is his seat, and his taking exception to leasing it out is understandable.

'I know what you're thinking,' he says. 'But it's still my palace; Ranibagh is the seat of my throne.' His voice quivers unsteadily.

I put the papers I have been scanning aside and lift myself from the lounge chair. I walk across the room, away from where he is seated, before turning back. I need to word this carefully.

'It stays in the family; it always will. It is your seat and will continue to be your seat, lease or no,' I say, bending over the desk and looking directly at him. 'But look at what we can give our people if we develop the land. It's livelihood, and it will always be your gesture to them. They need their king to work for them, Father.'

What I don't tell Father is that the Rathores need it, too. We need our land to work for us.

He nods. I use that as encouragement and press ahead.

'They will be appreciative that their maharaj is using all his resources to give them a better life; when opportunity and money come their way, they will be forever grateful,' I say. 'This is why a lease would work; we return the principal amount and get our property back at some point.'

Father looks out of the window. He has such an aversion to light, I wonder how he is handling so much of it.

'Do you know who this party is?' I ask.

'A foreign conglomerate. They acquire boutique properties and turn them into luxury hotels without altering the structure.'

'Is there a minimum period when we can break the lease?' I ask.

Father points at the papers I had set aside. 'I think twenty years. There's an out after ten, but that's in an extreme circumstance, and it comes with a huge penalty.'

I nod. 'Twenty years is enough time. We should be making good profits by then.'

Father smiles. I'm aware that the only reason he is considering the lease is because I'm pushing him to it.

Ranibagh is my most favourite corner on the globe. This is where I come to get away from everything. Navya and I rushed here to be with Grandfather on every school break. It is where I feel love, the ground below my feet and all it holds.

Some of my fondest memories growing up are at the maharaj's apartment, a floor above where I'm standing now.

In the spring, I used to sit on the swing on the terrace that overlooks an ornamental lake, thinking it was the brightest spot ever. In the winter, the water had a stealthy touch to it. The sun, bashful at that time of the year, came out later in the morning. Grandfather would point that out to me, and I would laugh hysterically.

'You look like the sun now, Veer,' he would tell me.

Ranibagh, with a living area of 80,000 square feet, is the largest palace in India. It has sixty bedrooms and ten ultra-luxurious royal suites, each with additional living areas and private balconies. It has nurseries, libraries, reception halls, dining and tea rooms, a movie theatre, games rooms and a sprawling spa and wellness centre. An economy by itself.

'We are not turning over Ranibagh in its entirety,' Father says.

I shake my head. 'The royal suites, the Maharaja's Library, a reception hall, the kitchens and dining spaces and the staff areas stay with us.'

'The sixty living rooms go to them.'

Ranibagh is built latitudinally, where the royal suites and the children's nurseries overlook a section of the waterbodies, while the other part of the construction, the area we will be leasing, runs alongside the grounds.

'The account books say Ranibagh is a strain on the finances,' I say, swallowing guilt.

'I found a way to manage.'

We have to do better than manage, and Father knows that. 'If, for the time being, a part of it becomes someone else's problem,' I say, 'it will work for us.'

He is non-committal, but as I turn to him, I see the blood rush to his face.

'We should wait,' he says.

I nod. That he hadn't said no is a victory.

Raj Kiran opens the door, and Navya walks in, armed with her sunglasses.

She settles into the seat I vacated and tells Father that she is also considering marriage, maybe in a year. Her tone is casual, like she is telling us about the next pair of glasses she wants to buy.

'Wedding.' Father considers the word like it is a collector's item he is turning over to check its veracity. 'We have Veer's first.'

As a family, we don't do emotions very well. Definitely not that part of the family that is in the room. Drama is never far away.

'When do you want to get married, Rajkumari?' Father asks.

'I'm giving you advance notice,' she says.

Father looks pointedly at me, and I turn to the window. It is my turn to take some sun.

I'm finally able to read between the lines of his reluctance. The wedding celebrations are high on the list of reasons he is so at odds with leasing the property. He has made elaborate plans in his head to get both his children married in pomp and style. And scaling down isn't him.

'Aaditha and you are all over social media after the interview, brother,' Navya says. 'Everyone is swooning, saying "how sweet", "how cute", "how into each other they are" and all the rest of it.'

'Yes!' Father is finally smiling. 'I saw that, too!' His laugh is a roar. 'And here I'm worrying that Vedveer has lost his charm!'

'You are blushing, brother!' Navya is pointing at me and laughing.

I turn to the door, looking to make haste.

'I have a favour to return,' I tell Navya.

Father taps his fingers on his desk, calling the attention of the room.

'Yuvraj,' he says slowly. 'Choti Holi is yours. You will light the first Holika next week.'

'Why?' This is unexpected. I turn right back and return to the room.

'I will take your place on the dais and do the watching.

I want you to take over,' he says and takes a deep breath. 'You are the maharaj all over again. It's time you start taking over responsibilities.'

'This is a huge responsibility,' he adds, his hands around his head, motioning the crown. 'The best way to do it is slowly, when I'm still around and able to help you take over.'

'Why don't we invite Aaditha for Holika Dahan?' Navya is on her feet and looking at Father.

Mother walks into the room as Father gets on his feet, applauding his daughter. 'What's happening?' she asks, looking pointedly at me.

Father has already discussed my lighting the first Holika with his wife, and so he tells her about Navya's idea of inviting Aaditha.

'We must invite the whole family,' Mother says, 'all four of them, that's if Alia is in the country.'

'Goes without saying. She's hardly going to arrive here alone,' Navya says.

Mother is insistent that we share the dress code with them.

'We don't want a repeat of the polo game,' Navya says. 'They took it in their stride, but it's not fair; *TittleTattle* is mean.'

I agree. There's no harm in loose guidelines.

Father shakes his head. 'We should let them be, invite them and not issue a dress code.'

'Suit yourselves,' Navya says. 'I'm inviting Aaditha

for the Indian League game, which is the day after Holi. Hopefully, she can stay for an extra day. I'll tell her to bring an extra dress or two with her.'

'That's a good idea. She packs frugally. You'd think they're weighing her bags!' Mother rolls her eyes.

'Mother! No judging!' Navya is right on cue.

'She packs like the CEO she is, Mother!' I back my sister.

The remaining Rathores in the room roar.

12.

Aaditha

Holika!

I inform the Lakshmi Bar Devotees (aka LBDs) about my Jaipur trip only after we touch down in the Pink City.

I've been in such a funk in the days leading up to this that I forgot to tell them. Prescriptive traditions and elaborate ceremonies make me nervous.

Only Komal knows, and that is because we had a yoga session this morning.

Me: *Landed in Jaipur with parents. Back day after.*

Lavanya calls a minute later. 'Remind me again why you're in Jaipur,' she asks. She sounds like she's in the middle of a few things.

I mentioned the trip to Jaipur to her as soon as I slotted it in my calendar, but I hadn't told her why.

'Have you heard of Choti Holi?'

'Hmmm…'

'I didn't think so.'

Appa, who is sitting across from me, turns away, pretending like he hasn't heard.

Raju messages.

Raju: *Baby of the group is getting married.*

Me: *No one is getting married. I'll find a way to get out of this. Just you wait!*

I am deeply offended that my grand announcement of the opening of the COFFEE Before Books & Bras café just outside the gates of Ranibagh hasn't got the Rathores up in arms.

Vedveer raised an eyebrow ever so slightly during the interview that even damn *TittleTattle* didn't notice.

I shouldn't lose hope, though. Maybe the Rathores are saving it for when we are here.

Navya messaged me two days ago, asking me to bring an extra set of clothes. I've been invited to the T20 league game that her boyfriend is playing in. In the following text, she says Choti Holi is a big evening for Vedveer; he'll be lighting the Holika for the first time.

Appa thinks Gaurav Rathore Singh is rolling out succession plans. Apparently, it is not common for a king to entrust royal duties to the next in line when he is still healthy.

I'm stretching out the fingers of my right hand and balling them up. I repeat.

There will be more cameras, a whole crowd of people, endless staff, talk of heritage, culture, practices… I tell myself this isn't about me, not this moment. I have to show up for my family now. Later, there will be an out. There has to be one at some point.

I spot the Rathores – father, mother and son – flanked by a small army of uniformed staff, waiting at the palace foyer as we step out of the vehicles that ferried us from the airport.

The parents are caught up in polite greetings. Then, from behind them, Vedveer appears, cutting through the stillness with purposeful strides.

My heart stumbles in my chest.

'Aaditha,' he says, his voice low. His right hand brushes my forearm. His face is drawn, almost pale, like he hasn't slept. The noise around us – conversations, murmurs, shuffling footsteps, clanking luggage – fades. For a second, it's just him and me, caught in the quiet tension of something unsaid.

'The staff will show you to your chambers,' the senior Rathore says. Vedveer insists on escorting me to my room.

He is wearing a white shirt on blue jeans, with sleeves pushed back just enough, giving his gait a workman-like edge. He has thrown my tote over his shoulder without ceremony, having taken it from one of the staff.

We walk side by side, the silence between us taut, not awkward. Like a thread that connects two people.

'Apologies for pulling you away from work and disrupting your routine,' he says.

I nod, mostly because I can't quite find my voice.

Does he actually believe COFFEE Before Books & Bras is my baby and not a venture Appa funded to shore up an offspring? Or is he just being gracious? If he means it, really means it, when did that shift happen?

Was it the award?

'How are you doing?' I ask, glancing at him.

He turns slightly, meets my eye and smiles. A small, unreadable thing.

'Not bad,' he says.

I make a conscious effort not to look around me. I could drown in the sheer massiveness of the place. One foot in front of the other, eyes only on what is before me. That, however, lasts until the room door opens. My eyes widen at the expanse around me. A ginormous space, then another room, comparatively smaller, an open-air sit-out, more doors that lead to… more rooms?

Vedveer places my tote on a table and points at the three chambermaids and a young woman wearing a corporate uniform. They bow in unison. Knees bent, torsos angled.

He gestures to the lady in the grey skirt and waistcoat that carries the Rathore insignia.

'This is Reema Barmer,' he says. 'She's been hired to help you with anything you may need in the lead up to the…' A loud pause, a sharp intake of breath. 'Wedding,' he finishes.

Anything I may need... Wedding...

Reema's smile stretches from ear to ear; she couldn't wear it any wider, even if she tried.

How many queries would one have? Did they need to hire someone to answer my questions? There are already one too many people running around this place anyway.

I wait for Reema to walk away.

'I could just call you if I need anything,' I say. 'I mean, I could just ask you, no?'

Vedveer raises an eyebrow before his face breaks into a smile. 'Sure,' he says, 'you can, anytime.'

I nod. There's a question I cannot quite read in his eyes.

'Are you nervous about lighting the Holika for the first time tonight?' I ask.

'What's there to be nervous about?' he scoffs. 'Just centuries of tradition and everyone's eyes on me and the very real possibility that I trip and set my kurta on fire.'

I grin. 'Wow! I like the confidence. Should I keep a bucket of water handy?'

Vedveer's smile falters as his eyes darken. 'It's a lot. Not just the lighting of the fire or the people watching; it's what it means. Like carrying something bigger than me, something that's supposed to bring light after darkness. I... I don't want to mess up.'

My eyes are on Vedveer. The weight of tradition and expectation is a complicated maths sum.

'You won't mess up,' I say quietly.

'But keep that bucket of water ready, just in case?' he says and turns briefly before making his way out.

'Is there anything you need, Rajkumari?' Reema asks.

I need to be left alone. The only thing on my wish list at the moment.

I tell Reema I will call if I need anything. She leaves her card on the table.

Two of the maids are young and all smiles; the older lady's gaze is firm. I meet her eyes squarely.

The two younger maids start moving my baggage around, giving an already pristine space more order, if that is even possible. They then disappear into the bathroom and return giggling.

They want to unpack my bags, but I'm not unpacking.

I haven't packed my entire wardrobe – just a couple of options for the events and outings that are planned. The extras are only because of Alia, who is sitting in the United States and running my life.

'A girl needs to have options', she says.

Gauri Elena isn't taking chances and has ordered my outfit for this evening, the idea of which has me in splits.

My suitcase is open, and one of the maids is tugging at my undergarment bag. This is nonsense! I put out my hand, signalling for them to stop.

'I can manage on my own,' I tell the maids. 'If you tell me how the shower works, I'm good.'

The prying twosome are wearing shocked expressions. They change tracks. One of them insists on showing me where the night clothes are (I have brought my own night clothes) while the other one runs the bath.

There are satin sets, in my size, in the walk-in wardrobe. They are wrapped in crisp tissue that are in three different shades of pink. There are style options, too. Pyjamas or shorts or a thigh-length chemise.

In a large box wrapped in metres and metres of tissue is my Rajputi Poshak in rose pink.

It is exquisite, but it is over-the-top grand. I run my hand over the fabric; it feels like satin silk. There's a scroll that has literature on the dress. It has taken thirty artisans to complete the gold thread work.

Just as well the Rathores took charge of what I am to wear this evening. I would never have gone for something this elaborate. I don't care what social media said about how I dressed, but it obviously matters to these people; theirs is a mighty platform. My option (which I have carried courtesy Alia) is a Mysore silk *lehenga* with an ornate dupatta. Amma says, in her day, it was called a half-sari.

The girls join hands to lift the poshak out of the box and put it on a hanger. I'm grateful for that help. They say it is heavy; it looks like something one might employ a crane to move.

Just before exiting the apartment, the youngest apologizes.

I don't know what she is apologizing for, but I don't ask either. I want to be alone.

I shut my eyes, trying to extricate myself from the lavishness of everything around me. I'm only a thousand nautical miles from home, and my parents are a couple of doors from me, but the distance feels irretrievable.

My heart stills momentarily, and images of my parents, sister, her broken life and her expertly built bras, my baby,

COFFEE Before Books & Bras, dance before me. I think of my crazy group of friends – Lavanya, Komal and Raju.

That is my world. What am I doing here? What am I giving up?

A business I had built with sweat and wit.

Who am I doing this for? And for what?

I'm sobbing. I let myself have a good cry.

'Did you rest?' Navya Mrinalini asks. Her voice is soft and her tone gentle. She is seated next to me on an elevated platform, which faces the gathering.

I nod. My eyes are red. I'd rather the Rathores thought I had slept the afternoon off than cried it away.

'You're looking gorgeous,' she says. Her smile reaches her eyes.

She is adorned in a pink and orange poshak, every inch the princess. She's demure and savvy in equal portions and is suitably postured. Her back is straight, and her shoulders slope, just a wee bit.

'It's beautiful,' I say, my right hand on the *odhani*. 'Thank you!'

'It is my choice,' she says. 'Rani-pink for the rani-to-be. Fully cheesy!'

I choke back her compliment and try to smile.

I'm sandwiched between Gauri Elena and her daughter in an enormous courtyard on which the Aravallis gaze down. Appa is seated next to the senior Rathore, and Amma is by her husband.

The two men appear to be doing well together; every now and then, a laugh rises above the din.

In the centre of our row of seats is an opulent silver throne, on which Vedveer, whenever he appears, will be seated, I'm guessing.

I'm reading the room like it's a secret-agent movie, hunting for the subtle signals.

The setting sun has brushed the hills in a dull glow that lifts Ranibagh's sparkle. Every now and then, there is a rustle from the wind that brushes cheeks and pushes back errant strands. The sound system is playing heavy music, a genre of folk songs, perhaps.

Behind us is a row of men, four of whom hold the royal *chatta*s for the king and queen, while the others wave *chowrie*s – fans that finish in long, flowy fibres that don't give us relief from the weather but maybe allow the palace staff to participate in the ceremonies.

Open-air coolers are placed at strategic locations, away from the cameras. It isn't hot, but the sheer volume of people makes it stuffy.

Reema walked me down from my quarters, and on the way, she gave me a brief description of how the evening was expected to pan out.

'We are all waiting for Yuvraji to light the Holika,' she said. 'People love him, you know,' she added. In case there were any doubts.

In the middle of the courtyard is a mammoth construction of sticks and bricks, about fifteen feet in height. Around it is an elaborate floral decoration in marigold and desert jasmine.

Guests and dignitaries are seated across from us. The crowds are in the distance. Some wave their smartphone torchlights, while others record the space, which they will no doubt upload on social media. Their king is not lighting the Holika tonight; the prince is.

Despite the tension running through me and my reservations on royalty and its many reverberations, I'm appreciative of the ringside seat to what promises to be a hair-raising cultural show.

I'm so tempted to draw up my legs and watch the spectacle unfold that it takes all my determination to sit still.

I'm suddenly all there, all the bits and parts of me, just the way I am when I walk through the doors of COFFEE Before Books & Bras.

I hadn't seen or heard from Vedveer after he showed me to my room earlier in the afternoon, but I know he is around somewhere by the arched hallways of the palace.

Men with big moustaches and tightly tied turbans, dressed in various shades of white, assemble along the corridor that leads to the courtyard. They are carrying silver staffs that glitter in the light.

The *dhol* is playing traditional *chaal*, an accompaniment

to the folk and devotional songs coming through the sound system.

My foot taps the floor unconsciously.

I inhale deeply, grounding myself in the moment. The hair on my arms stands on end.

It is an evening soaked in colour and sound; the air is charged. It could be the music or just the energy of the thronging masses awaiting the prince, who'll be king one day.

That's when I spot Vedveer, his presence seizing my gaze. The people standing in front of him instinctively part, swept aside by the power of his lengthy strides.

He is styled in a pearly ivory sherwani that gleams like the moonlight and is adorned with gold buttons. His *safa*, intricate and grand, rises from his head in a fan-like crest, crowned with a shining brooch. In his right hand, he wields a bejewelled purple sword sheath.

A shiver races down my spine, maybe awe or something undefinable. My jaw drops, perhaps stunned by the force of his presence.

Across the courtyard, our eyes lock, slicing through the throng, rising above the chaos of bobbing heads and swirling sound. His face, calm and unreadable, hides everything; mine, however, betrays the storm of emotions raging inside me, the charged pulse of the evening.

Just before he enters the courtyard, chants of '*Yuvraaaaj Maharaaaaj ki jai*' punch the air.

I feel the duet of love – that of the people and their leader.

There's another round of shouts and loud cheering, the decibel levels hitting new heights, but when Vedveer raises his head, the calls subside. That appears to be the cue for the drums to start rolling.

He strides in the direction of where we are seated. He looks first at his father and then his mother, his hands folded in prayer, before he steps forward and touches their feet, sword sheath in hand. He glances at his sister, his head slanting in a nod, before his eyes bore into mine, reaching deep. They hold a question I cannot read.

My breath catches in my throat, and I cough into my palms.

There's an unalloyed steel to Vedveer, hidden beneath his spark.

Sometimes, it feels like I can push him, really wade into him, risk provoking him... and he won't push back. But then, there's the other side, the one I saw in the Parivaar Suite at the Rathores' Delhi residence, when he dismissed the over-eager protocol execs. That side is cutting, composed and unmistakably cold.

This evening, I see another side, a fusion of both: the unwavering light and the icy edge. The command of a leader.

After a brief stop on the dais, Vedveer returns to complete the ceremonies.

He sits on a low silver stool and performs a puja, invoking blessings of divinity.

The songs and drums hit a fever pitch as he performs

the *arathi,* marking the start of an evening that celebrates the triumph of good over evil.

The ritual is completed with Vedveer lighting the torch at the holy pyre and carrying it around the bonfire. When he finally lays the torch on the stick and brick structure, the crowd erupts in a joyous chant that is in sync with the inner gates of the palace opening.

The bonfire rages quickly and aggressively, kissing the darkening night sky. Young boys and grown men light their sticks before merging in the distance, carrying the fire to their homes. There, they will light their own bonfires, which will burn to ashes, and with it, the idea of evil that threatens them.

It is dark outside, save for the lighting. In the distance, guests mingle.

Vedveer walks to where we are seated. His father is on his feet and envelops him in a hug. His mother tries to soothe the lines on his face.

Their boy carries an enormous weight with remarkable lightness.

My feet are steering the Poshak to my room. I walk the corridor of the floor we are living on like a drunk, swaying from side to side, trying to balance the weight around me.

I have the besotted Reema for company, and she can't stop drooling over her Yuvrajji.

Did you see the way he walked with that sword?
I love the way he walks. It is so royal!
His sherwani was the perfect fit.
Did you see his pearl-embellished juttis? *Oh my god!*

Every other sentence is an exclamation.

Meanwhile, I'm at the end of my tether. This skirt must weigh some thirty kilos at the very least. My hip feels dislocated; there's the harbinger of a gnarling pain. I enter the room and shut the door on Reema and immediately tug the cord of my *lehenga,* which comes down around me in a circle. I step over the fabric and toss away the *odhani* and blouse. I walk to the couch in a bra and panties, wondering why people would torture themselves so.

I told the maids that I didn't need help, but looking at the fabric sitting on the floor and considering its weight, I'm thinking I will need help after all.

I have twenty minutes to get ready for dinner.

The phone in my chamber rings. It is Manisha, the lady in charge of the chambermaids.

"Rajkumari,' she says, 'I hope I'm not disturbing you. I wanted to ask if you need our help with putting the Poshak away.'

I want to whoop with joy, but I control myself and behave like a rajkumari. 'Sure,' I say calmly, 'thank you, but please give me a few minutes.'

I put down the phone and race across the floor to my jeans, which I pull on, and reach for a white tee when the doorbell rings. Manisha has given me two minutes exactly.

Manisha and her two eager assistants take charge of the pile of fabric, clearing the room and putting away that mountain of a skirt.

As the girls disappear into the closet space, Manisha asks, 'Are you excited about Holi tomorrow? It is the happiest day in the palace for us; we have so much fun.'

I nod. What else can I do?

'You must put the first colour on Yuvrajji, and he must put the first colour on you!' she urges, her eyes bright.

I blink.

'This is our tradition, Rajkumari,' she says. 'This is how they have done things, maharajas and maharanis, for hundreds of years.'

I nod.

'The palace staff have a different Holi celebration; it is equal to the one you will go to. The Rathores have always been so kind to the workers,' she says. 'The family included my husband for our first Holi, and I hid myself until he found me. *Uske liye ise aasaan mat banao*!'

My guess is that Manisha is in her forties. She still wears a delightful blush when talking about her husband.

Amma will knock on my door in about ten minutes, after she changes saris, and we will go down together. Appa has dumped us for the senior Rathore.

I change into a deep olive embroidered Indo-Western wear, a fitted skirt and blouse.

I ask Amma what the men were discussing so animatedly earlier in the evening. She says it was cricket for the most part. On my way up, I heard voices in one of the rooms that I crossed; it might've been the senior Rathore. If it was Vedveer's father, then Appa was with him, and they were certainly not talking scores.

After the guests and dignitaries leave, the family, which includes the royal siblings and their offspring, gathers at the dining hall.

When Amma and I enter the hall downstairs, we find Appa in conversation with the senior Rathore.

Vedveer is across the room from where I am positioned. From what I can tell, he is the only man in the room who has changed.

The hall, like everything in this palace, is huge. A long dining table, which could comfortably seat twenty people, is the centrepiece of the space. At one end of the room is the bar, while the other end has a crockery cabinet. The room extends into a terrace with open-air seating.

The moment Vedveer sees me, he crosses the room and comes over.

'How are you doing?' he asks. His face is fresh. All the stress I noted earlier in the day has disappeared.

I nod. I smile.

I want to tell him that while I admire the lightness with which he bears his responsibilities, I'm caught between two worlds. Vedveer's and my own, both at a societal and personal level. The freedom of choice my life affords me... But that's hardly suitable conversation for a preprandial drink.

'I had the bucket ready,' I say, 'but it was a waste of effort.'

Our eyes meet, and Vedveer smiles. 'It is good to have got that done with. I have watched Father do this every year, and I feel like I know every move, but when you're doing it yourself, it is very different. Everything is new.'

Vedveer excuses himself to get Amma and me drinks, and as soon as he returns, the senior Rathore clinks a spoon to his whisky glass and says we will all be shown to our seats.

Appa and the senior Rathore continue their animated discussion, and it looks like one of Vedveer's uncles has joined them.

I wonder what they are talking about. It is not like they are friends. It's been all of fifteen minutes since they met.

I have Vedveer to my right and Amma to my left, and next to Amma is Appa. Gaurav Rathore Singh is at the head of the table; he is flanked by Vedveer on one side and his wife on the other.

Our drinks are replenished, and entrées follow. One of the plates is *dal baati* with its many sauces. Vedveer whispers '*dal baati*' in my ear, just in case I didn't know what I'm being served. As if.

I can't believe he actually remembered. On one of my trips to Jaipur, I had the yummiest *dal baati* ever, a favourite of mine. I told Vedveer that.

Gauri Elena looks dotingly at her son.

'It's Aaditha's favourite,' Vedveer says as I savour the first.

'*Ninage ishtana?*' Amma asks, smiling. Do you like it?

Navya Mrinalini, who is seated opposite me, is clearing her throat. 'Brother,' she calls, 'do you know what my favourite food is?'

'I know your allergens, sister,' Vedveer says.

I have never heard siblings call each other 'brother' and 'sister'. This is all too posh for us *akka-anna* folks.

'Favourites, brother?' she presses.

Vedveer is trying not to smile. He looks away from his sister, and his gaze strokes my cheeks. I'm trying to swallow that bit of food that is stuck in my throat.

13.

Vedveer
Talking Down Walls

I follow Aaditha to the terrace after dinner. Her hair cascades down her back like a silk curtain caught in a gentle breeze, until her hand snakes back and sweeps it over her shoulder.

It is just us. The families – immediate and extended – have all retired for the night.

I look around the sun deck. My eyes linger on the bar, the carefully scattered tables and chairs, the lone sofa and the stretch of bonsais. I like to think of this space as my benefaction to Ranibagh. This is where I spent long hours as a boy, my eyes transfixed on the Aravallis, which from this position are at eye level, or so it seems. Like a peer, almost.

Aaditha asks for a cup of coffee. She wants to make it two, but I'm not done with my vintage yet.

She rolls her eyes in response. I like that she still thinks I'm a coffee drinker. I have that edge over her; I know exactly how she likes her coffee.

'Apologies about the staff,' I say, referring to the fiasco earlier in the day.

I spoke to them before her arrival and made sure to underline her sensitivities, but their over-enthusiastic attempts to help her settle in ended up ruining it for her.

Aaditha's eyes are on my wrist. I'm holding a goblet.

'You notice them?' Aaditha asks about the staff on the terrace, her eyes darting to the corners. 'They try to be invisible, speaking softly and merging into the walls. I don't mean that in a feudal way.'

I laugh. What other way could it be?

'They all appear to be happy and very much at home here at Ranibagh. A bit bossy, too, especially the help at the chambers,' she says, her eyes dancing in the light. 'Again, they're not rude. It's just that I'm not used to so many people around me.'

Aaditha smiles and lets her shoulders drop before she turns to pick up her double-shot bone-dry cappuccino from Sagar, the server.

She waits for a couple of minutes, letting the staff settle into their spaces, which is a fair distance from where we are positioned.

'Do you want them to leave?' I ask.

'Not unless you want them to,' she comes back with a smile.

Aaditha's fitted calf-length skirt outlines her petite frame; her cropped V-neck vest reveals a sliver of her waist. Her dark hair sits on one shoulder; an errant silky strand falls over a cheek. I'm tempted to pick it up and tuck it behind her ears.

'When they reached for my bag of intimates, I kinda lost it,' she says. 'What next, I'm thinking. That's when I told them I can manage on my own.'

I apologize again.

She shrugs. Some of her hair slides from its perch and falls over her breast.

She takes deep breaths, and I try to regulate my breathing.

'Nothing to apologize for, Yuvrajji,' she teases. 'All is fair on the palace grounds.'

Aaditha's lips lift just a touch, like they had on a January evening, and for a moment, my mind goes back to that kiss. The one she has no recollection of, because of which I'm consigned to the heap of average kissers. There's no insult crueller than mediocre.

'Tell me,' she says, eyeing the place beside her, motioning for me to join her there.

'I would love to draw my legs up and sip my coffee,' she says, breaking from the train of the conversation. She does that sometimes, without missing a beat, then jumping right back to what she was saying earlier, dragging you back and forth like a yo-yo.

'Go ahead,' I say.

Aaditha shakes her head.

'My skirt is too tight.' She throws her head back and laughs. 'The thing about these fancy clothes is that they're not functional. They're not designed for multitasking working women like me.'

'Bourgeoisie, are we?' I ask, my gaze sweeping across her length.

'Are you checking me out, Your Highness!'

I can't help a sloppy smile.

'I was thinking, no, wishing, I could wear my favourite denims, which I've packed, by the way, for dinner! Maybe I should have! I would've embarrassed Mr Unflappable!'

She's laughing gayly at her own joke.

'You think me unflappable?' Is that how I come across to her?

She dismisses the question with a flick of her wrist. 'Is that what I said?' she asks.

'You should've given the denims a shot for dinner.'

'Threat or dare?' she asks, pushing out her chin, her eyes locking with mine. I sit back on the two-seater. It's all I can do to stay where I am.

My brows shift in a quiet motion.

'What I wanted to ask you earlier is that does someone actually pack your clothes for you when you travel?'

Guilty as charged. I nod.

'But how would they know what you'd want to wear on a particular day?' she asks, pointing her cup at my shirt. 'I mean, I get it. For men, what are your options – blue shirt or white shirt? Dress shirt or not so dressy or whatever descriptor you use for these clothes?'

She shakes her head dramatically, discombobulated by the nuances of fashion.

'What about your mother, or your sister?' she asks. 'Imagine landing in Mumbai or Dubai with the wrong pair of jeans in your suitcase! It would drive me crazy.'

'Navya packs her own bags. I'm not sure about Mother, though. I could ask her if you want. Aaditha is interested to know.'

I offer a small prayer every time I say her name. It's the phonetic roulette. There's thunder in her eyes each time I go over with the 'H'.

We sit quietly for a while, enjoying the breeze and the charged air that fills the silence. I refill my glass, but she's done with coffee for the night.

'I don't want to be walking up your palace walls!' she says.

I'm hunched over my knees, wine glass in hand, watching the colour of the night deepen.

'Is marriage something you have given a thought to?' I ask as a stiff wind tousles her hair.

Aaditha opens her mouth and then closes it before she speaks. 'Marriage in general?' she asks.

I nod.

'It's not something I want to think about,' she says after a while, her gaze meeting mine.

I'm not a man of a dozen questions, and in this case, I'm not even sure if it's okay to ask why, but I do.

'I didn't really have reason to,' she says.

I wonder about Arjun Mahesh, the dude from the *TittleTattle* posts, the sender of red roses.

'My parents' marriage is functional; nothing wrong with it. I don't think they have ever discussed divorce, but it's not something I would go to any length to replicate for myself,' she says.

The hollow of her neck sinks as she speaks. 'And Alia's marriage of eleven years will end in a divorce. It's only a matter of time.'

I had no idea about her sister's marriage. 'I'm sorry.'

'Don't be,' she says. 'She's better off single than being unhappily attached. Maybe the same for her husband.'

'I don't have great examples of happy marriages in my life, so yeah, it's not something that enthuses me. It makes me very nervous, actually.'

Aaditha's eyes are almost the colour of her hair.

'I don't mean to crib. Life has been good to me,' she says, 'but society, its views and opinions on women are so skewed, especially in the matter of marriage.'

Aaditha shakes her head like she wants to knock off a thought and preferably lose it.

'Look at the way I'm trolled for what I wear or what I don't wear, the way I look or walk. There's a national debate on stuff that is basically personal choice,' she says, 'but you, everything you wear is great. It's a different metric for a man, especially when he's as good-looking as you are…'

I'm caught between her point – something I had not really considered in the depth at which she articulates –

and a casual compliment she slides my way. A point that didn't make her pros list.

'Life has not been so kind to me on that count,' she says.

I nod.

'Tell me about America?' I ask.

What I really want to know is about the chap she went to college with, who keeps cropping up on social media.

'I had a dream, Vedveer,' she says. 'I was always massively trolled because I'm my father's daughter. It isn't the same for Alia, and thank god for that, maybe because she got married and moved to the US about the time Appa gained political prominence or because she is an IT professional.'

She exhales, and I feel her breath fan my face. She is sitting back on the sofa, her right elbow on the armrest.

'I went to a not-so-popular college so that I could get lost. I didn't want to be tracked down.'

'I wondered about that,' I say.

'I spent most of my time in college by myself, except for when I got into an unfortunate relationship not much before I abandoned my studies,' she says.

'What happened?' I want to know everything about her, what makes her tick, what she does every minute of the day.

'A guy, a vile gaslighter,' she says with a laugh. 'His name is Arjun Mahesh. *TittleTattle* had a picture of us having coffee the day you and I met in my office.'

Hmm... Why does she still meet him?

'Arjun thought I was just another Indian student trying to make it work in the United States,' she says.

I hold her gaze and say nothing.

'He must have figured otherwise much later, after COFFEE Before Books & Bras had taken off.'

I let her speak because she clearly wants to speak.

'He's probably the one providing *TittleTattle* photographs of me from my Ohio days. Arjun is the only other person who could have had those photos,' she says.

'Only other?'

'I'm the other, and I don't have any,' she shrugs.

I nod.

'I ended that relationship by throwing the remnants of a tepid cup of coffee on his face,' she says, her smile bright.

My eyes settle on the wine on the side table, and we both laugh out loud.

I lean back on the sofa after a while. We are sitting so close, it kills me to not be able to pull her into a rough embrace.

'Lavanya came into my life the day I ended things with Arjun, and she hasn't left.'

I hear her breathe.

'Good things also happened to me in America. Lavanya, and somewhere between running away from trolls and considering society's opinion of me, I became my own person,' she says, sitting up and squaring her shoulders.

Aaditha reaches for the wine glass in my hand, then pauses, fingertips grazing mine. She's undecided. I offer it to her. She takes it slowly, her lips brushing the rim as she sips, leaving a trace of lipstick behind.

'The idea of COFFEE Before Books & Bras was born on that campus in Ohio.'

COFFEE Before Books & Bras is her story. I let that sink in as I study the wine glass. Do I sip from the spot her lips just touched or turn it, pretend I didn't notice?

'My coffee is really good, no?' Aaditha's eyes light up. She's not asking a question.

'It's great,' I say and lift the glass to my mouth. My lips on her lipstick.

Aaditha's cheeks colour. The shade of her lipstick.

After a while, we move from our seats and stand by the parapet, from where we look down at the now-empty courtyard. We watch as the bonfire settles into the earth, whispering embers disappearing into the night.

A stiff breeze draws a shiver.

'My god, this view!' she says, turning to me. 'It's like I'm making eye contact with the Aravalli. Looking up at it from the courtyard is brilliant – brown, green, bold – but this is a whole different level of awe... It's like you can converse with it.'

'Why, hello, my friend!'

She stops talking and turns to me.

'Your friend for life,' I say.

She nods.

This balcony is my getaway in Ranibagh. It could be Aaditha's, too, if she wants it.

19.

Vedveer

Happy Holi, Your Highness!

I'm the first one from the family down at the Rang Mahal courtyard. We're playing true to form.

I stand in the centre, admiring the *jharokha*s, dressed in heavy strings of marigolds, in shades of happy and happier. Silken buntings in fuchsia and saffron flutter in the morning breeze.

Tall stalks of roses and desert jasmine, strung together thickly, decorate the archways in the corridor. Brass urns brimming with *gulal* line the marble steps at the entrance.

Ranibagh is ready.

The water fountain is already spouting colour, and Raj Kiran, the valet, can't take his eyes off it.

Holi in Ranibagh is chaotic – loud, bright and unapologetic. It never fails to lift the spirits. These are the only quiet moments when we can breathe easy.

In half an hour or less, the place will be a blur of colour and sound. The rhythmic beat of the *dhol* thrums my chest as I move through the crowd, smearing colour on the feet of elders. Even Father, stubbornly resistant to stepping out of his comfort zone, makes allowance for Holi. He wakes up early, pulls on a white kurta and joins in the celebrations.

I look at my watch. Father should be down any moment.

Aaditha and her parents are here. Holi will be different this time. *Even if it is just for this time.*

She has reservations about marriage in general and this match in particular.

My breath is rough; I feel it.

Raj Kiran turns to face me, a curious expression on his face.

My ringtone saves me. I wonder if it is Aaditha. I asked the nervous Ms Barmer to step back and give Aaditha space. I hope she hasn't forgotten her altogether.

It isn't Aaditha; it is Father calling.

When I return to the Rang Mahal courtyard some half hour later, after sorting out invites to foreign dignitaries who hadn't made our initial list, the place is a riot of colour.

In the last couple of years, we have started opening up our Holi celebrations outside the circle of family and friends. This is a joyous event, and I thought we should allow other communities in this country and beyond to get a feel of this vibrant festival.

I barely make it past the marble steps before my youngest cousin, all of thirteen, throws herself at me. She has a fistful of green, which I manage to avoid. I make my way into the crowd.

'I'll catch you, *bhaiyaji*!' Manvi shouts.

Somewhere on the grounds, Mother is laughing behind a veil of colour, and beside her is Mrs Gowda, dusting colour from her face. This is obviously Mrs Gowda's first Holi. She is standing with her hands knotted. Father is wielding a water syringe like a warrior. He is actually getting around on his feet, and Karnataka's genial finance minister has fallen in step. Beside them are a pair of tall silver mugs. I'm willing to bet that they don't contain bhang.

Then I spot her, decked in simple white separates with a red border. Her hair is tied in a bun, and an oxidized silver necklace sits on her dainty collarbone.

I sneak up behind her. 'Saving yourself for me?' I ask, keeping my tone casual.

She spins around, mock offended.

'Absolutely not,' she says. The double meaning registers, and sure enough, she pounces.

'Wow!' she says, deadpan, taking a step backwards. 'Did you rehearse that, or was it a spur-of-the-moment disaster?'

'Improv,' I shrug, moving with her, taking a step forward, 'but clearly underappreciated.'

'Oh, it's appreciated,' she says, 'just… quietly judged.'

'That feels fair.'

She grins, shaking her head.

'You do realize you're outnumbered today, right?' she asks, throwing a quick glance over her shoulder.

'Wouldn't have it any other way.'

We're standing face to face, a broad, cobbled pathway between us, and I realize this is the first time I'm seeing her with her hair pulled back and knotted. It suits her; everything suits her.

I move towards her, eyes locked. The legs are quick, but the heart is heavy. Strains from last evening are playing in my head.

I want to set it all aside for today, just for today, but the mind doesn't always do as it is told.

She's not considering marriage; she laid it out for me loud and clear.

'Where have you been?' she asks, moving further away, her hand in the silver bowl she carries.

I can't take my eyes off her.

This hairstyle highlights her features, particularly the lushness of her lips, which haunt me every night.

'Just fashionably late?' she teases, changing track and stepping closer to me.

'I was called away on work.'

She laughs.

'Brother!' Navya shouts. 'They've all arrived and are being taken care of. Ratanji is looking for you.'

Aaditha is smiling and walking up to me.

'She calls my clothes boring.' Aaditha is pointing at Navya.

'Nothing wrong with boring,' Navya says, winking at Aaditha. 'Brother adores boring.'

I'm trying hard not to laugh, and Miss Aaditha moves deftly and colours my cheek crimson.

'Happy Holi, Your Highness,' she says, backing up quickly. I go after her, just a few steps, but I check my stride. She notices and turns around.

'Maybe I should try my hand at polo,' she says, admiring her right hand. 'I have good aim.'

All it takes is a couple of seconds. She bends to admire her hand, and she has indigo on her forehead and hair.

'Happy Holi,' I return.

We stand there for a moment too long, surrounded by colour, chaos and family, trying not to stare.

It is closing on 8 p.m., but if the Coffee Queen needs her fix, who am I to tell her that her timing is off?

I message Ratan, who is also at the Jaipur Cricket Stadium, asking him to organize beverages. I settle for a cup of tea, though I'd have loved a glass of wine.

Navya is sitting in the same row as we are, a few seats away. She is with the wives and girlfriends and has Kairi for company.

Aaditha and I are here to support Navya's beau, Nalin Shah, who is captaining the Rajputana Royals in the Premier League. He is batting on 44. Not the best time for us to leave our seats as far as appearances go.

Aaditha leads the way as we head to the rear end of the VIP Pavilion.

Just as we step into the hospitality area, I spot Kairi, and Aaditha, who is beside me now, grips my wrist.

'What are you doing here?' I ask as Kairi wraps an arm around me in a hug.

'Getting a coffee for Her Highness,' she says, referring to my sister.

It must be said that Aaditha and Navya drink coffee at the weirdest hours, for reasons ranging from nerves to coping with boredom.

I introduce Aaditha to Kairi, who I make it a point to mention is engaged to a Kolkata industrialist. Aaditha nods; she is familiar with the Basu surname. Kairi apologizes for missing Ranibagh's Holika celebrations. She was in Delhi to see her grandparents.

I nod. Kairi would've been there if she could.

'I saw all the pictures, though, and you are looking every bit as lovely as you are,' Kairi says to Aaditha.

'Thank you,' Aaditha says. Kairi's words are heartfelt. I can tell by the tone.

Kairi's coffee arrives, and she excuses herself to join her friend, but not before warning. '50 is coming up,' she says, 'if only the man would give Nalin a chance to face the bowling!'

'Do you follow cricket?' I ask Aaditha, thinking that it is a bit late to be asking her that question.

'Now and then,' she says. 'If you mean, do I know the rules, yes, I do, but do I know the composition of all these outfits, the answer is no.'

Aaditha turns to our server, who has arrived with our order. She takes one look at the tray and turns to me. 'We both drink coffee,' she says, looking suitably offended.

'No,' I say slowly, unable to resist the smirk, 'you drink coffee, Aaditha. I drink tea.'

'What? No! Since when?' Her dark brown eyes have opened wide in an I-dare-you expression.

'For more than a decade easily.'

'Come on! You are only saying this because there's just one cappuccino on the tray. You had a cappuccino in Bengaluru, in my house, and then again, the next day with me!'

'I had a cappuccino with you, yes, but that was only because you didn't give me an option.'

'What? Noooo!' She is laughing hysterically and almost drops her head on my shoulder.

It is a while before she looks up and asks, 'Seriously?'

I nod. Never been more serious.

Aaditha can't stop laughing. 'Ved… veer, even I can't be this ridiculous!'

'So…' she says slowly, 'at my house, you were drinking tea; that's why a teacup.'

I nod.

All this is playing out, just as Nalin gets to his 50. The stands erupt, and the cameras are on Navya, who is on her feet and thumping her palms. In the next instant, it shifts to the hospitality area, where Aaditha and I are standing in the centre of the tiled floor laughing. Aaditha's head dips against my shoulder but straightens immediately.

The caption on the screen reads, 'Ranibagh royals beside themselves with joy.'

After the camera pans away from us, she picks up her coffee and I pick up my tea. We sip our respective beverages quietly. When we return to our seats, Aaditha asks me why I hadn't corrected her about my choice of beverage. I shrug.

'That's mean,' she says.

'I was sure we'd have an opportunity to make a joke of it as we got to know each other.'

Aaditha rolls her eyes.

After the Rajputana Royals' innings folds, Kairi moves down the row of seats to chat with us.

'Is this your first time in Jaipur?' she asks Aaditha.

Kairi is friendly and sociable. Aaditha is more of an introvert; she prefers to keep to herself. I am unsure where this association is headed, if indeed it is headed anywhere at all.

'No,' Aaditha says. She's smiling, and her shoulders are relaxed. 'I have been here a couple of times before.'

'You have to like it,' Kairi says. 'You don't have a choice, you know.'

Aaditha nods.

The three of us are on our feet and chatting when the camera finds us again.

Aaditha is in blue denims and a black dress top; her earlobes are bare because they are sore. She hadn't told me that, but the soft curve of her ear is a pinched red. If Aaditha had kohled her eyes, it is barely visible. She wears no make-up, if you discount the lip gloss. She looks fresh, though, even if she doesn't feel fresh.

Kairi is wearing a maroon dress and glitters in the evening light.

We are on the big screen, and there's a roar from the gallery; fans are waving in our direction. Aaditha flinches. I turn to her and suggest that maybe we should all go inside.

As we follow Kairi back into the enclosure, our eyes meet. Aaditha is so uncomfortable with this attention; she seems to be shrinking into herself.

'Let's watch the rest of the match from inside,' I say.

Aaditha nods. 'Let's find a place where the camera cannot reach us.'

TittleTattle

Gupshup Column

AADITHA IS LOVELY, BUT SHE NEEDS A STYLIST ASAP!

Curious so-and-so,

We hope you devoured the visual feast from Ranibagh's Holika celebrations - our Instagram page practically exploded, and yes, darlings, we flooded your feeds on purpose. At TT, restraint has never been our thing, and why should it be? A good moment demands the spotlight.

Let's start with Aaditha looking positively dreamlike in a lush, ripe-pink Rajputi Poshak from Jaipur's House of Sheeba, a designer also favoured by the new generation of royals. Price tag? A breezy INR 2.7 lakhs. HRH Vedveer wore a custom silk sherwani with 24-carat gold baubles for buttons. Because he can!

Together, they were a picture, the poised Prince beside his blushing bride-to-be.

This week, Vedveer took the ceremonial baton from his father for the first time and handled his duties with signature ease. Aaditha played the part well, standing by her man, smiling for the cameras, doing the rounds, dutiful, if slightly rehearsed.

She even turned up at the Rajputana Royals match the following evening - TT gives full marks for consistency. As you know, the Royals have a stake in the team (though they insist on being hands-off), and with the flamboyant *daamaad* now captain mid-season, the 'no interference' claim is getting harder to swallow.

But let's not stray; here comes the real tea.

During a mid-game break, Aaditha and Kairi Gaur, the royal ex, were snapped in the same frame. Kairi, in a ruby-pink tea-length dress, looked straight out of a glossy cover shoot. Aaditha? Zero make-up, and not even a hint of jewellery. Ears as bare as the day she was born... One word. Why?

Just 24 hours earlier, she had dazzled us all. We started to believe she might actually belong beside the Rathores. But the next day? Back to boardroom beige.

Was that a flicker of envy in her eyes when she

locked eyes with Kairi? TT won't say it loud, but we're thinking it.

Look, we get it. Aaditha's the Coffee Queen - bright, brilliant, built for the boardroom. But this isn't just any man. It's a prince. And she's stepping into a palace, not a quarterly assessment call. Kairi knows how to read a room. She knows when to turn up the sparkle, how to wield colour and cut. The quintessential fashionista. Meanwhile, Aaditha remains undercooked vanilla.

15.

Aaditha

JaiPour: COFFEE Before Books & Bras

COFFEE Before Books & Bras is about a week from debuting in Jaipur. I'm standing in the middle of the 5,000-square-foot café, looking around me at what resembles a wrecked construction site.

One half of the floor reflects the effort of the workers, who have tried to make it presentable – half-painted walls in a shade that is goat milk maybe or just primer – while the other side looks like a ransacked warehouse.

A worker on a ladder is engaged in a passive-aggressive struggle with a light fixture that is swinging like it is auditioning for a haunted house. The far corner is a mess. Carton boxes ripped apart, parts of tables yet to be assembled, with the instruction manual serving as a coaster for a half-empty plastic bottle with accented fingerprints that gives the illusion of a cup sleeve.

The espresso machine sits on the counter surrounded by the wreckage of screws, tape and six different sizes of screwdrivers. A worker in overalls is crouched behind the bar, making unintelligible grunting sounds.

Paint cans double as stools, and painters have used brand-new coffee mugs to dip brushes.

When I first visited the site seven months ago as a prospective customer, I was optimistic partly because of its prime location, directly opposite the gates of the iconic Ranibagh Palace, and partly because of the expansive open space. We ultimately chose this building because the area is a well-established tourist hub, which is always good for business. The palace, a deep source of local pride, naturally draws traffic, especially on weekends and holidays.

Even as someone from Bengaluru, where royalty isn't woven into the cultural fabric quite like it is in Mysuru, I could see the potential. We'd scouted several locations across the city, but market analysis pointed to this spot being well worth the investment. (All of this happened *well before* the Rathores sashayed into my life, back when I knew they were royalty, and Vedveer was a name I'd heard and read about. Our worlds hadn't crossed yet.)

I imagined the whole place with a warm, earthy ambience, a prominent wall adorned with intricate Jaipuri block prints. A mix of terracotta pinks and mustard yellows on the floor, and indigo tiles skirting the corners. Low-hanging lanterns made of coloured glass throwing golden shadows across the room. I wanted eclectic furniture, locally sourced, carved wooden chairs, distressed vintage tables, stand-alone pieces, a space balanced by aesthetics.

A section with cushioned floor seating in bold textile patterns, where caffeinators lounged with a book or lay on their backs, striking up conversations. A traditional charpoy could complete that space.

I want the uniforms to appeal as much to Rajasthanis as to tourists. I look at my watch. The uniforms are scheduled to arrive today. The coordinates are all black, with zardozi embroidery on the tips of collars, paired with pink aprons edged in mirror work.

I hitch up my jeans as I make my way across the store. The feel of denim in my hands brings a smile to my face; it feels familiar, a mix of hard and soft. *TittleTattle* would call it 'pageboy' attire, not fit to be photographed alongside the Rathores, who, if they wore denims, would come at the cost of all that lay locked in the treasury building. Royal backsides need so much more.

I'm walking to the back of the site, where the restrooms, the staff room and the manager's cabin are located. I say a small prayer as I put one foot in front of the other. 'Please, God, please, let some part of this store be done at least.'

I feel my jaw drop as I pause at the entrance. The room seems to be having an identity crisis; one wall has shiny new tiles, and the other is flaunting industrial décor, raw brick and no more. I poke at a brick, half-expecting it to shift, but it holds up. The mirror is leaning awkwardly on the white sink, like it just gave up and decided to sit down. Pipes peep out of walls.

I wanted this store to be different from my others

because of the flavour of the city, its distinct pink landscape, forts, palaces and vibrant bazaars. From where I'm standing now, it certainly looks different. It is a horror show.

We were initially supposed to launch in March, in time for Holi, but the work was badly stalled, because of which we were forced to push the opening to May.

We hired Bhanwar Lal, a reputed local contractor, in March, after we found that the initial team we signed with was dragging its feet. While there has been progress, we are clearly nowhere near where Bhanwar Lal is telling us we are in his daily updates. He had been briefing Mohit Mohan, my MVP in COFFEE Before Books & Bras, every evening, but he was obviously just painting a picture.

I'm scheduled to come in for the day, a week before the launch, like I usually do. I visit the site, tick boxes and make a list before I head home. Fortunately for me, maybe because Alia's 'a girl needs options' is playing in my head, I pulled out an overnight case and threw in extra clothes just in case.

I told Vedveer I would be in his city for the day before the staff from Bengaluru took over in the lead-up to the opening. The plan is for him to pick me up from the café and drive me to the airport. That seems unlikely this evening. There is too much to be done and even more to be monitored.

As I make my way across the floor, I consider calling Mohit. He is expected here a couple of days before the launch, but the sooner we fly him to Jaipur, the better it is for my mental health. He is the only person I can trust to take this space from a construction-site setting and drag it across the finish line in a week.

I need to find a place to sit down before I make the SOS call to him.

'*Sambhaal kar utaren, behen*!' someone barks as I duck just in time to avoid a swinging light fixture.

He speaks in Hindi, not Kannada. I'm far, far away from home; I feel the distance. I stumble sideways into a stack of chairs that are placed upside down; it clatters onto the floor like an applause track.

The air smells of paint fumes. Sawdust is everywhere, on countertops, in my hair, in my lungs, possibly.

Beside the man who had just called out to me, a girl whom I remember from the group chat as 'Simi with the coffee skills' has emerged out of thin air and is standing behind the espresso machine, wearing a random apron and a puzzled expression. She looks as stunned as I am.

She is the only local person we have hired for the café so far. That will, of course, change in the months ahead.

The other baristas and the pastry chef of the inaugural team are Bengaluru-based and will arrive in time to do the dry runs before the launch.

I step over an open box labelled 'FRAGILE', only to trip on an extension cord. I steady myself, feeling the sweat beads trickle down my face and settle on my clavicle.

'Aap kaun hain, behen?' a male voice asks. I look up to see an older man in a paint-splattered Calvin Klein shirt, grinning at me from behind a stack of unopened boxes.

I look at him blankly. I'm not sure what to say.

'Kya kar rahe hain, yaar? Sink ko ulta laga rahe hain?' he calls out to the man in overalls, who is lying on the floor.

The chaos is overwhelming, the noise echoing an unfinished story.

We started rolling out media campaigns last month, and in the next twenty-four hours, we start the one-week countdown on hoardings in prime locations in the city, just like we had done in Bengaluru.

What if we are not ready on the launch date? That looks more like a possibility at this point.

I need a few minutes to myself before I speak to anyone or make any decisions.

I settle on one of the dry paint buckets that has been turned upside down. From where I'm seated, I can see the palace gates – tall and symmetrical, studded with ironwork and flanked by sandstone pillars etched with floral motifs. We are there but not quite there.

I reach for my phone and message Lavanya.

Me: *I don't know when you'll see this message, but I'm totally panicking!!! I'm not sure if our Jaipur outlet will be ready by launch date!!! Yikes!*

Me: *Don't tell me to postpone the opening because the date has been announced in all the major publications, and the save-the-date exercise on social media is done!!!*

Me: *Fortunately for me, I packed a couple of extra clothes. I'm planning to stay on for a day or two. Will call Mohit. Hopefully he can get here soon and work his magic again.*

I decide against calling Bhanwar Lal and instead dial Mohit and tell him that he is needed here.

I shut the phone and exhale.

'Ma'am,' Simi calls. She's by my side now.

Her eyes are glazed. I want to ask if she is okay, but beside her, the man in the paint-stained tee is also on his feet and looking over me.

I do a 180-degree turn and face an open door where Vedveer stands. He is in a fawn-coloured suit, his shirt is open at the throat, and his hands are in his pockets.

This is the one person I do not need to see now. Behind him, a mini army battalion are shuffling their feet like they are preparing to attack.

Fortunately for me, he has the good sense to leave the unit outside. I don't need any more folks who don't know what they need to do in this space.

Vedveer walks carefully, avoiding the wires and the floor that resembles an abandoned obstacle race track.

I hear a sound right next to me, a crash, a thump. I swing around to see Simi on the floor.

She is standing next to me one moment and is sprawled on the floor the next.

The Calvin Klein tee, who is standing next to Simi, is bowing to Vedveer instead of helping the girl. 'Yuvraj Maharaj,' he says before turning his attention to Simi.

I remember I have a bottle of water in my bag. I pull it out and splash it on her. She flutters her eyelids as I kneel on the floor and help her sit up.

'What happened?' That's my voice.

She is resting her head on my arm and smiling at Vedveer's clean-shaven face now.

'Drink more water,' I say. Simi nods and licks her lips.

Vedveer, who had knelt beside me and looked her over, is back on his feet.

He dials his secretary, who is on the other side of the door, and asks that the lady be taken to the nearest emergency care. He asks Ratan Singh to accompany her, insisting that she be dropped home and that he keep him posted on her progress.

After Simi leaves with Vedveer's team, he tells the painters to carry on with their work.

'Are you okay?' Vedveer asks, his eyes on the hollow of my neck, before turning to the chairs.

He pulls out two from the pile that has crashed and lays them out for the two of us.

I stare at him for a moment before shaking my head. 'I'm okay,' I say, smiling. 'I'm really okay.'

Vedveer's smile is forced.

'Apologies for getting here earlier than I had said I would,' he says. His arms are on his knees, and his eyes are boring into me like he's trying to reach my soul.

I quickly draw in a breath.

'I had a business meeting, which finished sooner than

expected, and I thought I would swing by and see how you are doing.'

I nod.

Imagine realigning that entire regiment that goes with him everywhere when he has a change of plan. A logistical nightmare for the conductor of the show.

'Was your journey okay? Did you get here on time?' he asks, his eyes gentle on mine.

I nod.

My mind goes back to the evening on the terrace balcony, when I almost called him Ved but quickly managed to attach the Veer to it, like it were a surname. He didn't notice; at least, I don't think he did...

Over the last couple of months, something has shifted. Maybe it was the interview, but now, in my head, he's just *Ved*.

'Ved... Veer,' I say. The Freudian slip! Ugh! I notice a flicker in his eyes, a hint of a smile.

'Vedveer,' I repeat, forgetting what it is that I wanted to ask him.

'Vedveer is an intriguing combination for a name – not always easy to pull off together,' he says as he dips his shoulders to make eye contact.

I clear my throat, scrambling. 'My mind is all over the place,' I say, blaming it on the floor around me. 'I'm forgetting names!'

He chuckles, amusement flickering in his eyes. 'Ah, yes, the charming mishaps of the mind.'

'How are you doing?' he asks.

'Lost in the usual chaos,' I say with a shrug.

'Usual chaos sounds like a full-time job. Does it come with benefits?'

'Only if you like unpaid overtime and existential dread.'

He grins. 'Tempting.'

'I'll add you to the waiting list.'

'So exclusive?' he asks, his brow lifting.

'Naturally. Chaos doesn't just let anyone in.'

He nods, mock serious. 'And here I was thinking I had royal privileges.'

'Those expired the moment I called you *Ved*.'

His laugh this time is low and warm. 'Call me that again, and I might just forgive you.'

Vedveer turns slowly and looks around what will be a café in time. His face is fresh, and his shirt is stiff. The vibe of a presiding deity surveying the ruins around him.

'This place looks pretty basic,' he says.

I nod.

'There's a lot of work still to be done, but the good thing is that you have a week to go. You still have time.'

'What are you planning to do?' he asks, returning to his seat. 'About today?'

I can't leave this evening. 'I called the office and asked them to book a room in the hotel down the road. I will definitely be here tonight, maybe for one more night till Mohit arrives.'

I lied about the hotel booking, only because I don't want any drama. I was going to ask for a room to be booked when Vedveer arrived at my door.

'Why do you want to stay in a hotel and risk the prying paparazzi? They'll be shoving cameras into your face every morning at breakfast. You can stay at Ranibagh; there's ample space.'

Ranibagh is big enough, I know.

'Thank you! But I cannot ask my mother to chaperone me,' I say. 'You know how these things work.'

'I don't know how these things work, Aaditha. I'm not offering you a room; you can have a whole wing. There's nothing to worry!'

I hear some noise behind me, feet shuffling, and I wonder if it is Vedveer's army.

'Don't turn,' he says softly, leaning forward, his fingers warm on my arm. 'There's a bunch of photographers outside.'

I feel a shiver go down my spine. The interiors of my store is a mess, we are due to open in a week, and the paps are at the door waiting to pull me down.

Vedveer is standing in front of me. The air between us is so thick, it would take a knife to slice through.

It is his bloody convoy that called out to the paps, practically begged them to come snag us.

The Rathores cannot do anything quietly. Wear a wig, dress like a homeless person, disappear into a crowd.

'What do you say?' he asks about me staying at his palace.

I nod. I don't have much of a choice.

Tittle Tattle

Gupshup Column

AADITHA, VEDVEER & THE MATH

Curious so-and-so,

The pieces are finally falling in place about the story we've all been scratching our heads over. The why and how of this cross-country romance.

On a sultry Jaipur evening in May, Aaditha Prathap arrived at her COFFEE *Before Books & Bras* outlet, and dearies, you won't believe how bad the place looked with just about a week to go for the launch.

Aaditha was having palpitations. The work had ground to a halt, there was hardly a worker or two around, and the date for the inauguration is approaching.

In walks the suited HRH Vedveer and takes stock of the outlet. The walls may have been treated to a coat of primer, but wires were running everywhere and pipes popped out of every nook; the look was too raw for even industrial.

When Vedveer was taking stock of the place, one of the staff, perhaps thoroughly overworked, swooned at the sight of The Prince, who swept her up in his sculpted arms and rushed her to hospital.

It turns out that Aaditha has already moved into Ranibagh, where she'll stay as the Royals attempt to stitch the store together. They don't have much time, as we all know.

A little bird tells TT that Ranibagh's *bahu*-to-be has been so tight with the purse strings that the contractor has absolutely refused to work for her. He hasn't been paid for a month!

Has Daddy Dearest not been in a generous mood lately?

Prathap Gowda must know his daughter can fish in royal waters now, so this is as good a time as any to cut loose and walk.

From all that unfolded at the store two evenings ago, we are given to understand that HRH Vedveer is helping Aaditha with finances.

Of all the reasons, who would've thought money was why a thrifty billionaire father would hitch his daughter to India's most-landed Royal family?

That's exactly why Aaditha cherry-picked this strategic location for her store, just outside the

Palace gates. This way, she's in front of their eyes, and they'd know if she needed help! And she clearly does. *Chalaak ladki!*

The question TT is asking is: Has Aaditha gone from father to husband-to-be, asking for contributions to fund her dream for which she's winning awards?

Wooo...! Don't we love a theory!

16.

Aaditha

My Baby!

It is my second successive night at Ranibagh; that is one too many nights already!

I don't need to read the *TittleTattle piece* – the link for which Lavanya sent me – to feel like I have been tossed into a spin cycle.

The first thing I do as soon as I wake up is to shoot Lavanya a message about my anxiety, which has skyrocketed. I don't explain why I'm on the edge, assuming she'll connect the dots. The situation at the café, and also that I have no way of working off my anxiety here at Ranibagh. No one in this township of a thousand rooms I'm living in knows where the gym is. Working out helps me keep calm.

Lavanya unknowingly rubbishes *TittleTattle,* thinking the rag is the reason for my anxiety.

Lovey: *Please don't even bother with that. TT is too ridiculous!*

TittleTattle delights in highlighting my inadequacies,

and I have a few. I haven't gone on social media the last couple of days, and I don't know what stories they are spreading.

I make the mistake of asking which piece.

Lavanya sends me the link.

I click on it instinctively.

The slander these people pass as journalism. Shocking. Outside of the fact that 'Simi with-the-coffee-skills' had swooned at the sight of Vedveer, there is not a word of truth in it.

I visited her at home last evening. She told me that seeing the prince in real life for the first time unnerved her.

'I'm a big fan of the royal family, ma'am,' she said, pointing at a framed photograph of the Rathores on the rear wall. It is a relatively recent photograph, maybe from two or three years ago. 'I have only seen Yuvrajji on television. I was already feeling a little dizzy, and then I saw him walk through the door. He was so close, *main paagal ho rahi thi.*'

She was still gasping!

Simi had dropped by the store to click photographs and make videos of her first workplace before the rest of the crew arrived.

'We know you are engaged to Yuvrajji, and you are our rajkumari, but I wasn't expecting to see him at the shop,' she continued breathlessly.

It was a relief to see Simi up and about.

I'm genuinely thankful for how quickly Vedveer reacted to the medical situation. Then again, handling swooning women might be second nature to him by now.

The patriarchy scored again when Vedveer walked into my still-under-construction store. Just like that, I was the helpless heroine, and he was the gallant saviour, conveniently recast as my underwriter.

The *TittleTattle* reporter must've walked into the café after we had left, asking questions and coming to conclusions.

The good news is that Mohit, with his unique brand of magic, is arriving in a few hours, but why let solid facts come in the way of good gossip?

Like, who are your sources? These people are obviously smoking something *really* good; they are flying on a freaking twig.

Vedveer's words play in my head.

I'm not offering you a room; you can have a whole wing. There's nothing to worry.

A wing without a gym!

I asked the chambermaid (whom I forbid from touching my overnight case – I can't get over someone packing and unpacking your stuff) if there is a gym on the floor, and she didn't know what on earth I was talking about.

Kalari in the room is an option, but why give folks reason to institutionalize you?

Reema, who had been doing nothing but trailing me around, also didn't know the location of the gym on these grounds.

'For whom?' she asked and didn't wait for an answer. 'I think the ranisa works out regularly, Yuvrajji, too; he works so hard, and he runs every day. *Shaayad unke paas neeche gym ho.*'

I nod.

The palace gardens stretch for miles; there are peacocks wandering around marigold-lined paths. Beyond the sandstone arches, the city wears a bright morning glow, its rooftops reflecting a rosy hue.

I consider a walk in the garden, but I'm not sure what is okay and what is not on these grounds.

Yesterday, I had breakfast in my room – orange juice, coffee and two slices of toast.

This morning, Vedveer (who must've seen the *TittleTattle* piece but makes no mention of it) announces a breakfast meeting on chat.

VRS: *Aaditha, Mother would like to have breakfast with you at the Breakfast Room at about 8 o'clock? I would like to join you too, if you're ok with having company.*

Like I have a choice! I want to be on my own for a bit. I don't need company, but I have no option but to oblige. What can I say? I'm going to the market to buy… coffee powder?

Me: *Ok.* I was about to send a one-word message but quickly add: *See you soon.*

VRS: *Reema will meet you at your door at 8 and bring you across. See you there!*

Me: *See you!*

Just as well! I need help to navigate the path to this breakfast room.

It's not like I step out of this suite, in which I'm likely to get lost on the way to the shower, and fall into this breakfast room. (I refuse to capitalize the 'b' and 'r', like in his text; it's just a room where people eat breakfast, not a museum!)

There is a rap on my door at 8 a.m., and I'm escorted to the breakfast room on the seventh floor by a liveried gentleman who introduces himself as the butler. His name badge says Pranav. I wonder what happened to Reema, but I don't ask.

I'm in gym clothes – off-white Lululemon bottoms and a crop top, with a sports bra that peeps out of the wide neck. I'm carrying my gym bag, too. I'm protesting. The iPad is in the gym bag. I will open it to the *TittleTattle* page and very casually place it right where Vedveer Rathore can see it.

The door to the breakfast room opens, and I wade into a sun-kissed space; the warmth is tempered by an air conditioner in full blast. Sunlight pours through the sunroof, and the blinds cast a lace-like shadow on the marble floor.

The air is rich with the scent of roses and freshly brewed beans.

I take a seat where a chair is pulled out for me. The table is set, crockery and cutlery in china and gleaming copper.

Of the three people expected at this table, I'm the first to arrive. The room is full of help, who are standing with their hands behind their backs like an assembly line of schoolboys.

They are looking away, but keep an eye on me, just in case I call… for a cask of wine instead of morning brew!

The number of people who hover around you in this place is suffocating, to say the least. Imagine having to ask for a moment's privacy in your own home.

Gauri Elena walks into the room with her perfume, apologizing for being a couple of minutes late. She has no traffic to blame, if one discounts the lift.

'How are you, Ahdheeeta?' she asks, her scent filling the air around me at once.

There goes my name!

I smile and nod, not knowing what exactly to say to her. I don't know if her son, 'my financer', has told her why exactly I am partaking of their overgenerous hospitality.

'How are you doing?' I ask, returning her question with one of my own.

'I have been busy.' She turns to the staff waiting on us. 'Coffee,' she says, looking at me.

I nod.

Gauri Elena asks for two bone-dry, double-shot cappuccinos before adding, 'The rajkumari likes her coffee just like I have mine.' She asks if I want orange juice. She either knows my breakfast choices or we simply have similar tastes.

'Do you have eggs?' she asks me.

'Not today,' I say. 'Just plain toast will be good.'

'Give us both plain toast, yeah… Yuvraj will order his own breakfast when he arrives.'

Gauri Elena turns to me. 'I must apologize for Vedveer. He's going to need a few more minutes. My son works too hard.'

'Like I was telling you,' she continues without a pause. 'I've been busy. We have a few charities that I take care of, and now I'm managing Navya's, too, as she's been travelling a fair bit.'

My eyes are on Gauri Elena, and it looks to me like she has just worked out. She has showered and changed, of course, but her skin is without make-up, and her cheeks are flushed. She is wearing a white sleeveless linen shirt on dark blue linen bottoms. Her arms are superbly toned.

'Do you visit Jaipur often, Ranisa?' I ask.

'No,' she says. 'I'm generally here only when my husband visits, which is a couple of times a year, maybe thrice, but of late, I've been coming more often because of Vedveer. Not that we get too much time together.'

Maybe the senior Rathore is also in the building.

'Do you work out?' I get back to the subject that is tugging my insides.

'Religiously,' she says, adding, 'every day of the week. As I've grown older, it is something that I do for myself. I work out to keep my sanity.'

I nod.

'When I was your age, I hadn't seen the inside of a gym,' she says with a laugh. 'That had to change when the greys cropped up. I'm not a sporty person like Vedveer, so to get a routine going took a lot of effort, but both my children pushed me to it.'

Raju asked if I wanted him to travel with me. Had I said yes, I wouldn't have been sitting at this table... I'd be enjoying breakfast after a full workout. It would've been good to have Raju here in Jaipur; he's a stress buster. He had come to Kolkata with me when we were launching our café there, and we had so much fun. He drove me around the city on a scooter!

'What do you do?' I ask Gauri Elena about her workout.

'Pilates thrice a week, yoga twice, and I walk barefoot on the lawn twice a week. None of my workouts lasts over forty-five minutes, including the walks.'

'Do you have a gym here?' I have to ask.

Just as the words are out of my mouth, breakfast arrives. Behind the butler is the chef, carrying a third tray. As our breakfast orders are laid out before us, the chef puts down a plate that has avocado and a poached egg on a thin slice of bread.

'Ranisa,' the chef says, 'I think you should try it. The thin-crust sourdough is very good, and the avocado is perfect.'

Gauri Elena wears a broad smile and nods. 'You should ask the rajkumari, too. She eats very little at an age when one can digest stones.'

The chef turns to me and bows. 'I will get the rajkumari a fresh plate,' he offers with a broad smile.

'Thank you,' I come back quickly, 'but I'm good with what I've ordered.'

'Come now, you've disappointed the chef,' Gauri Elena teases.

As the staff step back, disappearing into the corners to let us eat, a random thought comes to me.

It would be impossible to binge in this kind of a set-up. How could you shovel food into your mouth with three grown men in the room, or if you had decided on a bag of chips when you retired for the day but had to contend with chambermaids running loops around you? There is always someone tailing you, asking if you want anything.

'Vedveer tells me you are in Jaipur for the opening of your café,' she says. 'I want to congratulate you. That's why I asked to have breakfast with you. It's an excellent business decision, a store in your *sasural*.'

Gauri Elena's accent is adorable.

'Where is the location of your store? I would love to visit once the inauguration is done, of course. Maybe we can have a coffee together there.'

What? She doesn't know?

Is that why they haven't bullied us to shut shop yet?

I pick up my coffee and feel my cheeks warm. 'Just here,' I say, looking in the direction of the window, 'just outside.'

'Is your store located in the palace?' Her voice is suddenly itchy. I like the sound of it.

'No, no, Ranisa,' I reply quickly. 'Just outside the palace gates, on the other side of the road, to be precise.'

'What? Right outside here?' she asks, looking around her and calling for a pot of sugar at the same time.

'That will not be a nice look for you. You should rethink this. The palace will dwarf your brand. Does Vedveer know? He should've advised you. He has a very good business brain; he thinks things through thoroughly.'

'I had decided...' I start talking when the butler reaches for the organic brown sugar and drops the ceramic pot.

I watch it crash to the floor; little brown crystals spread over white marble.

The palace will dwarf your brand.

I'm determined, more than ever, to keep the property opposite the gates of their precious palace. I'm going to stand my ground. The Rathores will push. The impasse could cause the break.

My head is a riptide of emotions. I swallow something that is not anger. It feels raw; it feels real. I don't want to contend with any of that at this point.

To add to the clutter, the door swings open and Vedveer walks into the room, his eyes on the floor, on which brown sugar crystals lie alongside broken glass.

'Yuvrajji,' the butlers mutter.

Help to clean the floor is on its way.

Vedveer turns to me and apologizes. 'I got dragged into a couple of meetings. It took me this long to get out.' His eyes are bright, and his smile is light.

He is in navy sweatpants and a matching hoody.

'Mother,' he says, turning to Gauri Elena, who looks a lot less enthusiastic about her breakfast now.

Vedveer orders his breakfast, which is all of what his mother is having, save for the coffee, which is replaced by tea.

I fish out my iPad and open it to the *TittleTattle* page. I push the tablet before Vedveer. His eyes wander over the story, which he has doubtlessly already read, before they meet mine. 'Has Mohan arrived?' he asks of Mohit.

'Mohit, my magician,' I say, looking at my watch. 'He should be landing any time now.'

'Aaditha is just telling me that her store is located here, outside the palace gates,' the ranisa says, leaning back in her seat. 'Don't you think it'll be a poor look? People will think Ranibagh has funded the place.'

Oh! I blink.

Either Gauri Elena has a great read on the play, or she has read *TittleTattle*.

'The poor girl has done such a great job of driving her brand. She should get all the credit; she deserves it.'

The poor girl. I lean back in my seat and exhale.

'This property deal was done well before the engagement,' I say, looking at my ring. 'I thought it would be great for business, given the number of tourists Ranibagh attracts.'

Vedveer, who is seated on the same side of the table as me, turns in my direction. 'I don't think we should bother about someone else's opinion, especially a gossip column.'

Gauri Elena is right that, in a sense, this is how the patriarchy sways. *TittleTattle* had spelt it out. They will always see it as me fumbling and Vedveer rescuing me.

'That's all very well, Vedveer,' she says, looking at her son. 'You should've warned her as soon as you knew. You have a great business brain. People are going to talk, and it is unfair to Ahdheeeta.'

Vedveer's breakfast arrives, and he takes a sip of his orange juice. 'Aaditha's store has a great location,' he says, his voice firm. 'If people think we are funding it, people are dumb. She has opened stores across the country. This is not her first rodeo.'

Gauri Elena smiles and nods. 'You are right about that!'

I take a sip of my coffee.

'No one can control how people think, Mom,' he adds. His tone is resigned.

Vedveer also calls his mother 'mom'.

He is looking at me now and, after a whole minute, pushes the iPad back at me.

'Besides, if anything, Aaditha's association with Ranibagh will power the COFFEE Before Books & Bras brand,' he says. 'It's a good thing that the store is located so close to the palace. It can feed off Ranibagh.'

TittleTattle

Gupshup Column

JAIPUR: HIS CAFÉ, HER COFFEE

Curious so-and-so,

We held our collective breath as Aaditha Prathap's COFFEE Before Books & Bras café in Jaipur raced the clock to be launch-ready by the weekend, and what a race it was.

As TT first reported, the space, perched just outside the grand gates of Ranibagh Palace, resembled a construction site mere days ago. But enter Prince Vedveer, flexing royal muscle in support of the Princess-to-be's venture, and suddenly, the narrative shifted. The one-time nepo baby, now being rebranded as an award-winning entrepreneur, is in full flight.

In true Rathore fashion, when the stakes are high, the impossible gets done. Overnight crews worked round the clock - painting walls, installing fixtures, unpacking furniture and completing restrooms that, days earlier, didn't exist. The place was practically conjured out of plaster dust and plywood.

TT was present for Friday's launch - yes, we made the cut - and were greeted with a full spread. The café opened its doors to the public (no velvet ropes here), serving up its entire menu to what looked like a thousand-strong crowd. The coffee? Excellent. The food? Surprisingly delightful.

Guests floated in and out freely. Some lingered, sipping iced lattes and working their angles for Instagram. The interiors were an aesthetic dream, right down to the staff uniforms, which were clearly styled to spotlight Rajasthani craftsmanship. We wouldn't be surprised if Maharaj Gaurav Rathore Singh had a hand in that - arts patron, after all.

As for Aaditha? Sources say she spent most of the day behind the scenes, presumably in the manager's room, phone in hand, tracking the café's sudden rise on social media.

She emerged briefly when Prince Vedveer arrived, flanked by his sister, HRH Navya Mrinalini, and staff. The trio vanished into the back rooms soon after and didn't resurface until much later in the evening.

Vedveer then reportedly drove Aaditha to the

airport himself, where she boarded the BBJ 787 - yes, the one with the Rathore insignia - back to Bengaluru.

Logistics, darlings. Royal ones.

17.

Vedveer

That Upside-Down Cake

I'm going through the Fiala Group proposal for Ranibagh. I have been at it since the crack of dawn. There's nothing I can pick on, outside of the 'minor structural changes' they are suggesting, which I'm going to insist they clear with us, but I can't stop reading and re-reading these papers.

This is my home. The noun Ranibagh Palace is in a bold font. Ranibagh and Palace are not words that collocate for me. I think of this most significant piece of real estate in my life as either Ranibagh or home; it isn't a palace to me.

Father thinks of it as the seat of his throne, though not necessarily as home. For Grandfather, it was his land and the place he returned to every evening; it was where he lived and ruled from. Rawal Rathore Singh and his wife, Pavitra Hansa, also enjoyed Aranya Mahal, our country retreat, where they were frequent visitors in their younger days. They were both excellent marksmen. Some even say Grandmother was the better of the two.

I'm in the library, on the third floor of Ranibagh, not far

from the royal suites. I ask for the curtains to be drawn on both sides of the room so that I can also use the morning light as I go through the papers. The bulbs in the room are bright, but I need all the assistance I can get.

At the other end of the room, Raj Kiran stands silently, watching me like the lines of books on the shelves. Now, almost three hours later, the sun's rays fuller, I have studied the document in such detail I feel like I can recite it.

We have decided to lease a part of Ranibagh at my insistence. At the very least, I need to be sure that these papers are only rentals and not a sale deed. There can be no opening that could possibly drag us down that path.

This is the first time, since my ancestor built the first version of it for his beloved wife, Rani Rasleen, in the early 1700s, that Ranibagh, even in part, will be out of our hands.

I pull myself out of the lounge chair and walk towards the rectangular window that looks out at Jaipur. The city twinkles against the late-morning sun, the sloping roofs reflecting the light. In the distance is the monsoon sky, clear blue for now, but the colour will change. It is raining somewhere; it is in the air.

An image of Aaditha flits through my head.

Her hair flowing down her back like a river of black silk. Her lips, lush and defiant, belonged to me in a fleeting claim, leaving me aching with a longing I cannot get out of my mind.

She uses charming descriptors like 'alien' and 'suffocating' for my world, says she doesn't have reason to believe in marriage, and maybe she doesn't, but those eyes, there are moments when they call out to me.

Her laughter bubbles up even amidst the chaos of her (then) soon-to-open store.

When her employee collapses, she doesn't hesitate. She sinks to the floor, holds her up with a fierce tenderness, and returns the next day, bearing gifts of fruits and chocolates. She's stubborn and unapologetically sassy, unafraid to make her point, even if she has to shove an iPad in my face, daring me to respond.

My fingers are itching. I want to pick up the phone and message, ask the question, but that is not a question to be asked. I have lived long enough to know that. The answer is to be arrived at. In the next kiss, maybe.

My eyes click back to the print in my hand. I flip through the twenty-something pages before putting them aside.

I walk around the table and click on the desktop. I start researching the Fiala Group and their various arms around the world. Not because our legal team hasn't looked into it but because I need to know every detail.

I run a few checks and see that the Czech group has tied up with an Indian extension – India Hotel and Resort Enterprise. There are a few distinguished names in the list of stakeholders of that company, but the major share is held by an entity called InspireDesign, on which there's nothing at all on the net. I dial Ratan and ask him to get me a brief on InspireDesign.

Ratan calls me ten minutes later. 'InspireDesign is owned by Prathap Gowda,' he says.

I hear the air escape my mouth.

I turn my attention to the Aravallis; they stretch across the horizon like ancient sentinels guarding the desert's edge.

I feel a shudder go down my spine.

Did Aaditha know about it?

There is no way Aaditha is in the know of whatever it is that her father is up to. That would be too easy, a set-up almost.

I walk around the table and flip through the pages of the morning newspaper, which I devour most days but have ignored today, when a headline catches my attention.

Karnataka Finance Minister Eyes National Stage Amid Rising Popularity

Bengaluru:

Karnataka's Finance Minister, Prathap Vedaranya Gowda, has become the latest political figure to stir national buzz after a string of high-profile appearances and reform-driven policies that have drawn both praise and scrutiny. Known for his technocratic approach and sharp rhetoric, Gowda has recently been making moves that many within his party interpret as an indication that his ambitions extend well beyond the Vidhana Soudha.

In the last six months, Gowda has made keynote appearances in Delhi, Mumbai, and Hyderabad, speaking on fiscal decentralization and digital innovation in public finance. His flagship policy – 'Namma Budget, Namma Future', which introduced participatory budgeting and AI-assisted expenditure tracking in Karnataka – has garnered attention from economists and party strategists alike. Party insiders say Gowda is being positioned as the 'modern face' of southern leadership, potentially to play a larger role in shaping national economic policy – or even as a contender for a top cabinet portfolio in the event of a political realignment post 2026.

While Gowda remains coy about his intentions, he told reporters last week, 'I serve Karnataka first, but I also believe the ideas born here can serve the nation.' Whether this is calibrated modesty or a carefully scripted prelude remains to be seen, but one thing is clear: the political winds are shifting, and Gowda seems ready to ride them.

On a personal note, Gowda seems to have positioned himself well to get the strategic nod in the north. He is believed to have played conductor in daughter Aaditha Asha's engagement to HRH Vedveer Rathore Singh, the crown prince of Jaipur. The Rathores are not just India's most landed royal family; they are even the most influential.

The engagement, reportedly a private ceremony at the Ranibagh Palace, has sent ripples through political circles, with many viewing the alliance as a calculated step in Gowda's quiet march towards national prominence. While the families have emphasized tradition and shared values, the political undertones of the match have not gone unnoticed.

Insiders suggest that the alliance, while rooted in genuine camaraderie between the two families, especially the fathers, also serves Gowda's growing ambition to be seen as a unifying figure across regional lines. With the Gowdas representing modern southern progressivism and the Rathores embodying north India's royal heritage, the engagement is being billed by some as the symbolic bridge between two influential worlds.

As murmurs grow louder about Gowda's role in the party's national future, this royal connection may prove to be more than just ceremonial – it could be his most strategic alliance yet.

I only read one-third of the article; that is as much as I can take.

My jaw is clenched so hard that my jawbone hurts.

I dial Aaditha. I have to ask if she knew.

I let the phone do its thing, but all I get is static at the other end. I dial again. Same result. I dial a third time. I decide to try later.

My eyes shift to the broadsheet. This is a national newspaper, which means Aaditha might have already read the story, given that she starts her day early and we are closing on 9 a.m.

I pick up the papers again a couple of hours later. This time, I'm breathing easy. I like what they are offering. I tick the rubrics, leaving nothing to chance.

Our legal team has already gone through it with a fine-tooth comb. It is only Father whom I need to talk to. He is on one of his rare visits to Jaipur. I look at the watch; he should be surfacing at any time.

I'm trying to lock out *that* fact about the lease that bothers me the most, but I just can't turn my back on it. It keeps coming back to me.

Did Aaditha know?

It's been three hours since I called her. I dial again. Once. Twice. Thrice. I wait and wait, but the call doesn't go through.

Where is she?

I feel my heart slipping little by little.

Aaditha is a businesswoman. Is it possible that she doesn't know what her father's business ventures are?

Was this all an act?

Aaditha wanted out of this alliance right from the start. She even wanted us to come up with a plan to break it off. She has no reason, she says, to believe in the institution of marriage.

Then, very casually, without word or warning, she announces that her café chain is launching in Jaipur. When she mentioned the location, my first thought was, *Great, brilliant idea*, but now, when I think about it, even though she signed off on this building, just outside the gates of Ranibagh, well before we met, she didn't tell me about it. Not before the public declaration at least, even though it was a well-thought-out decision.

What else is she hiding?

I exhale.

Is the chemistry a ploy, a hook? Is she in cahoots with her father?

I feel something in me break, and as I get on my feet, I feel the broken chips fall to the floor. A part of me, maybe.

I meet the smiling countenance of my father as I turn to the door. His expression changes as he eyes me with concern.

'Yuvraj,' he says.

I nod.

Father's valet brings him his afternoon drink, which he picks up from the tray, pushing back on the lounge chair. He points at the seat behind the large desk at the head of the room, which is his place whenever he's in Ranibagh. He asks me to sit there.

Father and I shadow box in the silence, each waiting for the other to speak.

I'd rather he start talking about anything, weather included.

'You are looking at the papers,' he says casually, gesturing at the papers on the table.

I nod. He has probably seen the papers, too.

'We should go ahead with this because it would be good for the people and also for the family.' Father picks his words carefully.

'My only request is that we finish yours and Navya's weddings before we give it away.'

I don't nod. 'We are not giving anything away, if I can help it, now or ever.' I taste the fury of my words. 'We are leasing it, Father. We are not giving it away. We are not selling!'

Father's smile is bright. It might've been the dark liquid that he just had a second sip of. 'I know, I know,' he says, his tone light.

I briefly consider asking Father about Prathap Gowda being the lead player of the conglomerate we are entertaining, but I quickly dismiss it. Is it even possible that Father didn't know? Gaurav Rathore Singh never makes a move without knowing every minuscule detail of the players in the game.

A silence descends on the room again. I can hear my thoughts.

Father is on his second drink. Beside the lounge chair on which he has settled is the newspaper I have read and tossed aside. He may have peeped at the open page, but he didn't pick it up. It occurs to me that nowhere in the report (that I had fully scanned) was there even a mention of Ranibagh being leased.

Father's eyes are on the wall before him when Mother and Navya walk into the room.

'Why is every curtain in the room drawn apart?' Navya asks.

Raj Kiran stumbles over a stool, trying to get to the window behind me.

'*Dheere se*,' Father says.

I'm on my feet, but Raj Kiran is nimble enough to halt the fall, which saves him from a few broken teeth.

Navya is looking for sunglasses, the ones she keeps in every room she visits. When she finally locates them, she brings down a pile of books with them.

'We are never short of entertainment when the family visits!' I say, making my way across the room.

I help Navya sort the pile of books that lands on her glasses, dislodging the temple on the right side. She picks up the broken spectacles and balances them on one side.

'Why are you so snarky?' she asks.

I shrug. 'Always happy to help, Sister!'

'I wanted to go to Aaditha's store for coffee this morning, but I got up really late,' Navya grumbles.

'There's a big difference in the coffee from our machine and the one in Aaditha's store,' Mother chimes in.

'Just as well that the store is just outside the gates,' Father says, smiling at his wife.

Mother launches into an offensive on Father's observation. She chides him for not being on social media enough to even know what is being said about their to-be daughter-in-law.

'There's talk,' she says, raising the timbre of her voice, 'that Ranibagh is financing her coffee shop.'

'It's very unfair,' she continues, stressing on the adverb.

'What Aaditha has done with this brand is just brilliant,' Navya says before she turns on me. 'Why are you just sitting there idly, brother? Why are you not defending Aaditha in the press? Such vile stuff is being said about her on social media.'

Father puts down his drink and repeats the three words that he has told us at different times in our lives. 'Ranibagh doesn't explain.'

'Yeah, yeah,' Navya says, 'we know that, but this is not about Ranibagh.'

Navya turns to me and raises a brow. 'Have you had a fight with Aaditha, Brother?'

'She has a great business brain,' I say, feeling compelled to speak.

I reach for my phone, which is on silent, wondering if Aaditha called me back.

There's no call or message, but I have a notification from an hour ago that says Aaditha's phone is available to take calls. She has obviously been notified, too.

Navya is staring at me.

'We need to start planning for the wedding,' Mother says. 'Everything has to be perfect – not just big and beautiful but completely meaningful. This is a north-meets-south wedding, so everything has to come together nicely. All the ceremonies must showcase our great traditions, but we must also make the Gowdas feel at home and highlight all their customs.'

Father nods before turning to his daughter, who is back to adjusting her broken glasses.

'We're not having two weddings in December,' she says, looking at Father. 'Nalin and I will wait until next March, before the start of the Premier League. Let's give Aaditha and Brother a moment to enjoy their wedding.'

I can barely think, never mind feel. My insides are ravaged by a fire that is burning everything in its wake.

18.

Aaditha

Coming Apart Beautifully

Aaditha's Journal

Bittersweet Brew: Notes from the In-Between

Was out all day yesterday. Mohit and I left for Kodagu early in the morning (4 a.m.) to look at coffee estates.

The plan has always been that COFFEE Before Books & Bras would eventually grow its own beans. Our search has narrowed down to two properties, and we're considering both. This drive was a last-minute decision; one of the estates just came up in the market, and I thought it was best to make a move.

I've been meaning to tell Vedveer about this, take his advice even. Maybe I'll chew his brains on it tomorrow now that I have the details.

Meanwhile, things are happening.

So, we finally know why Appa went for this proposal... to serve his political ambition. I, of all people, should've known. Like Appa, I dream big. Like Appa, I don't know when to stop; we keep going and going. There's always the possibility of reaching the top.

Appa probably sees the Rathores as a passage to political prominence on the national stage. He doesn't need to win an election in the north; his own brilliance and popularity here are enough, and he knows that. What he needs is approval in the corridors of power in New Delhi. That's where the Rathore nod might come into play.

I was so busy questioning why the Rathores would be okay with an alliance that's so culturally distant from them, I forgot to ask the same question of Appa (all in my head, of course; I wasn't knocking on doors, asking questions).

But the question about the Rathores still sticks: Why did they agree to this proposal? The truth is, they approached us. So why?

The newspaper report raised the question halfway through the story and answered it in the very next line. The alliance is linked to a friendship between the fathers.

What friendship? Alia and I were never introduced to this family. No mention was ever made of the Rathores of Jaipur, growing up or even in recent years. The Rathores of Jaipur were part of the curriculum; the section was called The Royal Families of Independent India, and the Rathores had an entire chapter to themselves.

I only read the article late last night after Alia alerted me to it. I wonder if Vedveer has read it too.

My heart feels heavy, like a boulder is sitting on it.

I lean back in my seat and listen to the rain for a bit.

It's almost 9 a.m., and the rain is behaving like a rebellious intern, showing up early and throwing everyone off. In Bengaluru, even the skies have a routine. A respectable drizzle around 6 p.m. or 7 p.m., just as half the city is trying to get home without becoming soup. Sometimes, we get a little early morning drama, but the skies usually clean up their act before we step out for work.

The rain is manageable when we start out, but en route, it comes down so hard we actually stop for twenty minutes.

I am appreciative of these Ikea wheels – that are carrying physical weight while supporting the heaviness inside me. There's a knock on the door. Before I swivel around in my chair, thinking, Whoever it is, I will ask them to come back later, the door opens.

Vedveer – in blue denims and a buttoned-up navy shirt, face wiped clean of a smile – is standing there.

I shake my head and exhale. In that moment, I'm grateful that it is him and he is here. I don't know why. My face reflects gratitude.

'Hello,' Vedveer says. His voice is rough, like the weather. It is a plain hello, no Aaditha… which is how he always greets me, saying my name like he is memorizing it.

'Hi!' I reply. 'What brings you to Bengaluru?' I ask, and before he can reply, I say, 'Not our best weather today.'

Do I need to come around my desk and greet him?

This morning, he and I are not a good vibe. Just as well that we have this massive mahogany desk between us.

Vedveer is looking at me like I'm a book, the pages of which he is trying hard to read.

He's probably here because of the newspaper article. If that's the case, I suppose it's decent of him to show up at my door – unannounced, sure – but still better than just calling. Though, to be honest, a phone call might've done the job just fine.

I'm opening and closing my palm, and Vedveer's eyes are on my hand.

He pulls back a chair and takes a seat; he is breathing hard. My feet are bare and are shifting under the table, looking for my kitten heels.

'Looking for your footwear?' he asks.

I laugh, and he finally smiles. He had fished out my sandals from under the table the last time he was here.

'Coffee?' I ask without thinking but correct myself quickly. 'Tea? Masala chai?'

Vedveer nods. His second attempt at a smile this morning is a shoddy half-effort. His eyes are without their characteristic sparkle; they look spent.

I should've maybe explained that the tea is freshly brewed, because who knows how these finicky folks drink their tea. I'm second-guessing myself.

Vedveer's eyes haven't left my face, nor has the troubled strain diluted. He clenches his jaw.

I pick up the intercom and place the order. 'One masala chai, one cappuccino, for me,' I say, before adding, 'and yes, the bakery basket.' Mohit is trying to tell me something, which I realize only after I disconnect the intercom.

'How have you been?' I ask.

'Things,' he says slowly. 'I've been busy.'

Things. He's always economical with words, but today, he is penurious.

You don't travel a thousand miles by air unless something's really eating at you.

The newspaper article?

Something else?

Is it etiquette that forbids him from bringing up whatever it is he has come here to talk about until the tray has come and gone? Is that a royal custom?

'I've been caught up with work,' he clarifies, looking around the room.

The silence is awkward, but I let it lie, allowing it to extend, seconds into minutes.

There is a knock on the door; the beverages arrive. I look at my watch; it has been seven minutes since I placed the order. The wait is longer than usual, because of the tea, I presume.

No sooner is the tray placed on the table than I notice Vedveer inhaling the aroma. I pat my back mentally; our tea is on par. I look more closely at the cup. It isn't masala chai; it is a yellowish liquid. Has Mohit served turmeric tea when I specifically asked for masala chai? Is that what he was trying to tell me, that we had run out of masala chai, when I hastily disconnected the phone?

Vedveer picks up his cup and raises it on a celebratory note before sipping his beverage.

'That's not masala chai,' I say. I'm sure he's aware; he's a connoisseur, but still, I should let him know.

'It's oolong,' he says with a flicker of a smile. 'You should try it sometime; it's very good.'

I nod. Drink tea, that is the only thing left for me to do!

Vedveer takes another sip of this 'very good' oolong tea, which I didn't know we had on our menu, and reaches for the banana bread cookie I'm eyeing.

There are three cookies, but only one is banana bread. He hasn't bothered offering me before helping himself. So what if he's the guest or if he is hungry?

I pick up the phone and ask for another banana bread cookie. Our eyes meet across the table for a brief moment.

I'm looking at Vedveer from the corner of my eye. I'm breathing hard, and the colour on my cheeks heightens. I feel the burn.

The single 60-gram banana bread cookie arrives on our signature cookie plate. I pick up the biscuit and bite into it.

I push back in my seat, draw one foot up on the chair and cradle the mug in my hand.

'Aadheethha.' He says my name for the first time in the morning. 'I called you yesterday.'

I blink. 'I didn't get a call from you,' I say.

Actually, I didn't get a call from anyone. I called Appa and then Alia later in the night.

Vedveer is locking and unlocking his fingers. 'It didn't ring,' he says, 'but you would have got notifications.'

For most of the day, wherever we were yesterday, the

reception was poor, but I didn't get any notifications. I pull out my phone to show him why I had no idea that he had called, when I find six missed call notifications from Vedveer. *Six*.

'I'm sorry, I was out on a day trip to Kodagu, and I didn't check the notifications after we returned,' I say, holding up my phone, acknowledging my mistake.

He nods. 'Why didn't you tell me?'

For a moment, I think he is asking why I hadn't told him I was going to Madikeri, when I realize that he's talking about the newspaper article. 'Because I didn't know.'

'How?' he asks, gesturing with his hands and shoulders, which rise in a befuddled expression.

'How would I know what Appa's political ambitions are?'

Vedveer is shaking his head disbelievingly.

'Too late,' he says, breathing hard. I watch his chest heave. 'I know what exactly you and your father are up to.'

My eyes widen with shock. I lift the mug to my mouth; my hand shakes, and a drop of coffee dribbles down the cup.

'It is in the newspapers!' I say slowly. 'If you've come all the way to tell me something, I hope it's worth my time at least.'

Vedveer leans back and takes another sip of his oolong tea. 'You could have just told me,' he says. The colour of his eyes doesn't appear different at this moment. They are both dark and distant.

'Co-conspirator and all…?'

How on earth could I have scripted Appa's political dreams? Seriously, is this who he thinks I am?

'First, you want me to come up with a break-up plan; you are so desperate to end things,' he says, his voice calm. 'Then you announce the location of your café in Jaipur during the interview without so much as mentioning it to me, even though you signed on that well before I came into your life.'

What is he saying? I shake my head.

'An elaborate, layered plan.'

A plainly worded accusation, that I positioned COFFEE Before Books & Bras just outside the gates of his precious palace to anchor myself in his life.

'No, Vedveer,' I finally say, my voice rising. 'I'll say this just once – you have got it all wrong.'

Vedveer's shoulders straighten, and he raps his right index finger on the table. 'As you already know, we have signed the papers for the lease. And I will say this just once. Ranibagh is mine; it's the home of the Rathores, and that's how it will stay.'

What lease papers? What is the man blabbering about? But I'd rather wilt in this seat than tell him I lost him at 'signed the papers'. He didn't even deserve my what-the-f#@k-are-you-talking-about comeback, because whatever it is he is raging on about, he has already pronounced me guilty.

'Yes, Your Royal Highness.' My voice is colder than the draught from the air conditioner.

'This is only a business deal,' he is saying. 'We are not selling or even thinking about selling. Father and I didn't want to waste that end of Ranibagh, which we are not using and haven't been using for generations. We want to put it to use, and that is all this is about.'

So, put it to use or let it go to seed. Who gives a flying fig? I pick up my coffee cup and take another sip of my double-shot, bone-dry cappuccino.

His eyes are on me; they stay on the nape of my neck.

'Is that your uniform?' he asks, waving his hands in my direction.

I'm wearing the same co-ord set I wore the last time he was sitting where he is seated now.

'Do you not approve of our uniforms, Your Highness?' I ask and take another bite of the cookie. The chewing distracts me.

I return the mug to the tray when I hear a commotion outside my door. Someone is being told I have a visitor.

The door opens, and Raju Mathew is standing in that space; his heavily tattooed arm is holding his helmet like it were a handbag. 'I want...'

Raju always puts a smile on my face. 'I'll speak to you later, okay?' I say.

'Okay! I'm waiting outside.'

Vedveer's eyes are on Raju. 'Who is he?'

'Someone very dear to me!' *Someone who would never charge me with manipulation, like you are doing now.*

Vedveer nods. His fingers are locked tight to keep them from fidgeting, maybe.

'If you are done with what you came here to say, please leave,' I say, getting on my feet.

'This is the celebration... for the deal, Pruh-thaap!'

'And for the record, it is not Pruh-thaap!' Their egregious phonetics are a saga I'll be well rid of.

Vedveer turns to the door. Just before he opens it, his eyes meet mine, and he says, 'We are done here.'

My shoulders are square, and my back is straight. I'm stunned by the happenings of the last half hour, to say the least, but I'll be damned if I'm going to let it show.

I give him enough time to exit my space before sitting.

My head is a crush of thoughts.

I pick up my coffee mug; my hands are shaking.

His words, *We are done here,* are on my mind.

I woke up this morning feeling a weight inside of me. My father's ambition put me in a difficult position. A few hours later, I am grateful for it. It has gotten me out of this shitstorm I had inadvertently found myself in.

But why had I stood there dumbstruck? Why hadn't I said something, anything?

My pleasure!

Do me the honour of letting the parents know!

Anything.

I should've been the one who dropped the mic, not him.

I exhale; it is a gale.

Vedveer knew that it was his father who had approached Appa with the marriage proposal. Appa, I'm sure, hula-hooped with joy, but *they* made the first move. *They*. It was Gaurav Rathore Singh (these names, like those poorly planned three-lane highways), not Prathap Gowda, who reached out.

Then again, those questions that came to me the moment I heard of this proposal: Why me? Why us?

I am in a bit of a shock and obviously not thinking clearly, but I have a feeling that the answer to that question is a crucial piece of the puzzle. I feel the blood rush to my head. My posture slackens, and my shoulders drop.

The more tightly I clasp the handle of my coffee mug, the more my hand shakes. I put the mug on the coaster. My head is darting in ten different directions; I feel it turn. I want a bag of potato wafers or banana chips. Several bags. I want to be busy, my mouth to keep pace with my thoughts.

When we first started here, I would stash bags and bags of crisps and chips, and each time I felt my nerves acting up, I would bolt the door and stuff my face. A couple of years ago, I had forgotten to lock the door, and Mohit walked into my binge fest. That is the last time I binged in the office.

I kick off my shoes, pull my right leg up on the chair and drop my head on the headrest of my seat.

We are done here!

What the hell just happened? This time, the question echoes a pain from deep inside.

This man, this impoverished (in more ways than one)

prince, who had signed some lease papers for a section of their precious palace, thinks Appa and I are trying to take over his however-many-bedrooms palace?

I have to see Appa. If I can somehow pull myself together and get off this chair my bum seems to be planted in.

Just as I dial his number, there is a knock on the door. The number of people knocking on my door in one morning! It is a slow, hesitant rap. I know the sound, but I can't place it. I shout, 'I'm busy!' I don't want to see anyone other than Appa at this moment.

The door doesn't heed my shout; it opens, and in walks Raju. His helmet is strapped around his sleeve tattoo; he has a coffee mug in one hand and a half-eaten apple muffin on a plate in the other. I have forgotten about Raju; he had said he would be waiting outside for me.

'I'm sorry,' Raju says. 'I had already opened the door when you said you were busy. I can wait outside until you are done.'

'No, no,' I say, waving for Raju to come in and take the chair that has just been vacated by the grasping royal.

I dial Appa's number for the third time. Still no response. Where is he when I need him?

Raju places his coffee mug on the spare coaster and moves the teacup to the side of the table. He then reaches for the coconut cinnamon cookie and puts it next to the apple muffin and stops to admire his art. The savoury cookie is placed on the side table next to the empty cup and saucer. No place on Raju Mathew's plate for a savoury cookie.

'I've been wanting to try coconut cinnamon,' he says, more to himself. My florid expression or heavy breathing haven't registered on Raju, who gobbles the giant cookie in two bites. That's how he enjoys his food.

Raju wipes his mouth and neatly folds the paper napkin before he speaks. 'You should have seen the drama outside.'

'Drama?' I ask as I hit Appa's number again. There are days when getting through to Appa is impossible, and this is proving to be one of them.

'As soon as the prince walks out of your office, he glares at me first,' says Raju, plumping himself up like he is a pillow while imitating the look Vedveer gave him.

Among Raju's many skills, he is not just a good raconteur but an accurate one.

'Mohit ran after the secretary and gave him a box. It had the rest of the teabags.'

'What bags? Why is he giving him the tea box? It's ours!'

'No! The prince brought his own teabags.' Raju is laughing hysterically now.

No wonder the tea looked so different from what we generally serve, and also his reaction... He was super pleased that we served him his tea at our café!

Vedveer's lackey had apparently handed the box of teabags to Mohit when he was getting the tray ready.

'I wanted to taste that tea, but Mohit gave me coffee.'

I need to learn from the staff how exactly it all played out this morning, but that will have to wait for now.

'The best thing is that the secretary was speaking to Mohit in Hindi, but Mohit is a total boss,' Raju says. 'He said, "Please, sir, I'm not following what exactly you're saying; please speak in English or Kannada."'

Good on him!

I'm on my feet. I have to see Appa. I need to figure out what exactly Vedveer is talking about. I look at my watch. If we leave now, my driver could beat the rush hour traffic. I could, maybe, catch Appa before the session starts.

I decide to drive. It will be better for my nerves; negotiating Bengaluru traffic actually calms me down.

I call our driver, Shashi, and ask him to bring the car to the rear entrance of Kempe Crown.

Raju and his helmet follow me into the car. 'You could've left your helmet in my office; it would've been safe,' I tell Raju.

He shrugs and places his Steelbird graffiti-adorned helmet on his lap. His baby. *Would he love anything more?* I wonder.

I check my phone. I have dialled Appa a dozen times. Shashi has adjusted the rearview mirror for me. 'Maybe I should call Appa's PA,' I tell myself.

I smile at my friend, who finally sees that I'm upset.

'Are you okay?' he asks.

'I will be okay,' I say as we turn out of the hotel.

The pettiness to talk about my clothes. I can wear whatever the shit I want to wear, whenever I want to wear it, in the boardroom or on the bloody beach.

I'm hanging on to the unemotional details because I don't want to think of things that really matter. All the times he looked at me, like I'm the only woman in the world… That Choti Holi evening when our eyes found each other's over bobbing heads, in the middle of thousands of people, sounds and songs. Later that evening, on the terrace… his lips on my lipstick.

The phone interrupts my thoughts. It is Kannan, Appa's smooth-as-silk PA. I tell him I'm on my way; I want to see Appa immediately.

'Boss is in his office; he's busy, madam.'

'I'll be there in ten minutes, and please ensure he is free.'

I don't wait for a response; I disconnect. Alia has taught me well.

I don't have to wait for Kannan to show me in because Raju took care of the PA. Kannan was Raju's first pal in Appa's team. He is the guy Raju broke bread with every morning when he worked here.

Appa's smile freezes when he sees me.

'Aashi,' he says, 'are you okay, *magale*?' His face crumples.

'Are you planning to take over Ranibagh?' I ask before I take a seat opposite him.

He nods instantly, and after a whole minute, he asks, 'How do you know?'

When he shook his head, I thought he was going to tell me he had no designs on Ranibagh Palace, but Appa's question explodes in my head like a parcel of crackers. So, this is what this morning was about?

Why has Appa put me in this position? My shoulders drop, and my throat burns.

'I won't go ahead with this proposal, Appa. I cannot,' I say. I speak slowly and clearly.

I didn't want to tell him that Vedveer had already called it off. That's for the Rathores to handle on their end. My reason for not telling Appa that Vedveer jetted into town this morning, convinced we were plotting to take over Ranibagh… is because my ego has taken a beating.

'It's not a big deal; they do not need our money. At least, not the way you think they need the money,' Appa says.

'How do I think they need the money?' I ask.

'They are not in debt or anything.'

I exhale. Thank god for small mercies, not that it mattered anyway.

'I'm out of this alliance,' I say. '*Heladha mathu keltha idhira?*' Are you listening to what I'm saying?

Appa is staring at me. If he is waiting for me to retract my words, he is going to be waiting for the rest of his life.

'Chinna,' he says, using one of my many nicknames like he is testing the keys of a piano, 'this is not an underhand deal; this is all above board. They are looking to lease a part of Ranibagh Palace, and we made an offer.'

Lease. The word stays in my mouth like a hard-boiled sweet.

'Why were they looking to lease?'

Appa explains that Vedveer is determined to convert their land into organic fields. That project requires heavy-duty financing, given how vast their holdings are. By leasing a section of Ranibagh, he could get on with the project without having to worry about the state of their finances.

I'm a businesswoman; I know what collateral is.

As I stretch my neck, I begin to see the situation for what it is. They want to lease a section of their palace, and we offered. It all came together with Gaurav Singh Rathore's blessings. But why is Vedveer pointing accusatory fingers? My eyes are now on Appa, when it finally dawns on me.

'I believe you,' I say after a while, summoning a vacant smile. 'I only wish you trusted me with the details. I deserve to know, especially because it's my life that we are talking about.'

'How did you know about the lease?'

'I read it somewhere. Maybe on the net,' I lie.

Appa nods. He isn't convinced.

'I want out of this engagement, Appa. I wanted no part in this from the beginning itself, but because of you, I went through with it. I cannot do this any more. Please be fair to me.'

Appa settles back in his seat and turns away from me.

I'm on my feet, carrying a sinking feeling in my heart. I should have been happy that Vedveer and I are over, but something stings at the back of my eyes.

19.

Aaditha

Done Here!

I told Appa I wanted out of the engagement, making my intentions clear, maybe even before Vedveer's jet hit Bengaluru's runway.

I stopped wearing the ring after that. No one noticed.

But I didn't follow through with my parents, not in the way they would've expected. I didn't storm into rooms, issue ultimatums or draw dramatic lines in the sand. In a family like mine, where we wait for storms to pass rather than confront them, it would've taken exactly that kind of force for anyone to believe I truly meant it.

From what I can tell, Vedveer hasn't moved either. Not really.

If he'd followed through on that cutting '*we are done here*', I'd have felt the aftershocks. I'd have known.

A month later, I decide to act on it. I start with a call to Alia.

I'm not telling her about how the prince came calling; I'm not ready to go there yet. Weeks have gone by, and it still feels raw.

'I don't think this engagement is working for me, Akka,' I say, two sentences into the conversation.

We are on a video call. She's doing her make-up, getting ready for work, while I'm lounging in my bed at the end of a workday.

'What do you mean, not working?' she asks, her mascara smudging her eyes.

I shrug. 'We are not really in touch, haven't been in a while... That's not exactly newly engaged couple vibes, right?'

'What is a while?'

'A month.'

'So message. Ask him what's up.'

I shake my head. 'I don't want to ask. I mean, why should I be the one who asks?'

'Because it takes two to clap,' she says, dropping her make-up brush and bringing her hands together in a clap.

'A relationship should be effortless.'

'Aadi,' Alia says, using one of the newer nicknames she has for me, the most obvious one I would think, 'an arranged marriage doesn't work like that. You need to make an effort. Both parties should.'

I want to say, *And where did that get you*? but that would be cruel.

'Anyway,' I say, exhaling, 'I'm going to tell Appa and Amma that I want out. I told Appa once already...'

'And?'

'You know how Appa is. He wasn't honest with me about stuff in the beginning; you know that.'

'Hmm… Those things don't mean anything. It's Appa. It's not a deal breaker,' Alia says.

Not for you.

'When do you plan to tell them?'

'Tonight. Appa is already home.'

I slip the ring on my ring finger before I walk into my parents' bedroom. They've just finished dinner and are getting ready to retire for the night. I make a show of relieving myself of the sizable emerald and give it to Amma, who starts turning it over, examining it like I may have lost a part of it.

'*Edu chennagide…*' It's fine, she says, wearing a perplexed expression.

Appa is rarely rattled, but this time, he is genuinely nonplussed.

He chalked up our last conversation about the engagement to a mood, something he believed would blow over. He clearly hasn't mentioned it to Amma. Even Alia didn't know.

'This engagement is over,' I say.

'Why? What happened suddenly?' Amma asks.

'I'm not comfortable in this relationship; this is not something I want for myself.'

'You can't just break off an engagement without giving us a good reason,' Amma says, her eyes sparking fire. 'What is uncomfortable about it?'

The last time I had seen Amma this angry was when I got 18 out of 100 for algebra in fourth grade.

Appa rescued me then.

'Yes,' Appa asks, sitting down on a single-seater sofa. 'What exactly do you mean by "not comfortable"?'

This is when I should tell them about Vedveer's visit, that he's the one who called off the engagement, but I don't say it. He wants to apologize. He sent a couple of texts saying so. I can't tell them half the story, and if I admit he wants to apologize, they'll be jumping through hoops for the prince all over again, with Alia cheering them on!

'You haven't been entirely honest with me about this proposal,' I say, looking at Appa, who is leaning back, arms folded across his chest in a stubborn posture.

'Is that what's making you uncomfortable?' Appa asks.

Amma glares at me while refusing to ask her husband what this is all about.

'Did I deceive you?' Appa asks.

Just like that, Appa turns the tables on me, playing the emotional card.

'I wouldn't do anything that isn't good for this family, you know that, right?' Appa says.

Amma nods.

He wouldn't jeopardize our lives knowingly. He is a good father and husband, not the most sensitive, but a decent man all the same.

'Has Vedveer hurt you? Harmed you in any way?' he asks, leaning forward in his seat.

I shake my head. 'He's not that important,' I say, settling myself on a stool.

'Then why?'

'Look at Akka's marriage; you found that boy,' I say. I hate doing this to Appa, but I need to make my point. 'Why are we going down this road again?'

'How do you plan to get married then?' Amma asks, before Appa shushes her with a look.

'I didn't pick the right boy for Alia. I am to blame, but your sister was of marriageable age and wasn't dating anyone. I did the best I could; I did all the background checks,' he says, holding my gaze. 'The same with you. If you were dating someone, I wouldn't have interfered. But you are of marriageable age, you have a great career, you are ready to move out of our home.'

'Ready to move out of home doesn't mean I'm ready to get married. Come on!'

'We are never ready to be married off, but when you reach a certain age, and if you are still single and a good proposal comes our way, I would be failing in my duty as a parent if I turned it away.'

I run my fingers through my hair and shake my head.

'This is a good proposal,' he says, adding that he wouldn't have considered any royalty for his daughter, let alone a north Indian one, people who are so different from us culturally, had he not been convinced of the kind of people the Rathores are.

'Look at the way they treat their staff; it is one of the first things I noticed when I visited the maharaj in Delhi. Most of them have been with him since he was a young boy. He knows them all by name, each and every one of them.'

'That's his father,' I say. My shoulders go up in a shrug.

'See how careful Vedveer is about you, especially where the tabloids are concerned,' he says, his eyes lighting up. 'He planned a small engagement and got the interview done even before I raised the safety issue. It was a security breach at that club, and he saw it and took action.'

'Anybody would do that,' I say. I'm flying a kite, and Appa's face colours.

'Don't tell me you don't love him, Chinna,' he says, pushing himself to his feet now. 'I have seen the way he looks at you and you at him. At Ranibagh, during Holi… you both are not just any two people. You're a couple.'

I exhale, relieved that Appa stops where he does in his description of Vedveer and me as a couple.

Tittle Tattle

Gupshup Column

THE AADITHA-VEDVEER ENGAGEMENT: PROBLEMS IN PARADISE?

Curious so-and-so,

We simply must ask: When was the last time you actually spotted Prince Vedveer and Aaditha Prathap together?

Hold your horses - our heads are swirling through the fog, too. It's been a solid six weeks since the Coffee Queen graced Jaipur for her grand store opening, masterminded entirely by the ever-obliging Ranibagh Palace.

Since then? Radio silence on the couple front. Makes you wonder, are they still 'a thing' or just a memory?

Meanwhile, Prince Vedveer has been spotted in Delhi, living it up with his crew. Among them, the dazzling Kairi Gaur, who apparently couldn't peel herself away from his side all evening at the Four Hundred Club. Cute, right? Especially since Kairi is engaged to Kolkata industrialist Vishal Basu. But hey, who counts hours when you're busy splitting time between Jaipur and New Delhi?

We've even got a photo – posted on our Instagram for your viewing pleasure – where Kairi is seated next to Prince Vedveer, rocking a sleeveless shirt dress and strappy Ralph Lauren heels. And the eyes locked on each other? Adorable. Or... telling.

So, what's the tea with Aaditha and Vedveer? One suspects South Indian thriftiness might've forced the Rathores to stop footing the bill. Aaditha wanted a new store in Jaipur, and surprise, surprise, she picked a spot just outside their gate. Naturally, the Rathores had to step in and save the day because watching her crash and burn? Not on their watch.

It's early days for Aaditha's COFFEE Before Books & Bras boutique in Jaipur, but whispers say business is brewing nicely. Hopefully, she's ready to stop mooching off family generosity and actually run the show herself.

But keep those fingers ready to click, darlings... a break-up announcement from the Palace might be next on the menu.

Meanwhile, busy yourselves with our poll. Have Vedveer and Aaditha broken up?

Aaditha
Worshipping at Lakshmi Bar

My fingers are in my hair, feeling my hairpiece, fixing what is already in place. I'm particularly fidgety this evening, more than usual.

I've worn this disguise for a while now. On most of these outings, I settle into it easily, like slipping into a second skin almost. But when my nerves fray, my hands betray me. They fidget, tugging at a collar or adjusting a sleeve, searching for something to anchor me. Tonight, unease clings to me like static. I can't shake the irrational fear that my wig might somehow grow legs, march off on its own and unravel the careful illusion I've spent a good time maintaining.

I reach for my glass of red wine; it isn't on point (considering we are paying ₹150 for a 350 ml bottle, I have hopes). I stall, eyeing the Bloody Mary that Lavanya ordered.

'*Oyi*, are you wasting everything today?' Raju asks, his eyes wide and cheeks puffed. 'You have to pay the bill!'

I'm not the only Nervous Nellie in the mix, but I'm sure as hell not letting Raju get away this time. He's squirming, trying to dodge paying the bill again. Three years, countless drinks and dinners, and the only man in the quartet hasn't paid a single time. Not once. I shoot him a look.

'How much Komal drinks?' He turns on Komal, a yoga guru who is friend and rival to Raju in the fitness industry. 'It's half a bottle already,' he says, pointing at her large glass of gin and tonic.

'You cannot be this obvious, not even you!' I'm looking at Raju and laughing. 'You are policing only because you are paying!'

'I'll take care of this,' Lavanya says, winking at a delighted Raju and grabbing my glass of red at the same time.

Raju is on his feet, trying to high-five Lavanya, whose hands are already taken. Wine glass and onion pakora.

Tucked away in an unremarkable alley – with bric-a-brac shops, garishly refurbished pre-Independence passages and a couple of hole-in-the-wall fabric units – in Chamarajpet, six kilometres from MG Road, Lakshmi Bar is our *adda*.

The location is ideal, a short distance from the lights of the main thoroughfares, posh bars and gourmet restaurants but close enough for all of us to get there and for Lavanya to drop us all back. Everyone, except for Raju, who always rides his bike home after eating most of the snacks, washed down with his trusty 650 ml beer.

Lakshmi Bar is Raju's discovery. He had gone there with a college friend who lives in the area.

I roll my eyes at Komal the first evening we walk through that shabby doorway some three summers ago. A lopsided nameboard that hangs on a twisted, barely holding wire, with fading neon lights that cast a dim glow on the uneven pavement below, marking the entry point.

'No judging,' Komal whispers. That has been the spirit of these outings.

Lakshmi Bar, despite the assiduous planning, is where we let our hair down. It's Khadus Komal's getaway, where she doesn't have to think about the chores and responsibilities she won't talk about. For Lavanya, it's where she just *is,* not the heiress, not the businesswoman, not the warrior daughter in a Patil-versus-the-world stance. And me? No one notices the girl with the baseball cap worn backwards, from under which black-brown curls cascade.

The menu is wallet-friendly, and the drinks cost a fraction of what upscale counters charge.

The bar itself, the centrepiece of the room, is a rickety trestle, lined with bottles of affordable liquor and discoloured shot glasses. The furnishings, if you could call it that, have seen too many nights. Mismatched tables and chairs are scattered haphazardly across the room. There have been evenings when we had a table which we hung around but only gathered the chairs to sit on as the night grew old...

The clientele are mostly local traders. Their countenances, when illuminated by the lighting, appear familiar in that you have seen that face in this space before. They recognize us, too, especially Lavanya, the fashionista, who, despite turning out in an ordinary salwar kurta for our Lakshmi Bar outings, gets a lot of looks.

'Is it really over with Vedveer?' Komal asks. She tugs at my shirt, the sleeves of which I have rolled in a clump. 'Actually over?'

It is Komal, of all the people in this mix, who read the *TittleTattle* piece that literally screams that Vedveer and I are over. He's given them good reason to believe!

Komal put it on the group: *It's time to sue these people. Look at that poll. 80 per cent think they've broken up.*

Me: *I'm so done with this relationship!*

Komal: *What do you mean?*

A minute later, she called.

She is the first person I tell about Vedveer's Bengaluru visit a month ago. I didn't mean to spill the tea, but I felt ready to talk about it in this circle. Later, I filled the blanks for Raju after our workout.

At first, I needed time to digest what had happened.

It came from left field, and I couldn't bring myself to talk about it. Not to Alia, not to Lavanya. I was shocked and hurt; still am. Vedveer and I had closed some distance since January, and yes, a part of me still wanted to break it off, but at the very least, I thought he respected me.

Had Lavanya been there when it happened, I would have spoken to her about it, but I just couldn't bring myself to introduce the topic. Work has been hectic (for both of us) these last weeks; there were decisions to take, and I couldn't afford a meltdown.

Lavanya messaged on the group chat a few hours later: *What?!*

My phone started ringing almost immediately.

I told her everything – from the accusations he hurled to telling me Ranibagh belonged to the Rathores, and that's how it would stay, and finally that, *we are done here*.'

She listened and cursed every now and then, all while initiating this LBD meeting and booking her flight from Delhi to Bengaluru.

Not once did Lavanya ask, *Why didn't you tell me? Komal did, but not my BFF.* Of all the people in my life, she's the one who believes in giving people space. Not because she doesn't have the time or couldn't be bothered, but because you need it.

It's a different level of maturity; not everyone rises like that...

I turn to Komal to answer her question. 'No, not formally. My parents are still trying to convince me.'

'Was it four or five weeks ago you said that Vedveer was in Bengaluru? No word since?' Lavanya asks. Her messy bun is beginning to better the name.

There were a few missed calls. I open my WhatsApp and slide my phone to my friends.

VRS: *Hi Aaditha, I would like to speak to you. Please let me know when is a good time to call.*

This is from two weeks ago. There are two more.

VRS: *I was out of line. I want to apologize.*

VRS: *Please pick up the phone, Aaditha.*

'Did you reply?' Lavanya asks.

I shake my head.

'Good girl!' Komal comes back, slapping her palm on the table.

'Why?' Lavanya asks. She's holding a fork up, like she's looking to stab someone. 'Why don't you want to hear him out?' She's playing devil's advocate.

'He wants to apologize for his behaviour,' I say. 'Look at the messages: "I was out of line," not "I was wrong about you. Wrong about what I said about you."' I shrug. 'I am not interested in his sorry. It's not my job to help him feel better about what he did.'

'Yeah,' Lavanya nods, 'you are not his therapist or his parent to have to listen to the whys of his abhorrent behaviour.'

Lavanya puts down the fork and eyes the table, which resembles a taster's spread at a local fair, full of platters and plates. She pushes the chilly cheese fries towards Raju, urging him to eat.

This evening, food isn't disappearing from the plates as quickly as it normally does.

'Why exactly are the Rathores leasing their palace?' Raju asks.

I raise my brow in a question. Excuse me?

'Then what?' Raju's nostrils flare. 'You can't marry a pauper.'

I'm laughing, not Lavanya.

'Of all the things we need to worry about with this proposal, the Rathores having money or not isn't one of them,' she says.

'What does Alia say?' Komal asks.

'She wants me to speak to Vedveer; she thinks someone should be the bigger person,' I say, adding that Alia isn't in the know about his visit here.

'You guys should talk, and my feeling is you will eventually,' Lavanya says, shifting in her seat and getting up to her full height, 'but I think he should absolutely grovel.'

'Grovel is the word,' Komal agrees, grinding her teeth. 'Why should Aaditha give in?' she asks. 'Look at him, shameless! He has hitched up with his ex, Kairi, already. It's been but five minutes.'

Lavanya shakes her head. 'It's the angle of the photograph, I think. It could've been a perfectly innocent moment.'

'Could be,' Komal says, 'but we don't know!'

'The delicate, ever-so-perfect Kairi,' I say.

'I've heard there are cracks in Kairi's engagement,' Lavanya says, her eyes on me. 'I don't know if it is a rumour or if there's any truth in it.'

I shrug.

I've been on social media more in the last two weeks than I have in the past year, searching for signs of Vedveer.

Maybe it's because he reached out to apologize.

There was nothing, no new photos, no palace updates, until this photo popped up, and according to *TittleTattle*, he has been about town. And he has had Kairi for company.

I glance away from my friends and let my eyes drift around the room.

Earlier in the evening, the air buzzed with that desperate edge common to places where the drinking is hard and fast. But as the night stretches, the energy shifts. The crowd settles. There's a kind of glazed peace now, even though the voices are louder, and the bass still thuds beneath everything.

In one corner of the room, a battered jukebox crackles to life with a melancholic tune, *'Anisuthide yaako indu, neenenay nannavalendu'.*

There are times when the music provides a backdrop to the scenes playing out across this space. The occasional clink of pool cues or the shuffle of a deck of cards, the thump of a palm on the table, the look of a hopeless hand lending to the atmosphere. The diehards are at it at the two ends of the room, where the pool and card tables are placed. A small stage sits empty in the corner, a relic from a time when it was a more happening space.

'You are going to tug that wig off,' Lavanya says, reaching for me.

I turn the baseball cap on my head and smile at Komal, who is nodding at Lavanya.

I'm going incognito, I remind myself, and the night is still young. It is only in the safety of Lavanya's car, in a couple of hours, that I will pull off the wig and let my hair down, replace my Batas with my embellished ballet flats, unbutton my shirt, wear it like a shacket and apply some lipstick.

Raju breaks the moment, pointing at the freshly minted noticeboard that has a few new pointers in a bolder font.

The last order is at 12.30 a.m., and closing time is 1 a.m. (This is always at the top of the pile, I remember.)

I read the additions out loud lest anyone miss them.

It is mandatory to deposit cash before going out to smoke.

Vomit cleaning charges are ₹200.

The rest of us, except Raju, are hysterical.

'I've never seen anything like this,' I say, pulling out my phone to snag a photo.

'I would've charged at least five hundred for that,' Raju says, screwing up his nose.

Komal rings the bell, and Raju raises the price to ₹1,000.

'Have neither of you vomited in a pub?' That is Lavanya, trying to keep a straight face.

That's when I notice the new detail on the toilet sign; it says, 'Use of toilet – one person at a time'. The adjunction is in a bold font.

We are all over the table, laughing. I more than the others.

'Why don't we all go to Jaipur? All four of us?' Komal says, grabbing my arm so tight she has almost dislodged my wig. 'Let's take on this prince fellow.'

'Sounds like a plan,' Lavanya says. 'This prince fellow finally meets his match.'

Raju, who is busy on his phone, says, 'Round trip costs 7,333 each.'

'He has already worked out the rates!' Komal's laugh is laced with gin.

Lavanya does the slow clap for Raju. 'Let's ask this prince fellow why they want to lease their palace. What exactly is the reason?'

'He made the why perfectly clear when he was here,' I say.

Lavanya, who, like Komal, is also feeling the drinks downed, leans into me with a question. 'Does this mean his father trusts your dad more than Vedveer trusts you? Because the only one with ants in his pants is the prince fellow.'

I laugh out loud. Lavanya has a point. The question, though, is *why*... Could it be because Kairi Gaur is maybe newly single?

Tittle Tattle

Gupshup Column

GUESS WHO WE CAUGHT INDULGING IN COSPLAY?!

Curious so-and-so,

You are never going to believe this. Go through the pictures on the adjacent page carefully, one at a time. There are eight photographs in all, four people on this table at a bar in Bengaluru's Chamarajpet. It's called Lakshmi Bar.

We spoke to one of the customers to get an opinion on the place because there were no reviews! Come on, we're literally living in review raj! He gave the bar a five-star assessment, calling it '*pucca* local, *yella* basic'.

Okay. So can you recognize her? The girl with the black-brown ringlets, flannel shirt, Bata shoes and a cloth bag?

Behind the elaborate cosplay and curated mystery is none other than Aaditha Prathap – yes, that Aaditha, daughter of Karnataka's finance minister and fiancée to Jaipur's crown prince, Vedveer Rathore Singh. The latest addition to the celebrity circus seems to have forgotten that masks slip.

TT wonders if the Rathores are aware of the wild side of Karnataka's Coffee Queen.

We learnt that Aaditha and her gang of friends, which includes jewellery heiress Lavanya Patil and two others (a man and a woman) whom we couldn't identify, meet at this bar every once in a while. We wonder why, because there are at least two of them in the group who can buy the place with their loose change.

Nobody at Lakshmi Bar knew who this foursome was, but one of the customers, whom we tapped after he staggered out past midnight, took the piss out of us when he asked, 'Famous-ahh?'

Also, take the time to take in the details in the photographs; go ahead and zoom in. Aaditha isn't wearing the green bauble, obviously because that is hard to miss and would have given her away instantly. But also could be because Prince Vedveer has been otherwise busy, socializing with the lovely Kairi Gaur, who we hear is newly single.

When they were done with the evening, they clutched each other's hands, coming together in a circle, which sparked serious cult vibes.

It looks like the four of them ordered the whole bar and the kitchen, which isn't saying much because the wines cost 150 bucks for the 375 ml bottle, and the vodka is billed at 40 bucks a peg.

And finally, dearies, TT finds it hard to imagine HRH Vedveer in a place that charges 200 INR to clean vomit! Eeeiiiuwww! This may be a side of Aaditha the Rathores hadn't contended with.

21.

Vedveer
Colours of Autumn

Father is nursing his afternoon whisky, eyes fixed on an old photograph of mine that Mother had blown up on the wall.

I'm astride Bolt, my favourite steed. The wind is blowing through my hair, and my slightly angled back has soaked up the morning moisture.

'Remind me again, Veer, who took this photograph?' he asks.

Gyan, a stable boy who loves clicking photographs, particularly of horses, had caught that frame in a Canon Father gifted him.

Father nods and eyes my empty hands before turning to Bhanu, the butler.

'Yuvraj isn't thirsty, *hukum*,' he says.

It's that time of year when we retreat to our country home, Aranya Mahal, for a week's break before wading into the season's festivities. This time, the family has been busy, finalizing dates, circling ceremonies, altering guest lists and being difficult at food tastings, for a wedding neither Aaditha nor I want.

I haven't contributed to the wedding chatter since my Bengaluru visit four weeks ago, not in the family WhatsApp group or by replying to the emails Mother sends every other minute.

We haven't heard from the Gowdas, at least not in the way I expected. Had they reached out formally, Father would've descended on Ranibagh, where I have been for the most part until a couple of days ago, in a heartbeat.

October at Aranya Mahal, set on a bend of the Banas River, is addictive. The air is clean, and the light is bright. This property was hand-picked by my ancestor, Grandfather's grandfather, Amber Bishan Rathore Singh, in the latter years of his reign as a private hunting lodge and monsoon retreat for the family. It is the wildlife that drew him here.

About a week after I returned from Bengaluru, I caught myself scrolling through social media, looking for Aaditha. All I found were old reels and photos, some from that polo afternoon. Her hair was swept over one shoulder, her face without a smudge of make-up, except for a flush-pink lipstick. I stopped myself more than once. But the more I looked for her name, her face, even a passing mention, the more I regretted how I behaved.

I messaged her. I called her.

She read the messages. She didn't reply.

She doesn't pick up when I call.

'How exactly did this marriage proposal come about?' I ask Father, employing a casual tone.

Prathap Gowda owes me nothing beyond honouring the Ranibagh contract, which I've scrutinized thoroughly. His daughter, though, should tell me the truth. Because even if this began as an arranged match, it didn't stay that way. It became something more. Something real. Something that got under my skin (this is not her problem, I know). But none of that matters now. It's all in the past.

Father is taken aback for a moment, but his expression hardens quickly.

'I'm not sure if this is the time for that kind of a question, Veer,' he says. 'We've finalized dates with the Gowdas, and only the wedding invitations need to be done.'

'Curious,' I say, summoning a smile.

'Prathap Gowda is a top politician and a successful businessman; he and I met in Delhi,' Father says, pausing to take a sip from his glass. 'I invited him home, we met again over the next couple of days, and I brought up the alliance with him. We both thought it was an excellent idea.'

'Who broached the topic of marriage?' I ask.

'Why? And why *now*?' Father's face is florid.

'Why shouldn't I know the sequence of events?'

'I take credit. I thought it would work fabulously. And it is, right?'

'Was that also when you decided on Ranibagh?' I ask about his decision to lease, something he had been so reluctant to do, literally until now.

Father pushes back in his seat and stretches out his legs. 'Not right then. It is only after you convinced me that we should lease a section of Ranibagh that I took Prathap Gowda into confidence and asked for his opinion.'

'And he jumped at the idea, just like he did at the proposal?'

Father turns away, refusing to give my accusation the dignity of a response.

Father and I are at the Darikhana Pavilion, a long hall with arches and pillars, which probably served as an informal audience section in the old days. Mother has turned it into a family room. The wall is a busy space – shaded portraits, hand-drawn maps and hunting trophies – detailing the estate's story.

A striking oil portrait of a bejewelled Amber Bishan Rathore Singh, seated on his throne with a hawk perched on his gloved hand, is the centrepiece of the construction we face. Flanking him are photographs of princes and royal cousins in riding boots, polo sticks slung over their shoulders. Another painting, this one sourced by Mother, is colourful, with ladies in saris marching to the riverfront.

I'm looking at the art before me, trying to focus on it, but I'm shifting in my seat and shuffling thoughts in my head.

'Like me, Aaditha isn't in the know of the plans made by our fathers?'

Father moves forward in his seat. 'God, no! The princess-to-be has no idea.' His eyes widen, and he's shaking his head. 'I wanted to play safe with Ranibagh, Veer; that's why I went to Prathap Gowda.'

'How can you be so sure?' I ask. I have my doubts. Father is prone to assuming, especially when he trusts someone.

'We made that pact. Prathap and I.' Father's nostrils flare as he speaks.

Father looks away before turning to me. 'He is a man of his word,' he says, his right fist landing on his left palm in a punch. 'I know his ambition has earned him a reputation, but he's also known as an upright individual in the corridors of power. I have done my homework. You know I am diligent with that.'

My throat tightens, the kind of shock that doesn't show but stays.

'Are these questions the reason you haven't shaved?' Father asks. He is on his feet now.

My fingers are on my chin, sticking into my stubble.

'It doesn't suit you, Veer!'

I'm nodding, though I don't know at what exactly.

Father continues to speak, but my senses are shutting down. I can see him; his mouth is moving, but I no longer hear him.

What have I done? The insults I hurled at Aaditha come back in a steady stream.

I know what exactly you and your father are up to.

Co-conspirator and all...?

Ranibagh is mine; it's the home of the Rathores, and that's how it will stay.

As if that wasn't bad enough, I had some especially tardy ones, too.

Is that your uniform?

The worst, and the one that comes strongest at me, a left hook, is that she tried to make me understand.

No, Vedveer. I'll say this just once – you have got it all wrong.

It's not maths. It's not even logic. I wasn't thinking straight. Of course, I wasn't. Why?

When I walked into her office that morning, she was surprised to see me, as anyone would be when the person you're engaged to shows up unannounced. That's how she was seeing things. Yes, I had called her, but the call didn't go through, and she hadn't checked notifications, which, for me, was the final straw that morning.

Aaditha held up her phone and showed me that she hadn't checked the notifications that were right there.

She was being transparent; she was apologizing. I was bleeding. I was blind with fury.

Looking back at that morning now, she probably thought I was there because of the newspaper article.

When I launched into her – insults flying one after another – she was taken aback. I saw it play on her face then, but I thought she was pretending, manipulating the situation.

We are done here.

Those words have sat heavily on me these last weeks because I can't do anything about them.

I can't delete, I can't proceed.

I signed the lease papers and ploughed ahead with our Green Dream.

The wedding plans are in place, and fortunately for me, there is no move from the Gowdas to end things.

In quieter moments, I have asked myself whether I really couldn't do anything about breaking this alliance or was it that I did not want to do anything?

The truth is, I didn't want to follow up on my words, even when I felt that she was in cahoots with her father.

'Why are you asking me these questions?' Father asks, clapping his hands, reminding me that he is in the room.

'I should be in the know of details?'

'Fair enough,' he says, turning away from me.

Mother and Navya, who were out for another round of food tasting, this one for the one function we are having at Aranya Mahal, walk into the room. Navya with her sunglasses and Mother with her ever-flushed face.

'You have been extremely busy this past month. All work and no play is not a good thing, Yuvraj,' Father says. 'And please shave. You look like a grief-stricken *majnun*. You are getting married, not being sent to jail.'

Mother has been doing all the planning for the wedding celebrations, which are to extend across seven days from 16 to 22 December. Before we arrived at Aranya Mahal, Mother had Ratan Singh (possibly because I had stopped replying to her) mail me a tentative schedule, which read like the grand wedding extravaganza (starring the groom, co-starring culture, with a cameo by the bride and her family).

Even though she amended that quickly, coming up with a *swagatham sabha* – a welcome with honour on day two – she is now fretting about the food. She planned a ceremony after consultations with the palace head priest, blending customs of both sides, which was to be followed by a southern-style vegetarian lunch, served on banana leaves.

She is at her wits' end now because there is no chef in all of Rajasthan who can come up with authentic fare to serve on a banana leaf.

'We need to have cooks flown in from Bengaluru or other parts of Karnataka for the food tasting,' she says, sitting up straight. 'Maybe we'll invite a few gourmet caterers over the next couple of weeks and make a decision.'

'I will ask Neela for help; maybe she can fly in for a day or send Aaditha on her behalf,' Mother says, winking at me. 'Wouldn't you like that!'

'Why don't you just let the palace office take care of it?' I tell her.

'It is your wedding, Vedveer, the biggest event on the social calendar this year and maybe for a few years!'

I nod.

Navya takes off her sunglasses and looks pointedly at me. 'You look a mess! Are you unwell, Brother?'

Mother turns to Navya with a what-are-you-talking-about stare. 'He works too hard,' she says.

'You've lost weight! What's up?' Navya asks.

'I haven't shaved, that's all.'

'He doesn't have time,' Mother says.

'I'm sure it helps to know that your fiancée is living her best life,' Navya says.

How does she know? What does she know?

Navya's eyes shift between Father and me; she is gauging us.

'What? No one in this family has read *TittleTattle* in the last week?'

'It's not exactly the holy book!' Father says.

Nayva laughs out loud. 'It isn't,' she agrees, looking at Mother, who appears equally mystified.

I haven't been on social media for a couple of weeks. I had seen the picture with Kairi, typical *TittleTattle* garbage, but otherwise, I had steered clear. I was out on the field, getting projects on our various properties rolling.

Right now, my fingers are itching to click on the article. If I pull out my phone now, everyone will not only know what I'm doing, but they will also know that Aaditha and I haven't been in touch in this time.

The parents exchange glances, and Mother reaches for her phone, but Navya decides to put us out of our misery.

She pulls out her tablet, clicks the screen a couple of times and holds up her iPad like a school teacher before her class.

From where I'm seated, I read a headline about someone caught in cosplay.

I look out of the window at the rose garden – yellow, pink, orange and red blooms.

'You all are unable to read from this distance,' Navya says, putting her iPad down on her lap. 'But before I pass my tablet around, I have to say, I'm fascinated by my to-be sister's ability to live life. She absolutely refuses to be held back.'

The article carries a bunch of photos from Aaditha's late-evening outing with friends. The disguise is good. I try to keep a straight face. It's hard to tell it's her, at least in these pictures. Unless you know the location of the bar.

It is possible to identify her by elimination. The real giveaway is Lavanya Patil, recognizable in society circles. And by association, it won't take long before someone starts asking who the girl in the baseball cap is.

My first thought is that someone tipped off *TittleTattle*. Aaditha must be furious.

Father is beside himself with laughter.

'This is just great!' he says. 'The lady has a sense of humour. Who is that singer who walks around in disguises?'

Mother looks uncomfortable. 'I'm not sure I see the humour in this, Gaurav. I think it's reckless. You know I'm a fan of how she has managed her business as a woman, and she has done it all on her own.'

Navya shoots out of her chair. 'Come on, Mother! You,

of all people, should applaud her originality. You met Father when you walked the ramp in Milan.'

Mother blushes. 'She is original, I grant her that, but now, as Vedveer's fiancée, Ranibagh's bahu, she has responsibility, which goes beyond just being Aaditha, because of which she must be cautious of how she goes about her life. She's always in the public eye.'

'Mom, stop!' I hope Mother will not try this sermon on Aaditha. What I have done is bad enough.

'Do you have a problem with her disguise, Brother?' Navya turns to me; she's sizing me up. 'Not that Aaditha would pay heed; she's too much of her own woman.'

Navya's iPad is with me, and I zoom in on the photographs. The place looks like a dilapidated highway inn from another century. Her heavily tattooed friend is there, and so is his helmet.

'How come you didn't know about the disguise?' Navya nudges. 'Haven't you guys talked recently?'

I shut the iPad and turn away from Navya, and after what feels like perpetuity, I motion her with my eyes to the deck that overlooks the Banas.

The parents are discussing various ceremonies and how or whether to restrict invites for some events without offending anyone.

'I don't see why we have to restrict,' Father says, breaking from the conversational flow, 'Rathores don't restrict; we believe in big and bigger.'

'You can't be inviting the universe, Gaurav,' Mother

says as Navya and I move away from them and walk out into the late afternoon sun.

We lean against the newly polished brass railings and look out at the stone steps that descend into the river, flanked by *chhatris* and shaded neem trees. The monsoon has passed, leaving behind a freshly washed landscape, the river is full but calm, and the air is scented with the lush wilderness.

Even though I am still beating myself up for how I behaved in Bengaluru, this afternoon's conversation with Father has lifted a weight I've been carrying for weeks.

It isn't a ploy or a game. Her eyes didn't lie.

'I messed up big time,' I tell my sister, and proceed to lay it all out for her.

'That's so unlike you, Brother, losing your cool like that, showing your vulnerable side,' Navya says, turning to face me. Her fingers are on my wrist; her eyes hold my gaze.

A surge of emotion rises, long-buried, unfamiliar and so intense it rattles something deep within me, shaking my very foundation.

'Is this so-in-control Rathore lost in love?' She asks the question as her lips lift in a smile.

Navya has never had a problem expressing herself, her opinions, even her fears. Around her, more than with anyone else who carries the Rathore name, I feel inclined to hold a mirror to my inner self.

'What are you going to do about it?' she asks.

'I have messaged, called, but she hasn't responded.'

'She's hurt; give her time,' Navya says.

Maybe that, or Aaditha read my texts for what they were: that I wanted to apologize for my behaviour, not so much for blaming her.

'I'm not sure she wants to see me any time soon.'

Navya smiles. 'If I were you, I would take hope from the fact that she hasn't called off the wedding.'

I shake my head. I'm not sure Aaditha not calling it off means anything.

22.

Aaditha

Silk, Sequins and a Stubborn Silence

I'm seated on a divan placed at one end of a hall with a grand name – Sahitya Sabha. Gilded arches mark the entryways, one of which opens into the anteroom. I look carefully at the door and memorize it. I will need to escape this space at regular intervals.

Some of the finest designers in the country – along with their ever-present entourages – are swarming this part of the palace, a space usually reserved for literary events. Rolling racks of skirts and blouses, swathes of brocade in varying shades of gold and tangles of flimsy fabric are propped up in every corner of the room.

According to Reema Barmer, the intern, hired for the sole purpose of adding chaos to my life, we'll be trying on clothes all day for the 'crown prince's seven-day wedding celebration', which is set to take place in just about sixty days.

Amma and I arrived at Ranibagh late last evening because I insisted I would not leave Bengaluru until I completed the tasks I scheduled for the day. There wasn't much to be done, but I was determined I'd have a say, even if what time we left was the only choice I had.

'We don't have much time,' Reema says, speaking quickly.

'Ranisa was with the designers all day yesterday; she narrowed down options to make things easier for you. She knows you're busy; that's why she's helping. You are really lucky her taste is flawless,' she says, bending over me and adjusting my hair.

Gauri Elena called Amma two weeks ago to tell her that the palace had summoned top design houses for a three-day showcase so we could admire fabric swatches and pretend to make difficult choices for the seven days of wedding celebrations. She insisted we come to Ranibagh for at least a couple of days so the bride's outfits could be finalized.

'What do you do when I'm not around?' I ask Reema. I'm genuinely curious.

'I don't know, Rajkumari,' she says. She is breathing hard. 'I try to help Yuvrajji. I check with him all the time to see if he needs anything, but he's too busy.'

'Doing what?'

Reema breaks into peals of laughter. Her blush is bold, a new colour in the palette.

Maybe I should suggest to the Rathores that Reema could help at the coffee store just outside their palace gates, the same one they 'funded'. That'll inspire *TittleTattle* to run another piece on south Indian stingy. This one will be earned at least.

Thrift like the Gowdas.

How Aaditha uses a palace employee (who basically does nothing, outside of triggering my anxiety levels) to cut back CB3's expenses.

I'm in Ranibagh only because I couldn't escape (credit to my family for that). Ever since I told my parents I wanted out, they've been pouring emotional persuasion over every conversation like it's gravy.

They coax, they plead, blow hot, blow cold and absolutely refuse to take no for an answer.

Appa roped in Alia for Team Prathap, and she was sticky with persistence, never confrontational, just endlessly gushing about Vedveer.

'He's a good person,' my older sister by a decade simpered two nights ago while driving to work in a different time zone.

She paused for a response, and when she didn't get one, she stepped on the accelerator.

'Vedveer is perfect for you,' Alia said. 'He's everything a girl could ever want – kind, funny, thoughtful. I don't understand why you are having second thoughts. And the way he looks at you... it's like you're the only person in the world.'

'Err... and when exactly did you see that?'

'At the polo game, Aadi! When he was talking to you, it was like nobody else mattered! It is so sweet, really!'

'I'm not so sure… He looks at a lot of girls like that.'

Appa called for a late-evening meeting with the security team at No. 5 MG Road to make an announcement, shortly after he caught wind of the *TittleTattle* story. A week after the Lakshmi Bar piece hit the stands.

'Effective from this evening, we keep separate logs for entry and exit – full names, addresses, whom they're meeting and the reason for their visit. We're fortunate that this incident,' Appa says, leaving out details deliberately, 'didn't result in a serious breach. But let this be a wake-up call for everyone. It is someone outside of not just this group but beyond these walls who noticed the disguise before any of you.'

A dozen nods and not a single response (according to Raju).

'Every two–three weeks, a *veshabhusana* (costume) walked out of these gates, but that *vesha* hadn't walked in. Didn't it occur to you to question?' he asked.

The disguise seemed to amuse Appa more than bother him. His only real issue with the Lakshmi Bar scene was the fact that security missed it.

I can bet my parents hadn't laid eyes on *TittleTattle* until the incognito story broke. They may have heard whispers of the kind of gossip that features on *TittleTattle*, especially after our association with the Rathores became a thing of national interest, but it isn't a page they would click to read ever.

I'm almost certain Alia is the one who told my parents about the article.

I had consciously kept the Lakshmi Bar meetings from my sister because I knew she'd lose it, and sure enough, she did the moment she saw the pictures.

'I don't understand why you're encouraging this rowdy behaviour,' Amma scolded Appa.

Appa took his cue and turned on me. 'What if a fight broke out?' he asked. 'What would you have done?'

Even restaurants where you pay two or three thousand bucks for a smooth cocktail have seen violence. If a fight had broken out, we would've left immediately; that's the plan always.

At first, the *TittleTattle* piece made me angry. I was outraged; it was an invasion of privacy. That this happened in the city I call home was hard to digest, not that boundaries haven't been violated in Bengaluru before, but this felt like a loss of ground.

Raju told me that Lakshmi Bar's clientele had doubled and trebled since the story broke. A neighbourhood watering hole had become a place of great curiosity, even in Bengaluru, where folks just go about their own business. A younger demographic in general, and more women, particularly, visit Lakshmi Bar these days.

I couldn't help thinking that to the LBDs, this hidey-hole was gone forever...

Raju did some digging and concluded that it was the watchman at the bar who may have unwittingly pointed the paps in my direction.

Apparently, there had been enquiries a few days earlier about an Aaditha Prathap, who had been frequenting Lakshmi Bar. Since no one there knew me, let alone as the finance minister's daughter, the answer was a firm no. But the question was floating in the wind. Eventually, the watchman, even if unknowingly, gave the game away by pointing at the group.

I was already mad at Vedveer before the *TittleTattle* piece dropped, and with good reason. But this, the uproar his presence in my life has caused, has taken it to a different level.

Stylists, designers and jewellers are reaching for me from every direction. Bangles are being replaced by armlets, somebody else is fixing anklets, I feel fingers on my earlobes and a pair of hands in my hair.

I'm nudged to a standing position, like I am a display doll. I'm half-draped in a cloud of silk, an outfit that covers one shoulder and falls to the floor in a heap. It is a lot of fabric, only some of which is on me.

I try to smile, looking for humour in a cluttered space that is steadily crushing my spirit.

Amma, whose allergy is threatening, is trying hard not to sneeze into a length of Banarasi tissue that stands next to her. She brushes her nostrils with her index finger, knuckling it, looking for relief.

There are *lehenga*s in every shade of gold – rose gold, dusky gold, champagne gold, confused gold – and I've been encouraged to 'feel the energy' of every colour before I make a choice.

There's a blouse on the railing that looks more like an upholstered cushion. I giggle, and Reema turns to ask if I need anything.

On my left, a slightly built man, dressed in a quilted skirt, grunts as he holds up a *lehenga*. I shudder; it must weigh a tonne.

'It's minimal by Rathore standards,' he cajoles, turning to face me.

I was introduced to the folks who are looking to dress me up as soon as I arrived: 'so, so and so from the House of Dadlanis,' or 'she, she and he from Malini & Mehta'. I stop trying to put names to the faces because of the numbers I'm dealing with.

Behind the quilted skirt, an employee from a couture line and a Kanjeevaram advocate with an accent are locked in a silent tussle, trying to stare down the other.

Reema is using a rose water sprinkler, which she came armed with, a little too generously.

She is stretched, managing delicate egos and rising decibels. She moves around the room slowly, brokering peace and pleading for patience; when nothing else works, she leans on the rose water.

'Ranisa said everybody will get a chance,' she implores.

'She should wear her heritage,' an anglicized accent declares. The Kanjeevaram advocate?

If I were ever to get married, I would definitely wear Amma's beloved yarn – Mysore and Kanjeevaram – for a couple of events, but I'm not going to finalize those drapes from this mix. That's like travelling to Jaipur to eat Mysore masala dosa.

It would be cruel to drop that on them now, so if they want to believe I am going to advertise their style and workmanship, I'm happy to humour them for the time being.

Never before in my life have I been held captive in the manner I am this morning. Every time my hand is free, I use it to reach for the glass of rose water, which is placed on a sparkling silver coaster. I even pull off a few neck rotations to ease the anxiety.

The room is quiet for the most part, save for the din of intermittent conversation. Instrumental music is playing in the background. Every once in a while, a newbie in the business buzzes into the room holding an iPad, saying, 'The embroidery's en route from Lucknow!' or 'The veil has reached Amritsar!' as if announcing positions of drivers in a cross-country rally.

I cough softly into my hand, feigning an allergy I obviously don't have, to keep the make-up artists at bay.

A lady whispers into my ear, 'Soft glam; we'll keep it light and make it quick.' I decline with another bout of coughing; this time, it's an exaggerated sound. 'It's persistent,' I say, brushing my nose with the back of my hand.

I have to dress up this evening, and there is no way I'm having someone paint my skin so early in the day, only to take it off and put it on a few hours later. It's my skin, not a brick wall waiting for a coat of primer.

I walked in wearing tinted sunscreen on blue jeans, and that is exactly how I'm going to walk out of this place in an hour or two, hopefully.

I have already warned: no nail extensions for me. I don't want to call out for help each time I need to peel off a sweat-soaked sports bra. I keep my nails short; they are shaped square always. That is non-negotiable.

I only have to nod, and they'll be fixing fake eyelashes on me.

I'm finally in the ivory *lehenga* I'd been eyeing since I walked into the room. It weighs as much as me.

I have diamonds on my neck and chandeliers in my ears. I get on my feet, only to sink back into the divan before pushing myself back on my feet.

I'm before a full-length mirror. I like how I look, except that it is laborious.

'Can you take the necklace and earrings off, please?' I request Reema.

I want to walk around in the *lehenga* and the warrior princess blouse, which goes perfectly with my mood.

'Rajkumari,' Reema says slowly, making no attempt to relieve me of the jewellery, '*aabh bahut pyaaree lag rahee ho*.'

I beam my brightest smile and point at my neck.

Amma is on her feet, adjusting her pleats. '*Nanu idhara sanna konege hoguttiddene*.' She has had enough of this demonstration and is retiring to the antechamber.

I'm going to follow her there as soon as I can lose these people. I want to FaceTime Alia and show her this outfit, without the over-the-top contraption around my neck. I'm not planning to give it away, though, rest assured; it could sponsor my next store.

If this wedding actually goes through (because you never know), I hope these folks understand I'm getting married, not walking the ramp for a jewellery store.

Reema works the sparkling necklace off me slowly, and I feel lighter instantly. Now all I need are pockets in my *lehenga* and a pair of kitten heels. I'd be good for a round of Kalari.

I wander out of the room barefoot through an unguarded back entrance, careful not to catch anyone's attention. I'm looking for the antechamber Amma disappeared into. I emerge at one end of a high-ceilinged corridor with old hunting swords mounted above long teak mirrors. In a corner, on a settee not far from where I'm standing, an embroiderer is hand-stitching the Rathore crest onto a silk pocket square.

As I make my way down the marbled flooring, looking for the door that could lead me to the antechamber, I notice some commotion down the other end. My step slows down, my heart is racing, people are rushing around, stepping over things and speaking in raised voices.

Someone has lost the turban pin that belonged to Vedveer's great-grandfather.

My eyes wander, and I spot him – Vedveer Rathore Singh – my obnoxious fiancé who didn't miss a beat before marching into my office and berating me six weeks ago. He is coming through a hallway wearing an ivory *bandhgala*. It is the first time, since he was in my office, that we are in the same postcode.

'It's on me,' he announces, and just like that, the rush around him recedes.

I'm right across from him. He hasn't seen me yet and is moving forward in my direction. There's a lengthy floor space between us.

It's the tinkle of the anklets I wear that catches his attention, and he looks up at my effortlessly contorted face. He's not smiling, his mouth is slightly open, and he's breathing hard. He waves to me, gesturing for me to stop.

I hitch the *lehenga* and hasten my step. I'm a couple of feet away from a door that I think might lead me to the antechamber, and Vedveer pauses mid-stride.

Our eyes meet for a split second.

His lips are a straight line, and my heart is hammering madly.

'Aaditha,' he says. I hear him breathe. 'You arrived last evening.'

These are the first words he has said to me after telling me, *We are done here*.

He called, sent me a few tepid messages that didn't really scream accountability or say I am sorry. In the last couple of weeks, there were more messages. I stopped reading them.

'Rajkumari.' I hear Reema; she is behind me somewhere.

I need my phone but realize that it is with Reema. I turn around to face her and use my right hand to signal telephone.

'Phone!' she exclaims and darts in the direction of the hall.

When I turn, I'm face to face with Vedveer. I hadn't realized, but I'd been walking on my toes to accommodate the length of the skirt, perhaps. I sway slightly to my right, trying to balance as I let myself down. Vedveer reaches out to steady me, and I instinctively take a step back.

'Aaditha,' he says softly, attempting a smile. The mid-morning light catches his eyes, only for a moment.

I feel the corners of my lips betray me before I clamp down on them and turn to the direction of what I think is the antechamber. It has to be one of these doors.

I want to say, *I thought we were done*, but I am not going to give him the satisfaction of knowing that those words singed.

As I open the door, I notice Vedveer's gaze has dropped

to my hand. At first, I think his eyes are on the armlet, but I realize his gaze is on my fingers. I lift my ring-free hand and wave a dismissive goodbye at him.

You and Kairi Gaur can waltz into the sunset for all I care!

I hope he knows he has lost me as a friend – and anything more we possibly could have been.

Amma is stretched out on a recliner sofa in the antechamber; her feet are bare, and her hands are toying with her phone. She is alone in the room.

Where is Reema? I need my phone.

'Reema,' I call, knowing fully well she is not around. As if on cue, the main door opens, and Reema, who is wearing a frazzled expression, stumbles into the light. She is clutching my phone.

'Where was it?' I ask.

'It was on the tray,' she says.

'What tray?'

'Jalebi tray!'

I laugh out loud even as I wonder what a tray of juicy jalebis is doing in a room full of pinched waistlines.

I sit down and click on WhatsApp.

Me: *Ran into VRS, trying to talk. Duh!*

Lavanya is online but takes a minute to start typing.

Lovey: *Why are you only messaging now? Worried sick! I was about to call Neela Aunty and check if you guys are ok.*

Lovey: *Reaction?*

Me: *Icy. I waved my ringless fingers at him! More later.*

I put my phone down and twirl for Amma, who is wearing an uncertain expression. It's the colour of the dupatta, she says, before dialling Alia.

I remove the third dupatta of the morning with a frustrated sigh that I hope echoes across these grounds and beyond. I'm annoyed, but I'm also feeling alive suddenly.

Reema picks up a peach dupatta with flap-happy birds in French knots and brings it to me.

Alia, who is nudged awake by her ringtone, says, 'Try that.' She is pointing at the fabric Reema is holding up.

'I've tried three shades of "sunset blush" in two hours,' I say.

'One more won't hurt then,' my sister comes back. She's sitting up on her king-sized bed, her body wrapped in a quilt. 'This is for the evening, yeah?'

I nod.

Reema leaves the room and returns with a different pair of earrings in the hope that they will make a difference.

'These earrings weigh more than my opinions.'

Alia laughs, sounding more like the sister I know.

'I can't really say if it's working. I'm not getting a full picture because when you step back, the image blurs,' she tells me, peering into her phone. 'I love the *lehenga*; you can't go wrong with ivory. It's the dupatta that I'm not sure about.'

I return to the Sahitya Sabha, and I try on *lehenga*s and

saris in every shade the human eye can register and a few it probably shouldn't.

Meanwhile, I'm one drape away from collapsing into a pile of sequins.

I'm fed bites of salad between my trials, but I need more. I stab my fork into a cherry tomato sitting on a pile of greens and shove it into my mouth. The salt in the crumbled feta is life-giving. I repeat the exercise twice, thrice before reaching for the rose water.

My eyes are on the doorway. I need to lose Reema and get out of here. A door opens, and late-afternoon light spills into a narrow passage. My eyes follow the light, and my feet respond to the cue. It's an opening. I look over my shoulder; I can't see Reema anywhere. I make a dash for the exit.

I cross another corridor. This one is narrower, and I enter a rectangular room. I'm welcomed by the soft scent of sandalwood. The room feels cooler than the space I just exited.

I settle on a sofa and look around me. The wall is lined with portraits of women, queens, maybe. I sigh and shut my eyes. Barely a minute passes when I hear the creak of the door, which is followed by a flood of light, as if to announce an entry.

'Here you are, Aaditha.' It is Gauri Elena's voice. 'That child, the intern, is running all over the palace looking for you.'

I blink.

'She must have told you I was looking for you and forgot all about it! She's just twenty-two but can't remember a thing!'

I'm on my feet, deferring to Gauri Elena, who takes a seat next to me. She's dressed in soft silks and pearls and is carrying a velvet box, which she flicks open before reaching over and placing it before me. An uncut *polki kada,* set in gold, fills the box.

'This was given to me by my mother-in-law,' she says. Her back is straight, and her eyes are soft. 'She gave it to me on the morning of my wedding.'

I nod.

'She didn't say much; she wasn't a woman of many words,' the ranisa continues, lifting the thick bangle and placing it on my wrist. 'But she reminded me that women like us carry a huge weight, but we must always bear it with grace.'

I wonder what the ranisa is getting at. Is this a reaction to the *TittleTattle* story?

'We don't expect you to wear it every day,' Gauri Elena says with a smile. 'But every time you look at it, let it remind you of who you are and who you represent.'

I'm being told off, and I'm not pleased.

I want to say, *I don't need this added weight. My own is more than enough, and I don't need a piece of jewellery to remind me of who I am.*

My eyes drop to my wrist and skim the gold; it is solid, full and slightly oversized. A perfect fit, somehow.

'Thank you,' I say reluctantly.

'Welcome to the family, Rajkumari,' she says, her fingers warm on my cheeks, when the door behind me opens.

'There you are, Rajkumari. I've been looking for you everywhere.' My phone is in Reema's hand.

The ranisa smiles. 'You are so forgetful. You told Aaditha to wait for me here but forgot all about it!'

Reema is confused. I could've clarified that I was running away from Reema, but I let it pass.

The door opens again. I almost curse. This time, it is Vedveer.

'Aaditha,' he exhales. His gaze goes over Reema but doesn't reach his mother.

Reema spins around, bows to the prince and rushes out of the room.

'Are you looking for your bride, Yuvraj?' Gauri Elena asks.

Vedveer nods and walks towards me. His eyes are dark, and regret is etched on his features.

I'm on my feet. 'We met earlier and had a long conversation,' I say, smiling at the mother first and then the son. 'I think he's looking for you.' My voice is honey-smooth.

Vedveer opens his mouth and then shuts it; his eyes are glued on me.

Gauri Elena is beaming. 'Yuvraj,' she says, directing her gaze at the sofa I just vacated.

'Now go and rest some before you head out for the evening. All eyes will be on the both of you,' she says of the grand premiere of the Hollywood epic that was shot in Jaipur. 'Go away before someone comes at you with another piece of cloth.'

Her laugh is rhythmic; it floats around me as I leave the room.

23.

Vedveer

Ring a Bell!

My eyes are fixed on Aaditha as I descend the curved staircase that leads to the foyer of the Durbar Hall.

She's a vision in a colour I struggle to pin down. Is it silver? A cool-toned sparkle? Polished. Composed. It shimmers under the light, a wintery richness complemented by a frosty aura. A form-fitting gown, the shade of which seems to change with every step I take, gaining in colour, from platinum to titanium.

I ignore my erratic heartbeat and put the hustle down to the glare of the chandelier.

Aaditha wants nothing to do with me; she makes that amply clear. During the day, she avoided me entirely, choosing to stay locked with the designers, who would normally bore her to tears. I spotted her once in the corridor, but she was gone before I could stop her. I found her again in Mother's visiting room, but she turns it on me, insisting we've already met, that it is Mother I was looking for, and scripts her escape.

Her gaze sweeps over me, then looks away unimpressed, like I wear tuxedos every Friday. But her breath catches in the hollow of her throat, betraying more than she intends.

'Shall we?' I ask, offering her my hand.

Aaditha puts her fingers to work, adjusting her skirt ever so slightly, just enough to give her hand an excuse.

'My hands are busy, Your Highness,' she says dryly.

I withdraw my hand and settle it at the small of her back, guiding her forward. She says nothing, but I can't help the smile she pointedly refuses to acknowledge the gesture.

I step closer and lower my voice to a murmur. 'Busy with what, exactly?' I have to ask.

Aaditha glances sideways, a flicker of amusement sparking her eyes.

'Contemplating appropriate punishment for your presumptuousness,' she says.

I chuckle, leaning in just enough for my breath to caress the top of her ear. 'I'm willing to accept any sentence you deem fit.'

She finally meets my gaze. 'Good. Then don't expect mercy.'

Aaditha's face, flawlessly made-up, gives nothing away, even when she's delivering a perfectly timed dismissal.

I walk slowly with her. Liquid silver, that's the colour of her gown. It flows with her, languidly, moving as she takes a step, taking her shape as she covers ground.

Her hands are on the front of her gown, pretending to coax the skirt. That's when I see it – no engagement ring.

Her fingers are bare, conspicuously so. It wasn't there this morning either.

The difficult part is that she won't engage – just that much and no more. I messed things up in Bengaluru, I get that, but she won't give me a chance to apologize and make it up to her.

I messaged. I called. I've been virtually stalking her. She refuses to take my calls. Hell, she refuses to look at me even.

She ignored me all morning and afternoon, and now we're walking side by side. My palm rests against the bare warmth of her back, but the silence between us is louder than ever. She's built a quiet boundary, and even in this closeness, I can feel the distance she's determined to keep.

I look at her hands again, needing to be sure. They are bare, completely. My heart slams against my chest, pushed towards a truth it's not ready to hold. My breath grows shallow.

Aaditha knows I have noticed; she looks up at me and smiles. The only piece of jewellery she has on is a pair of ornate earrings, which I may have seen on Mother.

I take a deep breath. I have to play the part for the next few minutes, and then we will talk. I'm determined.

Aaditha and I are the guests of honour at the premiere of the Hollywood movie shot in Jaipur.

The five-minute drive to the Art Deco Cinema is done in an unquiet silence. I can't make up my mind on how exactly to word the question playing on loop in my head.

Where is your engagement ring? That would be too direct. Borderline rude, maybe.

I'm staring at Aaditha's palm, which is opening and closing, maybe because I think that she has hidden it in her clasp.

Why aren't you wearing your engagement ring? Authoritarian?

I arrive at something somewhat cooler: Lost your ring?

By the time I pick the tone, we have reached.

I get around the hood of the car quickly, lending her a hand as she steps out onto the red carpet. This time, she mouths a thank you, her gaze holding mine. Her fragrance, jasmine in bloom, fills me.

We move together and wave at Jaipur. She isn't hitching the skirt of her gown now.

Aaditha wears her brightest smile for the people before turning sharply in the direction of the Art Deco Cinema.

The drone cameras are at work above us; searchlights sweep across the sky. At the other end, paparazzi bulbs flash at us.

Waves of 'Yuvraj, Rajkumari, Yuvraj, Rajkumari' charge the late-evening air.

My palm is on the small of her back. I feel her shudder.

We pose for the cameras, perfectly in sync. I'm standing by her, closer than usual, maybe because I want to make up for the fact that she isn't wearing her engagement ring or that the crowds are only 60–70 yards away from us, and I fear she will float away into the night.

As we pause one more time on the carpet, the photographers are shouting both our names. 'Yuvrajji, Rajkumari', 'please look here', *'ek baar aur'*.

Inside, the hall is a blur of velvet seats and champagne flutes. We take our places in the front row while the director makes his speech on 'the spirit of Jaipur' and 'how generous and gracious the royal family has been.'

'Have you lost your ring?' The tone is harsher than I intended it to be, and I regret it immediately.

'Which ring?' she asks, looking surprised and straightening her back, all at the same time. 'The one you put on me for the paparazzi?'

I hear myself exhale. She is being deliberately flippant. 'What are you saying?' I ask

She pats my hand gently, her eyes directed to the screen. 'We're at the cinema, Your Highness.'

I choke back a snort.

The lights dim, the film starts. A sweeping shot of the Aravallis fills the screen, but all I can see are Aaditha's naked fingers, which are now waving at me from the armrest between us.

Tittle Tattle

Gupshup Column

THE CASE OF THE MISSING RING. YIKES!

Curious so-and-so,

Well, well, well, did you all catch the drama at the *No Love in Pink City* premiere?

Of course, you did, because the real stars of the evening were HRH Vedveer and his fiancée, Coffee Queen, Aaditha Prathap.

Now, Vedveer was there, but let's be real, dearies, Aaditha *owned* that red carpet. She wasn't just making an entrance; she was staging a full-on performance.

Waves, kisses, smiles, she had it all down to an art. And Jaipur lapped it up.

Meanwhile, the Prince, dashing in a black tuxedo, appeared to be in a bit of a rush. We don't know. Maybe he had a meeting with the Royal Bureau of Speed Walking.

But back to Aaditha, who completely *stole* the show in that silver gown. It was backless and had a neckline daring enough to cause a traffic jam. We couldn't stop staring at her, and it wasn't just because her gown was the physical embodiment of 'wow'.

No, it was also the little detail of her *ringless* hand, which had the crowd buzzing. She was waving her digits around so much, we have to ask if she was making a point!

Now, we know some of you might argue, maybe the emerald ring didn't match the gown. Or that it didn't fit with the other piece of jewellery she wore, the chandelier earrings (last seen on HRH Navya Mrinalini's lobes). And you might have a point.

According to Palace talk, she was not wearing the ring at her *dress fitting* at Ranibagh earlier either.

Let's just say, we're raising an eyebrow.

The question is, what's going on? *Trouble in paradise*? Is Kairi Gaur the reason?

Or is it just Princess-to-be Aaditha thinking, *who needs a ring when you've already got a Prince*?

We'll keep our eyes on this one, because something tells us there's more to the story than just missing jewels.

21.

Vedveer

Where the Heart Is!

A COFFEE Before Books & Bras creative flutters in the early-evening easterly at the entrance of the heritage hotel that is home to Bengaluru's Literature Festival. Aaditha's brand is the sponsor of the event.

It hadn't occurred to me until this moment, as we glide past the gates of the colourfully decorated venue, why Robert Kaminski wants a Bengaluru launch for his last season's release – *The Rathores of Ranibagh*. It is because of Aaditha, her association with me and the festival. Cognitive jam.

When Father asked Navya and me if we could make ourselves available for Bob's Bengaluru launch, I agreed without a thought because it is Bengaluru. This is where I've been living this past month, in my head at least. Obsessing over Aaditha.

What is she doing?

Where does she *now* go to let her hair down?

How can I reach her?

I have been messaging her daily these last couple of weeks, the length of the messages shortening with every passing day until it is reduced to *Hey Aaditha*.

My eyes are going through the descriptor for our session:

A Regal Rendezvous: A day in the life of the Ranibagh Royals – Vedveer Rathore Singh and Navya Mrinalini will be in conversation with author Robert Kaminski, a former diplomat with a passion for words and photography.

The Rathores of Ranibagh is a richly illustrated hardbound that traces the journey of the Rathores – custodians of tradition, fashion icons and celebrities by inheritance in a modern republic. The book has rare archival photographs, hand-painted family trees and never-before-seen glimpses of palace life.

My smile is nervous; it has nothing to do with what I have just read or the session ahead. My thoughts are flirting with the image of Aaditha, dressed in a shade of white, floating around these grounds, coffee cup in hand.

'Did Aaditha reply?' Navya asks as the wheels come to a halt at the entrance of the hotel.

I had sent Aaditha an invite to our session the moment I confirmed.

'No,' I answer.

A huge crowd mills around the lobby.

'She'll be here,' Navya says. 'She may not give you the time of day, Brother, but she'll be here. She hasn't broken it off, remember.'

I nod, more to myself, as the car door opens. Knowing Aaditha, she may have tried to break it off; her silence is eloquent.

Anna Maria Menon, the festival director, meets us at the lobby. She's the picture of poise, trying to steer us into the VIP room, but the gathered bodies aren't in the mood to give.

Anna Maria talks as loudly as she can, urging people to clear the passage, but her voice doesn't carry. A younger woman grabs the imaginary baton from Anna, tapping her shoulder. She uses the boom in her voice to maximum effect.

'The prince and princess will be available for a limited period after the session, but now, you have to let them pass.'

Her voice forces the pack to part.

In the relative quiet of the air-conditioned lounge, the festival director tells us we cut our arrival so fine it almost gave her a heart attack.

'Too close for comfort,' she says. Her smile matches the crispness of her starched sari. She looks as far from a cardiac episode as the clouds are from breaking.

In the interval, my eyes dart around the room. Aaditha is somewhere around. Her perfume is in the air.

'I know,' Anna Maria says, 'but I can't help worrying. What if...'

'What if the cattle stretch themselves across the road and aren't in the mood to move?' Navya says with a laugh before enveloping Anna Maria in a hug. I had no idea they knew each other.

Navya's eyes shift to the room.

'Don't worry, Robert will be here any moment,' she says.

My eyes finally find Aaditha; she's in blue jeans and a Breton stripe shirt. She's deep in conversation with two people, a man and a woman. I wonder if she knows I'm in the room. She probably does, but is ignoring me.

I turn in the direction of my strong-willed fiancée.

'Those are two top literary agents; they have been hovering around Aaditha all evening. They're trying to get a book out of her,' Anna Maria says.

I feel my chest swell.

'Let them talk,' she adds. Her hand is on the sleeve of my blazer. 'Besides, you will have time with your fiancée after your session. I'm assuming you are staying on here in Bengaluru, Your Highness.'

I nod, but I can't stop my feet from moving towards Aaditha. 'I'm allowed a quick hello,' I tell Anna Maria, who is all smiles.

Aaditha turns to face me just as I close in on her. Her smile is tight, but I can see that she's breathing hard. Her hair is swept over her shoulder, and her eyes are heavily kohled. Her hand is opening and closing. I take it in mine and drop a kiss on her lips.

The eyes of the room are on us; I can tell by the way the place has quietened.

'Please make time for me later in the evening?' I'm not asking. I'm pleading.

Now that I am close enough, I can see that her eyes are fatigued.

'Don't you have a session just now, Your Highness?' she asks, exhaling. I leave her hand reluctantly and walk back to Anna Maria.

'Coffee, tea or water before you get on stage?' she asks.

I would've liked a cup of the expertly harvested Oolong, not any tea, so I let it drop.

We walk on stage at exactly 6 p.m. Anna Maria's show runs like clockwork.

It is an impressive turnout – rows and rows of people under a massive canopy. My eyes find Aaditha; she's seated in the first row. She's wearing her emerald ring. I want to whistle.

The session is off to a strong start. Navya, the more interesting by far of the Ranibagh siblings, is in her element today.

'Being royal isn't sipping coffee under marble arches,' she says, looking at Aaditha. 'It wouldn't hurt my sister's pockets, though, but in all seriousness, it's about dodging family politics, committee meetings and your mother's opinion on your Instagram posts.'

I chuckle. Aaditha is smiling, looking at Navya. There's a movement to Aaditha's right. Mr Tattooed Arm, helmet in hand, is actually nudging her.

She says he is someone dear to her, but who is he? I'm not jealous; I'm curious.

Kaminski asks about my Green Dream – the hours I spend on the land, what time I go out each morning and what time I return and all that happens in between. I detail my day, speaking extensively on organic farming and boring everyone, particularly Aaditha.

Thankfully for me and the audience, Navya's soon-to-be-launched fashion label, RaniLine, takes over the rest of the interaction.

The session then opens for questions from the audience – something about what it means to be born into a legacy – then one about palaces – if living in one feels surreal or suffocating. A student from a law school asks if we feel obligated to be 'inspiring'. And where does royalty stand in the age of democracy?

All good questions. We take turns answering, until I'm tossed one that takes me by surprise in gentle Bengaluru.

'Your Highness, have you and Miss Aaditha Prathap signed a prenup?'

I take a second to react. My gaze shifts to Aaditha, who turns away the moment her eyes meet mine.

'Considering that she's the one who is moving into a relic of a residence a couple of centuries old, with an ancestral sword collection no one's allowed to touch, I'm fairly certain she's making the bigger gamble,' I say, my eyes on Aaditha.

She's smiling; the cameras are on her.

'Jokes aside, we both believe in being open and honest. Whatever we sign, or don't sign, is immaterial because of the mutual trust. What is important for both of us is how we protect and honour each other's journeys.'

'Will Aaditha Prathap change her name to Rathore after marriage, Your Highness?'

Aaditha flinches. Navya's face is inscrutable. The question has upset both women.

'I find questions of this nature offensive, more so when they are posed to the man because it is not his decision,' I say. I'm irked, and I don't hide it. 'If Aaditha wants to change her name or initials, it's her choice. I'm not the one who christened her, and I have no plans to rechristen her.'

There's a round of cheers. Someone shouts, 'Well said.'

Sometimes, applause is necessary, even if it is for calling out basic societal issues. The indiscretions need to be highlighted, over and over again.

The moment Navya and I get off the stage, we are surrounded by people requesting photos and autographs. I have an eye on Aaditha.

A thousand clicks later, I realize I have lost her.

Ratan extricates me from the crowd and nudges me along in the direction of a waiting vehicle at the rear entrance of the hotel.

'Vedveer.' I hear my name being called. I almost turn because of the familiarity of the address. It's probably another Vedveer, I decide, and keep going.

'Vedveer.' It's an American accent. It is Bengaluru, where Shanky, my bud from school, lives. I turn.

A tall man, almost my height and definitely not Shanky,

is approaching us even as Ratan puts out his hand to keep him at bay.

'Do I know you?' I ask. He looks familiar; I have seen him somewhere.

'I'm Arjun,' he says, putting out his hand. 'You don't know me, but we have a common friend, Aaditha.'

I nod. This is the man in the photographs. The one who sent her roses, the one she emptied a mug of coffee on.

'Aaditha and I go back a long time. We are friends… more than friends, actually,' he says.

The smile is sly.

'Nice meeting you, Arjun,' I say, without shaking his hand, allowing security to move me along.

The moment I spot Prathap Gowda's silver-grey Mercedes, I take off my blazer, loosen my tie and roll up my sleeves. I tell Ratan, 'I'm driving.'

I make my way through Aaditha's office quietly, unlike the last time I was here.

I approach the store manager. He's the one I asked to keep the change two months ago. He was in Jaipur, too, but I have forgotten his name. His name badge says 'Manager'.

'I would like to meet Aaditha. Is she here?' I ask.

He doesn't nod. No yes or no either; he reaches for the intercom behind him. I don't hear him speak, but a few seconds later, he directs me to the door. He isn't smiling.

Good, loyal team.

I like that I knew where Aaditha would be. Ratan had lost her, too, so I took a wild guess! Maybe not so wild.

I know so little about her daily routine, I could maybe count them on one hand – coffee connoisseur, wine drinker, lover of denims, likes to hang out at Lakshmi Bar, is not opposed to hiding behind a costume to avoid attention. Though the last two are not a part of her regular regimen.

The manager holds the door open for me before pulling it shut behind him.

'Did you just get back?' I ask Aaditha's back.

'I didn't hear you,' she says, spinning around. 'Mohit, whom you've met before, just called. I couldn't hear him clearly. I thought you were on the way.'

I'm exhaling a storm, offering libations in my head. She hasn't thrown me out!

'Apologies,' I say quickly. 'I knocked.'

'How did you know I was here?'

'I took a chance,' I say.

Her face is as blank as an untouched school board on the first day of the year, but the dip at the base of her neck is pronounced.

'I drove your father's car,' I say.

She smiles; the light catches her eye. 'I'm impressed! First taste of my city's infamous traffic snarls?'

Her smile is infectious. 'It's not so bad, actually,' I say.

She exhales, and her shoulders drop a tad as she points at the chair beside me.

Between us stands a heavy mahogany desk, and heavier still, the weight of unspoken confessions.

'I want to talk to you, Aaditha.'

She nods. 'Can I get you something to eat or drink?'

Yamazaki on the rocks would've been good. 'I'll have a coffee,' I say.

'You don't have to punish yourself,' she says. 'We have tea, too – the bags you left behind the last time you were here.'

'My behaviour is inexcusable.' I stop, the words catching in my throat. I shake my head, voice barely steady. 'And that's just the beginning.'

Her shoulders shift in a gentle motion. She leans back in her seat. Her tiny frame has taken up all the space in my head.

'Would those bags be stale? It's a couple of months already,' she asks.

'It will hold,' I say.

'Tea, then?'

'No, your coffee.' A cup of my to-be-wife's coffee every once in a while would be good for the system.

Aaditha orders just the one coffee.

'Do you not want a cup for yourself?'

'I have had six cups already!'

The double-shot, bone-dry cappuccino arrives, and I take a sip immediately.

I clear my throat and clutch the cup. 'Aaditha, I'm sorry for my behaviour,' I say, holding her gaze.

There's a heaviness behind her gaze, untethered somewhat by an effort to appear unbothered.

'I want to tell you what happened… My actions… were wrong, and my words were awful. But we're about to build a marriage based on honesty, and that means no unspoken truths. Even if what I'm going to say comes across like justifying the unjustifiable.'

I see Aaditha swallow before she speaks. 'You don't owe me anything.'

Her words land heavy on my shoulders, in my chest, sinking straight to the pit of my stomach. But I don't let it shake me. Her trust is delicate, and I'm already standing on cracked ice.

'I was going through the papers of the Ranibagh deal the day before I arrived in Bengaluru. It looked really good,' I say, exhaling, 'then I figured your father was at the other end of it… I called to ask if you knew about it, but I couldn't get through. I waited the day out, but I was already losing my mind.'

'Why? Because my father cannot be trusted? Or I couldn't be trusted?'

'No, neither your father nor you,' I say, drawing a deep breath, my eyes pleading with hers. 'I trust you implicitly. It is me…'

I hesitate, then the words spill out. 'Thoughts of you have consumed me, Aaditha… Your eyes, the fall of your hair, how it settles on your shoulders before slipping away, the curve of your lips, the colour that rises in your cheeks… You are my sunshine, Aaditha. I cannot fathom losing your light.'

Aaditha's gaze drops; it settles on the table that is polished to a shine.

'When I saw your dad was tied to the Ranibagh deal, I couldn't help wondering… was that the point of us? Were those moments we shared on the terrace, during Holi, all that your eyes told me… was it a part of some bigger plan?'

'You are so full of yourself,' she says, shaking her head.

Her voice is barely audible – flat and hollow. Like the feeling has been drained from it.

'I have tried to deny this feeling, Aaditha. I have tried to convince myself it is nothing more than admiration or fleeting fancy, but the truth is undeniable,' I say.

The air I exhale is cyclonic.

'The moment you entered my life, everything shifted – the colour of the blossoms was brighter, the weight I carried felt lighter. I woke up to thoughts of you and slept with thoughts of you. You have stirred a passion in me I did not know I was capable of feeling, and now, I can no longer brush it aside.'

Her eyes widen, and her cheeks peak to a wild rose.

'I have spent nights wrestling with my own heart, trying to discern whether what I feel is mere infatuation or something deeper,' I say, moving forward in my seat. 'And now, sitting here before you, I don't want to deny it any longer; I don't want to hide, Aaditha. I will chase you to the ends of the world if I have to… but I cannot be without you.'

Aaditha wraps her arms tightly around herself.

In the silence, her eyes speak first, something that looks like hope.

I step around her desk and crouch, close enough to feel her breath on my skin. Taking her hands in mine, I say, 'I love you, not as a fleeting spark but as a steady flame. I love you with a vulnerability I have never allowed myself to show, with a sincerity borne from my deepest being.'

When Aaditha inhales, the hollow at the base of her throat sinks so deep her skin is almost pale.

'I know the road ahead will test us. Life in the palace will take some adjusting for you, but I will relax everything around you, everything but security, so that you can live life like you have always lived it.'

She blinks. Maybe to hide the emotions playing out in her eyes.

'Shadows will fall, but know this, I am yours if you will have me. I promise to love you in all the ways that matter, to protect you, to celebrate you and to be there when you need me.'

Aaditha's eyes are on mine.

'I hope you know what you are doing, Ved,' she says after what feels like an eternity, 'because I seem to be slipping.'

25.

Aaditha
Circle of Love

The Presidential Suite is a ginormous space, big enough to host an empire and its cousins.

Vedveer opens the door, holds it open and follows me in. My eyes roam the rooms before I turn to face him.

My heart is hammering madly.

He shrugs off his blazer lazily, his eyes caressing my bare arms.

For a moment, I stand before him transfixed. The devilish grin he wears snaps me awake. I dash around and relieve him of his coat.

'At your service, Your Highness,' I say, tossing his blazer aside and wrapping my arms around him from behind.

I hold him tight, crushing him to me. I want to devour him.

This ache of wanting to be around him, feel his warmth, touch his taut muscles, knot fingers, brush lips… say everything, say nothing, scares me.

I never allowed myself to acknowledge what I feel for

Vedveer, the attraction, the desire, the electricity… It was crazy, but I controlled it.

Maybe because I didn't have a good enough answer to *why me*. Not until he walked through my door this evening, breaking walls and putting his heart on the line.

Is this how love feels?

'I was thinking of changing, but I'm having second thoughts,' he says, breaking my hold.

He pulls me up on his back; my legs flap behind us as he heads in the direction of the bedroom.

I nibble at his ear. 'Go on, change. I don't want to be accused of being unfair.'

Vedveer puts me down and grabs me by the waist. He looks at me, not like he's reaching into my soul but like he is stoking a fire that is already wild with longing… I feel my heart, but I shush it.

'Feel free to join me,' he says, stretching out his hand.

I shake my head. 'At the very least, I hope I'm marrying a man capable of throwing on his own clothes.'

Vedveer's laugh is a hoot. 'I enjoy conversations about ability and capability.'

'I rather prefer the action,' I say, pulling the door hard behind me.

I look around me. The place is so roomy, the million impulses running riot in me have enough space to get lost here.

Soft amber light pools from wall sconces that wash over the polished wooden floor. Cream curtains frame tall windows that look out onto busy thoroughfares scattered with gold dots.

The air smells of sandalwood and candle wax.

I make my way into the lounge.

At one end is a heavy bar counter on which a matt gold ice bucket sits. It carries three bottles of wine. Different brands of the same grape.

Vedveer joins me in the lounge area. He is wearing a dark-chocolate linen shirt on blue denims. He has sports sliders on his feet.

'Who'd have thought you royals know how to dress like regular people!'

'I'm regular.'

'Very regular.'

As I move further into the room, Vedveer clicks on the remote, and the curtains pull away. A plunge pool is chilling in the evening light.

Norah Jones's 'Come Away With Me' comes alive on the sound system.

Vedveer stretches his hand out, asking me for a dance.

My heart stills, and my stomach turns as I put my hand in his. He tugs me, and I fall into him. His chest is hard, and his arms are tight as they wrap around me. There's just enough space for air to pass between us.

His breath warms my neck as we turn, slow and close.

The thickness of my fitted denims clings to me, and I feel the pressure of his hand on my waist. We aren't dancing – not really – just swaying, lost in rhythm, in sentiment, in what we've said... and maybe something unsaid.

Come away with me, and we'll kiss

On a mountaintop

Come away with me, and I'll never stop loving you

Vedveer adjusts my hair, moving invisible strands behind my ears as we move. He's looking into my eyes, and I look at his coloured irises.

He's a spectacular physical specimen.

The more we move, the more I get into him. His tall frame, his lithe step, his warm breath and his freshly worn fragrance.

I could run away with him, but right now, it feels like I have run to him.

Norah's sweet notes run out of words, and Vedveer takes a deep breath. I wonder if he's inhaling fragrant Jasmine.

He leans into me and kisses my lip.

His groan makes me giddy. I giggle.

'I can't get over how you have no recollection of the kiss,' he says.

I kiss his lips back and enjoy the luxury of gazing into his eyes.

'Lavanya, who was also quite high that evening, thought we had kissed, but she couldn't really tell,' I say.

'Should I take offence? Or maybe I'll just remind you.'

'You could just refresh the page,' I say.

Vedveer brushes my cheeks with the back of his hand.

The strokes aren't rushed; it is like he's memorizing texture, the physical and the emotional. Trying to mediate between every unspoken thought I have held these past weeks and months.

His eyes are bright.

He takes my hand in his, dropping kisses on the inside of my wrists, on my bare shoulders, on the corner of my mouth and on the tips of my clavicle.

I feel a rush of stirrings inside me. I'm delirious with desire and longing and everything in between.

Vedveer lifts me onto his lap, and we kiss, his lips taking mine in an urgency I recognize inside me.

He is telling me something that can't be communicated in words, awakening sweet sensations that lie entrenched in my visceral being. It isn't delicate or hesitant – it's a tempest taking shape, flying free and wild. I'm making little noises that seem to encourage Vedveer, and just when I think there's nowhere else in me for him to go, he reaches for more before pulling back slowly. His palms frame my face; our eyes lock in a barter until our mouths meet again.

The world around me drops like irrelevant bits of pottery.

This time, the discourse is fierce, the ache and the tenderness we are too wary to put into words. His arms are knotted tight around me. My breasts are buried in the brown of his shirt, and we cling to each other, determined that nothing will separate us.

'This is not the first time we're kissing,' he says, forcing a giggle out of me. Vedveer is on his feet, and I'm in his arms.

'You keep saying that,' I say, flirting with my body, 'but is there proof?'

'The proof is in the reminder,' he says. 'Delighted to remind you again and again.'

I swallow something, and it tastes like a rush of emotion.

'You want to try the bed?' he asks, his eyes darkening. I feel a shiver shoot up my thighs.

Vedveer strides across the room; I'm in his arms. He puts me down on the bed and sits next to me.

We are quiet beside each other, if you discount the breathing.

My breath is rough, something like the wind outside, which rustles through the trees, coaxing and stirring, while Vedveer may be panting. Like a runner who has just crossed the tape.

The city lights blink, casting a golden shadow across the marble floors of the bedroom and the crisp white of the hotel sheets. Vedveer picks me up again, climbs on the bed, strides across it and places me in the middle of the cloud of white.

He leans over me to unzip my dress. I inhale his deliciousness as he peels it off me.

I arch my back, pushing my finest lingerie, eyelash lace, maroon, at him.

His eyes widen in appreciation before they caress my body lazily.

Oxytocins are swimming vigorously inside me. I move forward and reach for his shirt. His fingers fumble as he helps me take it off. He leaves the bed for a moment, and I watch as his erection rises and his jeans fall around him with his underwear. In his nakedness, he is king.

My nerves are tied in messy knots, and my breathing is erratic. His eyes are devouring me, and I'm feeling self-conscious. 'Can you dim the lights?' I plead.

Vedveer laughs. 'She, the lover of bright and brighter lights, is asking for bulbs to be dimmed. How can I not oblige?'

'You remember our first meeting at your office? I wanted to sit out in the café, and you looked horrified?' he asks.

I laugh. 'You were so judging me!'

'I'm not going to pretend to deny it.'

He reaches around me and patiently unbuckles my bra before easing me onto the bed. I'm covered by his warmth, until he kneels to leave a trail of hot kisses from my lips, down my neck, to my scapula, before he moves inwards and finds the mounds of my breasts with his mouth and then his hands. He kisses my nipples after teasing them with his fingers. My body is burning. I moan, thrusting myself against him, and reach for his lips just as he whispers my name.

'I can't stop myself,' he says.

'I don't want you to hold back, Ved Rathore.' I have so many names for him, and I'm not holding back.

He groans. 'Ved,' he repeats. 'No one, literally no one, calls me Ved.'

I snuggle deeper into him in response.

'Ved,' he repeats. 'If it is a nickname, it is Veer.'

'That's the obvious one,' I say, 'but Ved is beautiful.'

'You are beautiful,' he says, sliding up against me.

'Ready?' he asks, pulling back and spreading my legs, his thumbs massaging the insides of my thighs before he relieves me of my underwear. I want to scream yessssss, not for the promises our families may have made to each other, his palaces or his position, but because, in that moment, his hands trembled slightly, just like mine, before they dug into his forearms with an intensity I didn't know I possessed.

I moan as his tongue flicks across my vagina, going back and forth, teasing me open before moving inside me. When he pulls out, my nails dig into his arms.

'Please,' I beg.

'*Jaan*,' he cajoles, his passion naked.

What has Ved just called me? *Jaan*. I feel my heart expand exponentially, balloon-like; my eyes are tearing up.

'I'm in love with you,' he says. 'I feel so full in this emotion that I don't think I could love you any more than I love you at this point. It is beyond anything I have ever felt in my life. I'm not sure it's a good thing in my position, but there's not a thing I can do to stop how I feel for you.'

I pull Ved down on me, throw my arms around his neck and listen to his heartbeat.

When he finally lies over me, length over length, our bodies meeting and moving almost instantly, my hips rising to envelop his thrust, it feels like a door we've both been waiting to walk through has opened.

There's a wildness to the movement. He's reaching further and further; he is deep, deep inside me when I hear myself call out, 'Ved… Veeed… Vee... eed…'

The night is still, and my voice echoes.

We move together like we've been holding our breath for weeks and have finally remembered how to exhale. It is tender, even a little shy, yet powered by the currents of the emotional tide we are wading into – it's the duality that makes it more real. More us.

I feel the hesitation, the hope, the unsung notes that press into that one lingering moment. And just like that, something shifts between us and explodes inside me, and I cry into the night.

It's just us – two humans, from worlds so apart you can't help but wonder how they may ever be bridged. Still, the only sensations are those of breath and skin and something that feels like an emotion that could stretch to infinity.

My parents don't know where I am, nor do Alia and Lavanya, but no one needs to know, because I'm home.

In this time we have together, I forget the weight of who we are – the Coffee Queen, the daughter of a senior politician, and the crown prince. There's no palace, no headlines, no eyes watching us from behind heavy curtains.

Just he and me, his lips on my cheek and the strange, aching beauty of being completed in this togetherness.

I smile against his mouth, tasting relief, nerves and the beginning of something neither of us has the words for yet.

'I love you, Aaditha,' he says, trying to steady his ragged breath. The space between us has slowly melted – layer by layer, kiss by kiss.

My heartbeat knocks on my ears, louder than the city outside.

'I love you, Ved,' I reply as his fingers stroke my naked leg, pressing against the inside of my thigh.

Later, in the hush that follows, I realize it isn't fireworks; it is something quieter and softer, but it is everything. It is where I feel safe. Wanted. Loved – not for the version of me people imagine but for the girl I am underneath it all. The girl who fled to Ohio and returned with a dream, a girl who was burned by love but is now inhaling it and twirling around in it like it were a dress that has given her room to move.

When I open my eyes, I'm naked under a sheet and Ved's leg is over mine.

'*Jaan*,' he calls, sensing I have opened my eyes. 'This is how I want to wake up every morning of my life.'

I reach up and place a kiss on his lips. 'Have we kissed before? If we have, I have no recollection.'

I hear Vedveer's moan as he rolls me over him and pulls me up against his erection. 'I'm good with reminders, and prompts, too,' he says.

Tittle Tattle

NORTH MEETS SOUTH: INSIDE THE WEDDING OF THE YEAR

The coming together of Prince Vedveer and Aaditha Prathap is more than a synergy of cultures; it's the rumba of contrasting, often colliding worlds. None of which seems to have got in the way of this darling twosome.

A love story for the ages played out before high-powered guests at the brilliantly lit Ranibagh Palace last weekend.

The toothsome Rajput Prince Vedveer Rathore Singh and Aaditha Asha Prathap - the sparky Coffee Queen - tied the knot, following week-long celebrations that culminated in the holy ritual where they were pronounced man and wife. An array of ceremonies honoured both cultures, highlighting the union of families and communities from different corners of the country, with the abiding message of togetherness. Live, and let love grow.

TT was inside the wedding and the reception that followed the next evening, but before we drool about those gorgeous, scrumptious affairs, we wanted to tell you that almost every attendee was a known name.

There are big-ticket weddings that go on and on, and then there are those unions with moments for which time seems to slow down. The heart is racing, but everything around is moving perfectly slowly - fragrant orchid trees, in shades from purple to light pink, hold firm despite the flush of the winter breeze; the bride and groom locking eyes, communicating silently, but the soundless exchange is audible across the room. The Prince's adoring look at his glowing bride while adjusting her *maang tikka* adorned with an uncut pink diamond.

The daytime ritual sparkled as much with the opulent grandeur you've come to expect of the Rathores. And the love shared by the beautiful couple, has forever smudged boundaries of region, language and culture. A bookmark for society, a reminder for all to rejoice in the wealth of our great differences.

Aaditha was luminous in a custom-made, pastel-pink Kanjeevaram silk that shimmered in the late-afternoon light. Gold *zari* traced across the heavy temple border, while the pallu, tightly arranged, fell in geometrical lines, lifting the look. Her blouse, a classic cut, blended into the six yards.

India's Coffee Queen wore statement jewellery on her big day.

The centrepiece was a dazzling uncut diamond and ruby choker with matching earrings. The set had the Rathore stamp all over it, but the Palace declined to comment on our query. Aaditha's elaborate Rani Haar was designed by her BFF Lavanya Patil. Her waist belt, the holding piece for the jewellery she wore, was a manifestation of prosperity. It featured Goddess Lakshmi seated in grace, flanked by peacocks, flowers, and coins.

TT has long commented on Aaditha's choice of clothing and make-up (not always positively), but there wasn't a colour out of place on the day. She went with minimalist, where the focus was on her radiant skin and elegantly styled hair.

The bride's entry into Ranibagh's sun-drenched Rang Mahal courtyard to the rich strains of the *nadaswaram* set the tone for the wedding. She had everyone in wraps from the moment her mehndi-stained feet touched the ground.

Aaditha walked under a pearl-embellished *phoolon ki chaadar* that was dressed with baby's-breath blooms and sizable pink roses.

The Rajkumari did away with time-honoured practices and had her sister, the lovely Alia, along with two female friends - Lavanya Patil, a jewellery chain heiress, and Komal Rao, a yoga instructor - along with Raju Mathew, the heavily tattooed Kalari expert, carry her exquisitely woven *chaadar*.

The *chaadar* is conventionally held by the bride's brothers, but who is to question the Coffee Queen?

The society debate leading up to this wedding of distinct halves was about what the bride would wear. She was, after all, marrying into royalty, and there would be lines she dared not cross.

Would Aaditha walk out in a Rajputi Poshak, or would it be a *lehenga*? That it was neither must tell you who exactly Aaditha Asha Prathap is.

At the end of the aisle was His Royal Highness Vedveer - drop-dead gorgeous in a perfectly tailored ivory sherwani. His pink turban was the soft rebellion in his otherwise classic look, a private conversation of colour between his bride and him.

Earlier, the groom arrived on a Marwari stallion that saw a section of the guests swooning.

Gasps of 'lucky Aaditha' filled the air as he swung off the steed and made his way to the centre, while words like 'hawt' floated around the courtyard.

It was obvious by the look on Vedveer's face that Aaditha's choice of attire took him by surprise, a breathtaking surprise. He had no idea that she would go with Kanjeevaram silk for her big day, but as she walked up to him, emerging from under the *chaadar*, his nod said he should have expected it.

The newest member of Rathore royalty will forever be Aaditha Asha Prathap. She's not changing, she's not trying to fit in, and the King-in-waiting wouldn't have it any other way.

The way HRH Vedveer looked at Aaditha, checking to see if she was okay every now and then, it looked like he would storm every fort in the land to keep her safe - saying more than any oath could.

Throughout the ceremony, Aaditha and Vedveer exchanged glances and subtle touches. Whether it was the Prince lifting and then adjusting Aaditha's *pallu* after they exchanged garlands or Aaditha holding on to Vedveer's arm during the rituals, even sharing a passionate kiss after the ceremony.

The wedding was a more intimate affair, with only a thousand guests in attendance.

The Rathores, the last word in grandeur, laid it all out there, wooing the Gowdas from Bengaluru, who, for all their achievements and money, stood out for their simplicity.

The royal side shimmered like a living gallery of jewels and heirlooms; the bride's family - parents, sister, extended family and three of her dearest friends - brought a different kind of grace to the ceremony.

They wore Kanjeevaram and Mysore silks in shades of red, while the men wore silk kurtas of an earthen hue on white dhotis. They also draped a dupatta-like fabric called the *angavastra* on their shoulders.

The mélange of stunning southern silks was reportedly sourced directly from the weavers. TT is in the know that for a weekend, Kanchipuram was transported to the Gowda home on MG Road in Bengaluru.

Shaahi Shaam

Ranibagh at night transformed into a living dream.

Garlands of fresh marigold and fragrant jasmine cascaded down baroque balconies, the scent spiking the chilly evening air. Rangoli patterns in bursts of pinks, blues and golds adorned the marbled courtyards. The durbar halls glowed in the light of chandeliers dripping with crystals. Brocade drapes in wine red and navy, carrying the Ranibagh insignia, framed the doorways. Antique silver vases with tuberoses and native desert blooms decorated the passageways.

The garden was strung with fairy lights, and notes of '*Kesariya Balam*' claimed the air.

The newlyweds - Rajkumari Aaditha and Crown Prince Vedveer - walked into the reception hand in hand, meeting and greeting guests.

Aaditha's bespoke ivory *lehenga*, crafted from mulberry silk, came alive with a quiet shimmer every time she moved. The embroidery was done in threads of dull silver and gold. The sheer veil in a sunset blush, with embroidered borders, draped over her head, and one shoulder trailed behind her like a confidant trying to keep pace. She wore her waist-length hair loose. The blouse, with thread work in dull gold, carried sequins and pearls, echoing the patterns of the skirt. The deep neckline and cap sleeves added a contemporary twist to the traditional attire.

In the last month, Aaditha's reception *lehenga* was the topic of conversation at Kitty Party News Hours around the country. Would the Princess-to-be wear a traditional *lehenga*, or would she walk in in a gown? A little bird tells us a gown was never even part of the conversation.

The lehenga, designed by Sara Khiani, required 30 pairs of hands and 700 work hours, costing upwards of INR 20 lakhs.

Aaditha, who stands at 5 ft 3", while the Crown Prince towers at a commanding 6 ft 3", owned her height, wearing flat-as-pancake *juttis*.

Vedveer was in a daring blush pink *bandhgala* with work in dull gold that complemented the bride's attire. A pearl chain with a ruby pendant added to the opulence. Vedveer wore a matching *safa*, adorned with an elaborate ruby brooch. Embroidered *mojris* completed his look.

According to Palace gossip, the only thing the groom and his stylists knew about the Rajkumari's wedding wardrobe was what colour she would wear on each of the days.

Every few minutes when they took a break from the meeting and greeting of people, the bride and groom appeared lost in themselves, Vedveer taking Aaditha's hands in his, opening up her palm or simply adjusting her hair that was already in order, or the Princess getting up on her toes to brush aside the gold dust on his face or laughing at jokes they were only telling each other.

The royals - Maharaj Gaurav Rathore Singh and the stunning Maharani Gauri Elena - were quite the presence. HRH Navya Mrinalini and her beau, cricketer Nalin Shah - who are expected to wed in the coming months - were very much the picture-perfect couple.

Navya Mrinalini dazzled in a midnight blue velvet lehenga, hand-embroidered with silver *zardozi*. Her blouse was sharply tailored, with a dramatic high neck and sheer sleeves. A statement diamond choker and her signature confidence rounded off the look. Her lehenga was from her own RaniLine, which is expected to launch in the new year.

The Ranisa wore an elegant ivory saree, threaded with pearls and silver sequins. Her heirloom emerald necklace - once worn by her mother-in-law - sat like a crown on her collarbone.

The Maharaj kept it classic in a deep charcoal *bandhgala* with hand-embroidered cuffs and antique gold buttons, paired with a matching churidar. A large oval-shaped blue sapphire pendant hung around his neck. A silk pocket square in Jaipur pink and his father's vintage diamond-studded gold watch were his only nods to flamboyance.

The glitter of the royals was balanced by the method and order the Gowdas brought to the evening.

Neela Gowda was draped in a deep maroon Mysore silk sari with a narrow gold border. She wore two strings of garnet and diamonds on her neck and matching earrings. Her hair was tied in a bun that was decorated with fresh jasmine. Karnataka's finance minister was in a black tuxedo, and his smile, like his leather shoes, was polished.

There was food and drink everywhere. Entrées - Laal Maas sliders, Sulemani Murgh Tikkas, Quail Kebabs, Tandoor Machli, and Dal Baati bites - were doing the rounds.

As the guests took their designated seats, the Maharaj clinked his glass and called for the attention of the floor. He held up a glass in one hand and took hold of the microphone in the other.

Ladies and gentlemen, friends, family and dear guests,

As we come to the end of this wedding celebration, I stand not just as king but as a father - a very proud and slightly sentimental old man. Watching my son today, standing beside the woman he loves, I am reminded of how time has flown. One minute he was running in and bowling cricket balls in the palace corridors, and the next, he's here, marrying the one who has clearly stolen his heart.

To our new daughter - brave, wise and strong - you've brought warmth and joy into our family. And to my son - may you lead with love, not ego; may your crown sit lighter with Aaditha Asha beside you.

May your life together be rich with experiences and memories and the laughter of children.

He finished by raising a glass in the direction of the guests.

While people debated if COFFEE Before Books & Bras was really Aaditha's baby or if she was just the face for her father's newest business venture, the Crown Prince and Prathapji *ki beti* were writing their own script.

Once the guests settled into seats, with waiters swarming around tables with replenishments - food and drink - it became easier to spot people.

Royal cousins draped in vintage jewels, business tycoons, film stars, art collectors and a few notorious socialites, each seemingly trying to outdo the next in designer couture and ancestral bling. Oscar-winning actress Olivia Beckenbaur, who is believed to be a friend of the Prince, stunned in a breathtaking ivory sari. Shankar 'Shanky' Renu, a global tech supremo, was seen awkwardly adjusting his Nehru jacket, and supermodel Samantha Ferrer did some heavy lifting, effortlessly carrying six kilos of hand embroidery.

On an evening when Ranibagh also glittered with the kind of guest list that made seasoned society editors clutch their pearls, the sentiment that infused fresh energy into the winter air was the audacious celebration of differences. Done in Rathore-Gowda style.

PSSST… What we heard between sips.

Why did Aaditha name her brand COFFEE Before Books & Bras?

'Books' because she thought it goes well with coffee, like cinnamon cookies. 'Bras' because of her sister Alia's knack and her own feminist vein to put the globes out in the public domain. Boobs wear bras. Say it bold, say it loud.

ACKNOWLEDGEMENTS

Jaipur and its distinct culture have long intrigued me, ever since my first *namkeen lassi* in a clay cup.

It's been a joy to anchor this north–south novel in two remarkable cities: the Pink City, Jaipur, and the Garden City, Bengaluru. *You Can't Be Serious!* challenged me as I explored cultural nuance, lifestyle, society, language and topography, forcing me out of my comfort zone.

Dear reader, I hope you enjoyed it as much as I did putting it together. Thank you for picking up *You Can't Be Serious!* and giving a relative newbie romance author your precious time. It is valued.

My deepest gratitude to my editor at Hachette India, Abhivyakti Singh, who has gone above and beyond – the best cues and comments, and at just the right time, that firm '*I hope you'll rethink this*' nudge, which still haunts me late at night.

A special thank you to Thomas Abraham and the entire team at Hachette India – especially my meticulous copyeditor Vinita Nayar, as well as Ajith Iyer for typesetting,

Sai Prasanna for proofreading, and the talented Damini Gupta for the cover.

To my friends – these past years haven't been easy, and I'm deeply appreciative of the fact that you stuck with me. Some of you read my drafts, some offered advice just when I needed it, some I see often, others less so – but every time we connect, it feels like no time has passed. This is for all of you, girls and boys, who stayed.

Mummy and Papa, you are my whole and soul. And always, Sanjay – the calm in the middle of my storms. I couldn't have done this without you.

VEDVEER RECOMMENDS

My friends still tease me that I spend more time with books than with my wife, but Aaditha insists it's one of the few indulgences she'll never compete with, as long as I make her coffee first! This year's reading has been unexpectedly delightful. I started with *Pitch: How to Captivate and Convince Any Audience on the Planet* by Danny Fontaine. *The Act of Living* by Frank Tallis followed, and I found myself thinking about how easily we forget to just *be* – something Aaditha, with her startup chaos and boundless energy, manages far better than I do.

Lone Pine by Siddhartha Menon gave me compassion about displacement and anomalies, while *Watershed* by Mridula Ramesh and *Climate Capitalism* by Akshat Rathi reignited my sense of purpose toward sustainability. Aaditha keeps saying we should make our estates fully solar – she's right, as usual. *City of Kashmir* by Sameer Hamdani was exquisite; its blend of art, history and devotion reminded me how beauty can endure, even in fragile places.

Of course, *A History of Test Cricket* by Tim Wigmore felt like coming home – I found myself reading passages aloud to Aaditha, who pretended not to listen while sipping her third Double-shot Bone Dry Cappuccino. *The Call of Music* by Priya Purushothaman added a lyrical note to the year, and *Running behind Lakshmi* by Aadil Rustomjee, about India's turbulent love affair with the stock market, had me in a thrall. Aaditha, ever the investor, called it 'required reading for princes who still think land is the only asset worth having.'

Then came *Raj Khosla: An Authorized Biography*, a reminder that reinvention is the soul of creativity; *565: The Dramatic Story of Unifying India* by Mallika Ravikumar stirred something deeply patriotic in me; and *Lives of the Stoics* by Ryan Holiday and Stephen Hanselman brought a sense of calm to it all.

It's been a good year!

AADITHA RECOMMENDS

They say opposites attract – and maybe that's why my husband disappears into history and cricket while I chase stories of women who built, broke and began again. This year, my reading list has been my version of a board meeting for the soul. I began with *Opinions* by Roxane Gay – sharp, honest and impossible to skim through without a dozen underlined sentences. Then *My Life in Full* by Indra Nooyi reminded me why I started my company in the first place: to build something that could outlast both ambition and burnout. *Limitless* by Radhika Gupta was a burst of energy – I found myself nodding through every chapter, then texting half my team to read it immediately.

The Dig by Sowmiya Ashok drew me into the necessity of uncovering the past, while *17, Morris Road* by Parul Sharma offered that perfect balance of wit and emotional truth I crave after a long day of meetings. *Eden Abandoned* by Shinie Antony left me thoughtful and a little heartbroken; *Notes on Heartbreak* by Annie Lord reminded me how love – like a startup pitch – requires both risk and reinvention.

Called by the Hills by Anuradha Roy made me pause and breathe; her writing always feels like the literary equivalent of monsoon air. *The New York Years* by Patricia Highsmith and *A Memoir of My Former Self* by Hilary Mantel were fascinating studies in creative restlessness – something I know too well. And when I wanted to laugh, I turned to *Have I Told You This Already?* by Lauren Graham, who somehow manages to sound like your best friend and your wiser self at once.

Finally, *The Dilemmas of Working Women* by Fumio Yamamoto tied it all together – it was like reading the subtext of every coffee-fuelled conversation I've had with other women founders.

This year, I was reminded that balance isn't something you find – it's something you keep remaking, one page, one conversation, one quiet moment at a time.

Sometimes
The end is just
The beginning
THE WAY WE WERE
AB
MORNING HERALD
PRAJWAL HEGDE

ALSO FROM HACHETTE INDIA
and
PRAJWAL HEGDE

Bitter rivals.
Reluctant colleagues.
Tormented ex-lovers.

Myra Rai is living her best life. At twenty-eight, she is a prominent journalist at the precipice of dreamy success and her dating life is the envy of the town. After all, jealous heads stir to probe her almost engagement to Ravi Rao, the gentleman heir to a roaring political legacy! Myra is well on her course. Until comes knocking the broad-shouldered, devastatingly dishy ghost from her past…

Andrew Brown is a headstrong political activist, unexpectedly back in the city after a winning stint in the US. Set to take over as the executive editor of *Morning Herald*, he is determined to revisit his past and reconnect with that one feisty journalist at work who hates his guts, hates that he is back, and hates that he never called…

Both Myra and Andrew have lost a lot over the years, including each other. But in the fierce race to best one another while pretending not to seethe in the hellfire of jealousy and suppressed passion, can they keep their barbs (and hands) to themselves? Right from the centre of a smouldering passion-fest, Prajwal Hegde tugs compellingly at the heartstrings and delivers a stormy rom-com that is all love (AND a whole lot of lust)!

ABOUT THE AUTHOR

Prajwal Hegde is the author of *The Way We Were* (2023) and *What's Good About Falling* (2018) and has been the *Times of India's* tennis editor since July 2005. She began her journalism career with *Mid-Day* in Mumbai, before moving to *Deccan Herald* in Bengaluru. Prajwal has reported on all four Grand Slams – Australian Open, French Open, Wimbledon and US Open – for several years. She is on the International Tennis Federation's Media Commission and is also a member of the International Tennis Writers Association. The Association of Tennis Professionals awarded Prajwal the 2021 Ron Bookman Media Excellence Award, making her the first Indian and second Asian to receive the honour. She was given the Media Excellence Award 2025, by Vijay Amritraj and the Tamil Nadu Tennis Association. She wrote the 'Steffi Graf' chapter in *Sportstars 40,* published by *The Hindu* in January 2020. She features in *Break Point,* the Leander Paes–Mahesh Bhupathi docuseries. Prajwal lives in Bengaluru with her husband, Dr Sanjay Hegde, a senior orthopaedic surgeon with Medicover Hospitals.